I thought of the words long ago that mama said to me, while standing there in front of the old farmhouse, getting that last glimpse of the farm. I will never forget her parting words, now ingrained in my memory forever, as they resounded over and over in my head on that seemingly long and silent drive. "Benny, leaving things behind will never be as hard as leaving those you love!"

And how I wish I could still be there,
Up in the house built in the air

LITTLE RIVER

Dadfire

Paperback ISBN: 978-1-64719-157-3
Hardcover ISBN: 978-1-64719-158-0
Epub ISBN: 978-1-64719-159-7
Mobi ISBN: 978-1-64719-160-3

Published by BookLocker.com, Inc., St. Petersburg, Florida.

The characters and events in this book are fictitious. Any similarity to real persons, living or dead, is coincidental and not intended by the author.

Library of Congress Cataloging in Publication Data
Dadfire
Little River by Dadfire
Library of Congress Control Number: 2020921977

Printed on acid-free paper.

BookLocker.com, Inc.
2020

First Edition

Dedication

Daniel Farmer
author
A K A DADfire

For my dad, mama and little brother Mack, whom I miss every day, yet remain in my heart forever. The characters created in the pages of this book help fill the blank page left in my soul since their absence, as anyone who has experienced loss understands. But to my daughter Abby and son Jordan; may you be granted the fortune of love as I have been privileged to know as your dad.

Danny
Mack
Lynda
Dorthy
Dale

Acknowledgments

A special thanks to my sister Lynda, my son Jordan, and my lifelong friend Bobby for their invaluable help and unwavering support in completing this project. Many thanks to the friends, teachers and other individuals that had so much influence on my young life. Without their inspiration and encouragement, this book would not be possible.

A special salute to all the little towns tucked away in forgotten places across our land that shape who we are, with memories of the lives we lived and of stories to tell.

Table of Contents

Part One

CHAPTER ONE
The Trouble With Beans

In so many ways it was truly the best time to be a kid. I'm not talking about money or material things at all. No, I'm talking about the day, the moment. There wasn't any big plan for the future. Heck, we didn't even think much about that. We just thought of the day we had on "that" day, not the next. It all came down to one word - simple. We lived in a simple house with simple things, living our lives like most other people around us.

I suppose it could be broken down to just simple purpose. What we had then we didn't know was so special. Life was so uncomplicated and so easy. All you had to do was put on your clothes and go out the door. It didn't matter where to; school, work, play, with no big plan to figure it all out. We would just come home to the same dusty old house each night, with that big, noisy attic fan blowing, and go to sleep with anticipation of the next day.

Every story has a beginning, but this one will start with how I got the name that most folks knew me by.

My given name was Benjamin Franklin Barnes. John F. Kennedy had just been elected president. People would often make a comment to me of how I was named after a president. I would usually only respond, "Reckon so," even though I had learned in school that Benjamin Franklin was never actually a president of the United States. It's funny how older people can believe something for so long, when it is so easy to find out the truth. I could tell them they were wrong about him being president and sometimes I actually did, but most adults don't like being corrected, especially from a kid. So I usually didn't say anything. Besides, why would I want to spoil my pride of having been named after a "president."

I was just called Benny until I was about six years old. That was when people around town also started calling me the nickname Beanie or Bean for short. It started out as a joke mostly, but later folks called me that in a natural sort of way. I didn't mind and even got to liking the nickname Bean. I thought it was cool to have a nickname like that and for a reason to be explained, made me famous around town. As it happens, when spoken, Beanie sounds like Benny and Bean sounds like Ben, and so it really didn't make much difference. Having some kind of real history attached to your name, made it more special than just being named after some old famous person.

But back to my story of how I got the nickname Bean. It was because of what happened when I was playing down at the old big barn that wasn't too far from our house. You could always find something to do around the barn when you might be bored of sitting around the house. Jack and I could play in the hay, in the loft, and make up lots of games using the big barn as our prop. Sometimes we would climb around on a tractor, a combine or some other big piece of farm machinery, chasing each other around. It was especially fun playing in the cotton and bean trailers that were usually there as well.

I happened to be by myself on this particular day. When I arrived, I saw the most wonderful thing. There it was! A trailer full of fresh soybeans, waiting for me to jump in and play around in. Being able to jump down in those beans and swim around in them, especially in a big trailer that is full, is like having this huge playground all to yourself. I didn't have to share it with anyone or sit in a line to get my turn. It was just me and the beans, and I had it all to myself. I would climb up to the top of the trailer, jumping into my pool of beans, dozens of times. I would lie there, swimming in them like I was in the biggest, city swimming pool you could imagine.

Just like in water, pulling your arms and moving your legs through those millions of beans, it could tire you out very quickly. I was having so much fun, but it didn't take long to wear myself out. I found myself stuck in the middle, sinking down and struggling to keep my head above the beans so I could breathe. The weight of the beans just kept pushing me down toward the bottom. I would reach my arm up as far as I could to try to clear the beans away to get some air. They would fill back in faster than any air was getting in. I had beans jammed up my nose too, so the only way I could breathe was to open my mouth. The more I struggled to get out, the farther down I sank. I was sinking in a quicksand made of soybeans.

I couldn't yell or scream out in any way. If I opened my mouth at all to yell for help, the beans would just come pouring in and start choking me. I remember getting really weak, thinking to myself, 'this just might be it for me.' But for some reason, I wasn't filled with panic.

The last thing I could remember was lying there buried in those beans, and hearing this faint voice. It was calling my name in a slow, drawn out manner, over and over, "Bennn'-ny... Bennn'-ny… Bennn'-ny." It was a reassuring, gentle voice, and it made me feel at peace about my dilemma.

The next thing I remembered, I woke up to an ambulance beside me, with an oxygen mask over my nose and mouth. Dr. Thombs from town was telling me to take slow, deep breaths. Daddy and mama were right there too when I woke up.

Mama said, "Son, you scared the living daylights out of us," and was very understanding about the whole thing.

But, daddy admonished, "Boy, I got enough people to worry about without you getting into a whole bunch of trouble with beans!"

I heard mama thanking our neighbors the Wilsons, and Dr. Thombs, for what they had done. They had probably saved my life. Mama knew I usually told her if I was going very far from the house. My bike was still there, but I had been gone for several hours. It was getting late, and she was getting worried. Mama asked Jack if he had seen me, but Jack just shook his head. She began calling out my name, making her way down to check at the barn. She knew it was a favorite place to play. Mama had been looking all around the barn when she stopped Mr. Wilson and his wife Martha who were driving by. They told mama they didn't see me while driving down the road. The Wilson's joined the search and they all began calling out my name.

Mama knew we loved playing in the trailers and asked Mr. Wilson to check them. He climbed up and down several trailers peeking in for any sight of me. Finally, in one full of soybeans, he saw part of a shoe sticking out of the beans. He yelled, "I think he's in here," and he began to dig me out while his wife ran to the house and called for help. They told me that when they got me out, I was barely breathing and a little shade of blue.

I don't know how much longer I would have lasted if the Wilsons hadn't come by. Dr. Thombs told me I had passed out and almost suffocated, and claimed it was a miracle that I survived. They jokingly said they had gotten enough beans out of my nose, ears, and other places we don't want to mention, that they could have started an entire crop of soybeans.

For years, the voice I heard calling my name, while lying lifeless in the bottom of that trailer would haunt me, but I never mentioned it to anyone.

What had happened with me and the bean trailer, eventually had gotten around town. Mama, for a long time after the incident, would often stop me and playfully pull down hard on my ears. It would make me holler and think my ear was going to come off my head. Pretending to search intensely in my ear, she would exclaim, "We better check to make sure no bean stalks are growing down in there!" Thank goodness, none did!

From that time forward, the neighbors and some people around town would see me, and with a little snicker say, "How's it going, Beanie boy?"

So, the name just stuck, and I kinda liked being famous!

CHAPTER TWO
The Black Veil

We lived in mostly flat country. One could see for miles in any direction. It was the flatlands of northeast Arkansas, and we lived about two miles outside of the city limits. If you drove out of our town in any direction, there was nothing but cotton or bean fields. It was like the Lord Himself took streets and buildings and then dropped them right in the middle of nothing but farming fields. There wasn't much to see on either side of the highway out toward our house, except those fields of cotton or soybeans, with an occasional house or barn.

We lived in an old farmhouse that had been there for years, a little ways down a dirt road off the highway that went toward Dyess. It wouldn't take long to get back to town, maybe forty minutes walking time I suppose. Plus, it was a paved highway all the way back to town, once you got off our little dirt road that connected to the highway.

The small river in our town was very important to us, even though it was just a rain drop compared to that monster, the Mississippi. One branch of the river that ran through our town, curved all the way back out toward our house. Incidentally, the river's name was actually called "Little River", just like our town. Our little bank in town was called River Town Bank. I never had much experience with a bank and figured they were something made by rich people, so they would have a place to put all their money. I figured C.J. Potter, dad's boss, had a lot of money made off the sharecroppers saved up in that bank. He lived in a huge nice brick home, with water fountains, a swimming pool and this huge circle drive that went in front of his house. He had a maid's place to stay out back and hired people to tend to his house and his yard. His residence took up almost an entire city block. I was amazed every time I got to see it on the few times I went with dad to visit Mr. Potter about something at his home. I usually played outside and thought it was grand. I figured he must be a millionaire! I swore to myself, that one day, I was going to make a lot of money, come back and put it in that very bank, no matter where I might live at the time and build a house like Mr. Potter's as close to him as I could.

But for now, I thought I would be satisfied if someone would take a little money from that bank, and spend it on fixing the gravel road that led to our house. I didn't think that would be asking for much. The road would often be more dirt than an actual gravel road. There would only be a speck of gravel here and there, and the dirt always overtook the gravel eventually, especially when the road didn't get some regular maintenance. It would get so muddy when it rained, that cars would get stuck or slide off the road into the ditch. The county did grade it once in a while to smooth out the big ruts caused by all the tractors and farm machines coming and going.

Once in a while, after all the farmers pleaded with the county, they would bring loads of gravel out in some big dump trucks. I liked watching them when they would come and drop their huge loads of new gravel. The truck driver would raise the bed so high into the air to get the gravel to slide out, that I often thought the truck might flip right over backwards. It was one of my favorite things to watch.

There was this black layer of dirt just under the topsoil around our parts that we called gumbo. During heavy rains, if we managed to get much of this gumbo on our shoes, it would gather in clumps like drying cement on our feet. We would have to stomp, scrape and beat if off with whatever we had handy to get this clumpy, black, sticky stuff off. Dad informed me that the stuff was actually what geologists call a type of clay, which is mostly composed of water and that is why it was so sticky. During long dry spells, if the topsoil wore off, gumbo would get exposed to the top. As a result, the clay would dry out and cracks would form these zigzag lines. That made the land look like a giant, jigsaw puzzle. It was a total nuisance and was just something that we had to deal with constantly.

I heard that people down in Louisiana named a food after that black clay and they called it "Gumbo". I hoped it tasted better than our dirt! I think it was years before I ever had the hankering to try their 'gumbo', even when I got the chance!

The dirt road made a fork right at our old farmhouse. There were only a few houses past where we lived. The left fork of the road went right by the barn and on a little farther until it dead ended at a cotton field. That direction was where the Wilsons and the Handleys also lived. Both families were some of the sharecropper tenants that dad looked over as farm manager for C.J. Potter. Dad really liked the Wilsons. They were very hard workers and were great stewards of the land. They would visit us sometimes and Martha Wilson would on occasion drop off my favorite treat, a homemade cherry pie. She was known for that famous cherry pie. She sold it to the local cafe in town to earn a little extra money, so I was lucky to get it for free. Besides, I didn't get to eat at that cafe very often anyway.

On the other hand, I often heard dad complain about Mr. Handley for one reason or another, like not taking care of the farm equipment or always complaining to dad about something around the farm, or how he wasn't being treated right. Dad pretty much told me he just tolerated Mr. Handley as best he could, since the man had a family to feed.

The other fork to the right went about half a mile, all the way down to a branch of the river where teenagers loved to hang out. It was truly a beautiful spot. It was far away from town, so there were no lights, no noise at all, except for the constant chirping of crickets, frogs and creatures of the night. On a clear, starry night, it was a great place to sit on the hood of a car and watch for falling stars. This made it an ideal spot for teens to come to and especially for guys that had a car and perhaps a girlfriend.

Donny Hobson was telling me that if you were there with a girl and saw a falling star, she was obligated to give you a kiss. Donny was a few grades ahead of me in school and was always talking about girls, "Girls this and girls that!" He would tell us about how all the girls loved him. How he was a real ladies' man and that the Black Veil, as this spot was called, was his good luck charm and always worked to his advantage.

That is all Donny ever talked about. If I started talking about baseball, he would interrupt me, only to tell me about some girl that he claimed was crazy about him. I think he spent half his life down there at the Black Veil. He never talked about baseball, hunting, or fishing. At the time I thought he must have lived an awfully miserable life.

This fork of the road went just past an old abandoned house that had not been lived in for many years and was in the stage of falling down. The road continued for a few more yards and then ended beside this huge oak tree, right by the river bank. That tree was so huge, I figured it had to be at least a hundred years old.

Once when I happened to be there with some other kids from around the farm, we held hands in a big circle to see how many of us it took to go around the tree. It took six of us kids to accomplish the task. Sometimes we would make a game of it, while still holding hands, to start by walking slowly around the tree, then getting faster and faster, to see how long and how fast we could go, without breaking up the circle. It was quite exhilarating, as we would gain as much speed as possible before someone would fall, or get dragged in the dirt. On occasion, someone might get pulled into the tree and accounted for a few bruises from time to time, but it was worth the fun of doing it.

I always noticed these initials that had been carved into that ancient bark. The carvings looked to be pretty old, at least a few years or so, but you could still make them out. I figured whoever carved those initials, they might be thinking of it as a ledger of their existence, knowing that the tree with their initials in it, would still be there way after they were gone. From playing our little game and being there often, I had come to memorize those three sets of letters; RT, FH and JM, and at the time never gave them much thought.

I often overheard adults talking about the Black Veil and how they thought it was cursed. It was a known fact that on two different occasions, a young boy drowned trying to swim across the river at that exact place. If you could swim across at that spot, once you were on the other side, it would only take a few minutes to get into town. It saved a lot of time walking once you got through a little patch of woods on the other side. So folks often used this spot as a natural shortcut.

I later came to learn the names of the two boys that had drowned, trying to swim across the river at the Black Veil. Their names were Frank Hardin and Roy Thomas and both were mere teenagers. Dad knew both families and the Thomas family in particular.

He told me the story of how Roy's mother had asked him to take the shortcut to town across the river to buy something in town that she needed. It had recently rained heavily and the river was very high. The story goes that Roy made it about half way across the river, but getting tired, realizing he couldn't make it all the way, decided to turn back. With his mama waving him back from the bank, he got close enough for her to stretch out a tree branch for him to grab onto, but his grip on the end of the stick began to slip. She managed to grab hold of his long hair for a second before she watched him being carried away with the swift current and drown.

Dad told me that RT was the initials for Roy Thomas that had been carved into the tree after he drowned. He said that the other initials, FH, were for Frank Hardin, the other boy that had drowned at a later time, in a separate incident. He said it was the Thomas family who had once lived in the now old, decrepit house, there by the river.

Being haunted by the memory of their son's drowning, the family, not long after, moved farther north to a little town up in the hill country called Imboden. After that, no one else ever moved into that house. Dad instructed me to never go swimming in the river there and especially after it had rained. I think he knew after hearing all the stories told about it, he didn't have to worry too much about me doing that. With the tragedy of the two young boys drowning, it certainly didn't take any convincing. I might go down there to play or fish sometime, but I obeyed my dad and would not get in the water to swim.

There had even been a time or two of folk having too much to drink, who had driven right on over the bank of the river and into the water itself. A couple of posts and fencing was put up because of that happening but the fence usually stayed torn down after a while and nobody would fix it. I am sure if this magnificent old tree could talk, I could only imagine how many stories it would have to tell.

Another such story was how this place at the river got its name, the Black Veil, not long after the two boys had drowned there. It was said to be based on a tale about a young couple that had just gotten married and had left the wedding ceremony on their way to their honeymoon. The story goes that they were driving on a very dark night, after a heavy rain. They had gotten lost and were driving down this same road by our house, took that right fork, and continued on past the big oak tree, and drove straight into the river. The water again had been rising fast and had a lot of fast moving current. The car was quickly carried down the river in the strong current until it slammed into a curve of the river bank, coming to a stop. All the while, her new husband who managed to escape was trying to get to her, but only the top of the car was visible when he got to it. He was eventually able to get to her side of the vehicle but his young new bride was gone, somewhere drowned in the river.

It was said that her body was never found. People say that right after that, the initials JM suddenly appeared, and it was the girl's spirit who came back and carved her own initials into the oak tree. Rumor has it that on certain nights, when the moon is just right, a ghostly female figure can be seen in a flowing, white dress on the other side of the bank wearing a long black veil, holding her arms out, waving and crying out, pleading, "Come... Save Me... Please Come... Save Me... Save Me... Please!"

I never really believed the tale about the woman seen at the river. However, it still gave me a spooky, eerie feeling whenever I would hear that story told again or if I happened to be down there, seeing those carved initials, JM. On nights when the moon is full, it is said that one can hear all kinds of strange sounds down at the river, and one in particular around midnight, that sounds like the voice of that young woman crying out for help.

When I first asked my dad about that story after the first time I heard it, he replied,

"That sound that people say they hear down there is only a bunch of coyotes howling. The whole thing is an old wives' tale that keeps getting told over and over for the fun of it." I asked him about the JM initials on the tree and how some said it was for the name of the bride that drowned. He said no one ever figured out whose those were but certainly it wasn't done by any ghost!

I believed dad, but that still never gave me much comfort. If you were there after it got dark, combined with the whistling noises of the wind blowing through the trees, and the various animal sounds, it was always very unsettling. I knew that I didn't want to be around that place after the sun went down, and certainly not by myself.

I never liked thinking about the story of the young bride and how the Black Veil got its name, whether it was true or not. Whenever I heard that story being told again or I thought about it very much, I couldn't help but think about that helpless bride crashing into that raging current. I would visualize this beautiful young woman, trapped inside the car with her terrified face pressed against the window, screaming, trying to break free, with her in the car being carried by the current on down the river. I could see her lifeless body floating face down in the river with the current, until it slowly sank down into the dark depths of the water to never be seen again. All occurring in the still of the night, as the river claimed the woman as one of its own.

Then I imagined seeing her spirit re-appearing as a ghost on the other side of the river, pleading over and over to come save her, knowing it was too late!

The image of that event, whenever I was reminded of it, whether an old wives' tale or not, downright could keep me awake all night, and oftentimes;

It did!

CHAPTER THREE
Jack's Big Prize

Our little town was about fifty miles from the big city of Memphis, Tennessee, and I only remember going there a few times. On occasion when we did, I will never forget being awed by seeing the huge Mississippi River when it came into view. I would either peek my head out the window or in the cold winter time, I would press my face close up against the glass of the window, to get as much of a first-hand experience as possible to partake of its grandeur. It was something scary in one aspect but then so magnificent, a thing to be admired at the same time. It made me feel so small and insignificant in comparison to its immense presence. That big Mississippi River resembled more like something that was alive, that breathed, in constant motion and not just a thing of nature.

Halfway across the bridge was a sign that said you were leaving Arkansas and entering Tennessee. That always fascinated me that you left one state and entered another in the middle of a river. The halfway point was at the highest elevation of the bridge above the water. Especially at this highest spot, the muddy water below looked to be miles beneath me and felt that you were in a very precarious position. You began to wonder, what is holding all this up, this high in the sky, supporting hundreds of trucks and cars, and heck, the massive bridge itself. The steep banks and fast moving current below that mighty bridge always added a little more fear while on that bridge. I figured this must be what it would feel like to be in an airplane for the first time, peering at the sites so far below. I even had some inquisitive yet somewhat morbid thoughts, like how long would it take to fall from the bridge and then feel my helpless body hit that water below. That's when I suddenly thought of seeing Tarzan, who I remembered seeing on a Saturday TV show, jump off a very tall bridge like this one, except that bridge was in New York City, and of course, being Tarzan he survived unhurt. In the movie, it seemed like he was diving through the air forever, because it was so far down to the river below. For some reason, I always played that image of Tarzan diving off the bridge in my head, whenever we traveled over the gigantic bridge going to Memphis.

One time we had a very special occasion to go to Memphis, from which broadcast the three main TV stations we watched. Jonesboro, Arkansas, not far from our town, did have this one station, but we could only get it for a short period of time, under certain weather conditions. That channel was such a bad, snowy picture most of the time it usually wasn't worth straining our eyeballs trying to watch it. Most of our favorite shows were on channel three from Memphis. Jack and I were ardent watchers of afterschool TV shows, and never missed an episode of a show that was shown live from Memphis called The Happy Bill Hiller Show. Since their audience was kids, it started around four p.m. on weekdays, when they knew kids were just getting home from school.

It was a Friday, and Jack and I had not been home very long from school. We were so happy the school week was over and really enjoying playing outside, that we simply lost track of time. Jack suddenly in panic exclaimed, "I forgot today is when Happy Bill picks this week's lucky prize winner." We knew we didn't want to miss that, so we rushed into the house and went straight to the TV.

Mama was in the kitchen, and being totally ignored by us, exclaimed, "Well, y'all just go ahead, plop yourselves down and pretend you don't have a mama, as that television is more important than saying hi to your mama."

Not wanting to hurt her feelings, I answered, "We are sorry mama, but today is Friday when Happy Bill has the drawing, and you know we never like missing that."

She answered, "Oh that's right. Well, since we have gone to the trouble of sending in what seems like a hundred postcards with Jack's name on it, y'all might as well watch for the drawing of the winner."

It was always Jack's name we put on the postcard we sent in. I didn't mind anyway as we figured for some reason you had a better chance of winning if all the cards had the same name on them.

Mama, earlier in the afternoon, had been watching parts of one of those new daytime shows she said they called a soap opera on a different station. She rarely had time to just sit down and watch a show from beginning to end. She always had too many things to do but she wasn't watching anything now.

I had to turn the knob on the TV to get tuned to the channel three station that Happy Bill was broadcast on. When I turned the TV knob, it fell off onto the floor and I was panicking, trying to get it put back on properly. When I finally got the dial back on and tuned to the right station, it was a very bad picture, but Jack could hear the familiar Happy Bill intro song they always play at the beginning of the show.

Jack was very impatient and demanded, "Bean, hurry and get the station to come in better; we can't watch it like that, and the sound comes and goes."

So I went to turning and cranking those "rabbit ears" around in all kinds of directions, trying to get the best picture. One "rabbit ear" was broken and half of it was hanging down, but in spite of all my technical troubles, I somehow by a miracle, finally got a decent enough picture. I got it fixed just in time to hear Happy Bill say he was about to reveal what the prize was this week and to be sure and stay tuned for the drawing later in the show, to reveal the name of that one lucky winner. Usually toward the end, he would pick one card from the huge barrel full from all the cards that kids sent in with their names on them. Happy Bill would remind the audience that if their name was called, they had to call into the show during the commercial break to the phone number on the screen to claim the prize, or he would draw another name.

Happy Bill said this week's winner will receive a Superman costume, and get a tour of the studio with their parents. We always knew our chance of winning was slim, but it was always fun to listen to what name he would call out that he drew and to know where the winner was from. Every now and then, it would be a kid from a town not too far from us. We both loved the TV show Superman and probably never missed an episode. A superman costume sounded great but a visit to the studio would be unbelievable.

It finally got toward the end of the show, and it was time for the drawing and calling out the name of the winner. Bill plunged his hand into the huge jar of postcards, shuffled them around some, finally said, "I got it," and held up a card in front of the camera. He paused, and with anticipation in his voice said, "This week's lucky winner is... Jack Barnes from Little River, Arkansas. Jack, you or someone from your household needs to call before we come back from the upcoming commercial break to claim your prize."

Jack exploded in celebration, running around the room like Road Runner from the cartoon, and was jumping up and down in the air, off the couch shouting, "I won! I won! I won!"

Mama heard the commotion, and shouted out, "What in tarnation's going on in there?"

I went and grabbed mama by the hand to get her to the television to see for herself as quickly as possible. Mama was in total shock and disbelief for a moment, seeing Jack's name on the TV screen. We all three stood within inches of that television screen, reading the words over and over, repeating the words in near unison; "THIS WEEK'S WINNER, JACK BARNES, FROM LITTLE RIVER, ARKANSAS."

Mama was nervous and shaking, dialing the phone number on the screen to get all the details. I think she was more excited that something like this could happen than Jack and me. Mama wrote down all the details about the trip to the studio in Memphis. We were actually going to go to a real, live television studio. A time was set up for us to make the trip to the studio to claim Jack's prize, and get a tour of the TV setting. When dad got home, and we told him Jack was on TV, he couldn't believe it either. He thought we were pulling his leg, until mama assured him it was all true. I will never forget her telling daddy, "Yep, Jack's name was right there on that TV screen, as big as day. I still can't believe it."

The only thing dad said, knowing about sending in so many postcards with Jack's name on them was, "I guess it just shows you that persistence does pay off."

Getting to visit a real, live TV studio was one of the best trips we ever took as a family, and Jack got to feel like a TV star. No vacation ever matched the raw excitement of that experience. We got to meet Happy Bill, the host of the show for a few minutes, his puppet L'il Mo, and some other characters on the show. Of course, we kids had never experienced anything like that, and neither had mama or dad. I think they enjoyed it as much as Jack and I did. It was something that was so foreign and so far removed from those cotton fields we might as well have gone to Mars.

It was a very long time after that, before we ever missed another Happy Bill Hiller Show. From then on, whenever we had an occasion to cross that big Mississippi River, I more often than not, thought of that trip to visit the television studio, meeting all the stars of that show, and not nearly as much about Tarzan jumping off that bridge.

CHAPTER FOUR
What's In A Bale?

All the land around us was pure Mississippi River delta country. Heavy rains would often cause the river to swell and overrun its banks, depositing silt and other nutrients into the soil, creating rich farmland, thanks to thousands of years of the Big Old Muddy's meandering. So naturally, most folks in this part of the country were farmers of some sort or the other, mostly growing cotton or soybeans.

Being a kid, I didn't exactly know what people did with soybeans, but I sure knew a bunch about cotton. For one thing, I never heard of anybody wearing a shirt or a pair of pants made out of beans. Cotton was downright practical and as far as I knew, everybody had to have clothes to wear.

The land was rotated with growing soybeans and cotton for the most part. I learned later in life that this rotation preserved the soil and the nutrients in the soil for growing the best harvest of crops, without hurting the soil. Some of the fields would be planted with beans, others with cotton, and the farmers would switch that around every so often. Each would be grown at the same time, only in a different field.

But dad loved to grow cotton. It was his thing. I would always have so much fun playing in those huge trailers full of the white, fluffy pickings, but I would never be caught again playing in one full of beans; no sir. Besides, the beans were not comfortable to lie in like cotton. I don't think I ever slept on a bed that was as comfortable as a big pile of cotton. I loved the smell of fresh picked cotton loaded in a trailer. I would climb up to the top corner of a trailer, jump off and land in that big fluffy soft, pile of whiteness, and just keep doing it over and over again. It was the best fun a kid on a farm could ever have. I never had to worry about getting hurt and Mama didn't mind

21

my playground being one of cotton, as long as it kept me out of the bean trailers. When I got tired of jumping over and over in the cotton, I would lie there, hands propped under my head snuggled in comfort, staring up at the blue sky, thinking how great life was. Being sunken down in the cotton below the top of the trailer, the rest of the world simply disappeared. The sides of the trailer above me formed a barrier that shielded me from any distraction the outside had to offer. It created my own little isolated world of only me, the sky above and my thoughts. I could still get a peek of that world out of the top of the trailer, looking down on all around me when I wanted to. But more often than not, I would fall asleep in such tranquil comfort. I felt as though I could lie there forever in a house that was so pure and clean.

I always hated it when daddy's hands took the trailers away to the gin. It was like they were taking away my best friend. A trailer full of cotton was like a giant free toy that offered fun that I never grew tired of. I would rather give up some old toy I got for Christmas, than see the last of the cotton trailers taken to the gin. But I also knew what those trailers meant to my family and the other farmers. It would bring the money everyone needed to provide for their families. So, of course, I was very happy about that, but I got to use those same trailers for my own free playground in the meantime.

Sometimes I overheard farmers talking about bales of cotton when getting it to the gin. People in other parts of the country were used to seeing bales of hay rather than seeing actual bales of cotton. They might see the hay bales lying out in the fields all winter long, however, cotton was not like that. We planted it, grew it, chopped it, picked it, and finally got it to the gin as quickly as we could to have it ginned into those bales. We didn't leave cotton out in the weather any longer than we really had to because it could mold and rot under the wrong conditions, which meant a loss of money and perhaps one's own livelihood.

I considered a bale of cotton a thing of beauty; a piece of art. It had been transformed from that one little white boll I could hold in my hand, to this massive compressed giant that overshadowed anyone standing next to it. Going from hanging on a stalk in the field, to a perfectly shaped, giant square white bundle, was truly a thing to admire.

I always had wondered how much cotton went into making that one bale. I visualized lots of pickers in the field putting in all that hard back-breaking work and wondered how many days of picking it would take to produce that single bale.

But my dad was the expert, and when he dropped by the house for a few minutes one afternoon, knowing that he had that knowledge, I asked him that exact question. He told me he hasn't thought about a bale in that way in a long time, only about the finished product. He said he had figured on it at one time but hadn't thought about it until I brought it up. He stood there for a minute and put his hand under his chin gently rubbing it, like I had really put him in some deep thought.

He finally answered, "Hmm, well let's see, I would have to figure out how many pickers it took; then how many total hours they all spent picking that went into getting enough cotton to end up as a bale after ginning all the bad stuff out and seed out. Now remember, all the stems, seed bolls and other stuff that got in people's sacks, even dirt, while picking, would have to be removed from the cotton at the gin."

With an impressed look on his face by my question, he added, "Benny, you ask the darndest questions sometimes, but they are really good questions. How in the world do you think of these things? I will have to do some figuring on it. Maybe check some old notes on that one though and get back to ya!"

I was actually proud that I could tell dad thought I had asked such a smart question. Then I followed up with one more inquiry. "Dad, I got one more question."

"Okay, Bean...," in somewhat of a weary tone and by him using my nickname, I knew I was about to reach the end of my being the inquisitor for the day. He continued, "What's your question now?"

"Well, how much cotton exactly is in each bale, like how much does it weigh?"

Now I could tell this time I had asked something he would have a quick answer for and he was thinking he could get this inquisition over with.

The way he put it, he said, "A bale of cotton is several feet wide, about as tall as a man, and each weighs around 500 to 600 pounds."

Then I asked, "Well, why isn't it exactly the same weight for every bale?"

"You see, Bean it's because..." And, after pausing and then in a little bit of frustration added, "Right now, I got something pressing I need to go do and I'll tell ya about that later, okay? But hey, I just thought of a picture you may not have seen of one proud bale from the tenants around here, you want to see it?"

He reached into his billfold, took out an old worn out picture with a big crease down one side of it. It was a picture someone had taken of him and C.J. Potter, the land owner whom dad was the farm manager for, standing next to a beautiful white bale of cotton. It was all wrapped in a symmetrical, cross work patch of strings, around the bale, from top to bottom. On the front of the bale was a handwritten sign, with faded words which I slowly was trying to make out.

Dad said, "This picture is getting old and worn. The words on the sign are getting hard to read but I remember exactly what they say," and he began to read them:

Winner,
First bale grown in Dyess
Mississippi County

Producer, C.J. Potter
Farm manager, Bill Barnes
DP Variety 15
Weight 672 lbs

He was holding the picture, and as I careened my neck over to see it, I could hear the pride in his voice as he read those words. It was a big deal to get the first bale ginned in the county and he said the farmer's co-op or some such group usually had a five hundred dollar prize reward for whoever got the first bale ginned. He went on to say if everything worked out right, our farmland could sometimes produce around two bales per acre. He said that is really good, compared to a lot of other farming communities.

Getting a little impatient, he exclaimed, "Benny, I got to go check on something with a tractor that Mr. Wilson told me about. He said the Pto or something was messing up and I told him I was heading over to check that out. We'll have to finish this cotton lesson later son."

I understood that I was keeping him from something he needed to get done and was apologizing for asking so many questions. Dad told me, "No son, don't worry about it. I am glad that you take interest in what goes on with my work and how we make a living. The more you understand about it, the more you will appreciate what it takes to make it in this world as you get older. And don't ever stop asking questions!"

I was again feeling pride in that although I'm sure it nagged him a little with all the stuff I kept asking him about, and taking time out to talk to me, he also was proud of me for being interested in what he did.

Then dad happily added, "Bean, want to ride over with me to the Wilsons to take a look at that tractor, that is, if you don't have something else more pressing to do?"

With a big smile coming over me, without hesitation I answered, "You betcha dad. Let's go!"

Dad instructed, "Well run in and tell your mama you're coming with me to go see the Wilsons about something and that I'll have you back before supper."

I ran in the house, told mama what dad said and she asked, "Well, what about Jack? He's out back playing by himself. He will probably want to go too."

I wanted this time with dad all by myself. Jack was usually always there around dad too every time I was, and I didn't want anything spoiling this chance to be just dad and me.

I replied, "Dad said to tell you we needed to get going and couldn't waste any more time and Jack could go some other time."

I couldn't believe the words coming out of my mouth. I just made up a complete, awful lie to tell my mama. How could I have done that, especially to a parent. I was taught to never lie; always tell the truth. But then I thought of being with dad all by myself and thought, "One little white lie ain't gonna hurt nobody!"

Then as I hopped in the truck with dad, of all things, he said, "I guess we could let Jack go too if he wanted."

I thought, huh oh, now I am in big trouble. But I couldn't believe how quickly I responded, "No, I asked Jack if he wanted to go with us and he said he was having fun playing with the rabbits and wanted to stay home."

Now I went and did it again. I was telling another huge lie. I thought, oh no, I am becoming a regular lying machine. I was telling so many lies I was thinking that was too much for even my baptism to cover! But I got to figuring about it, as I took my seat in dad's truck, and I began to feel much better justifying my getting to spend time alone with dad. I figured I could do a little extra praying that night and maybe that would make up for it!

As dad and I were heading down the dirt road, raising a trail of dust on that dry day, I looked back and saw Jack poking his head up spotting us in dad's truck, mosey on down the road. I ducked down low in my seat, hoping he wouldn't see me. Then I wondered if I didn't want to be seen with dad because I didn't want Jack to feel left behind or was I hiding to keep me out of trouble for finding out all the lies I told? I thought, with all this extra time I'll be spending praying at bedtime for my constant sin of lying today, it's going to be a long night!

A little later that month at school, around the peak of cotton picking time, my teacher gave every student the assignment of finding out how many and what things could be made out of only one single bale of cotton. I couldn't believe she was giving out something I looked forward to doing. This caused a big smile to come over my face and I think my classmates noticed I was overjoyed to get the assignment. They were all giving me a look as to why homework could possibly make a person so happy. I was very interested in learning the answer, since this was my dad's livelihood and we had recently talked about that very subject. I knew this was exactly the kind of homework assignment I couldn't wait to get started on. I thought that instead of hounding dad with **so** many questions this time, I would study up on the subject and impress him with my learning as well as my teacher with all my vast new found knowledge. I proceeded to visit the school library to find a book that would help me find all the answers I was looking for.

The lady in charge that day was Mrs. Tuggles. As I approached her, in a quiet voice, I politely requested, "I need to find a book that tells me everything about things made from cotton."

Then with a little chuckle, she replied, "Bean, I thought you would be more interested only in soybeans?"

Of course, I knew exactly why she said that. I now began to think that the bean trailer incident was going to follow me for the rest of my life. I figured if I was elected President of the United States one day, the very first question some news reporter would ask me would be about that dang bean trailer.

But I nicely answered Mrs. Tuggles, "No mam, I have an assignment from my teacher to find out what things are made from cotton and its many uses. I know clothes are made out of it, but that is about all I know."

Mrs. Tuggles told me she would be glad to help me and said she hoped I didn't mind her bringing that up about the beans. I assured her, "No, that's okay. I am totally used to that by now. The worst part, is having to explain to people that don't know the story when they ask me... How did you get the nickname Bean? Then I have to go into the whole event that happened and I get kind of tired telling the same thing over and over. Sometimes I think some people already generally know what happened, they ask the question to hear me tell the story with a personal touch."

She went on explaining, "Well look at it this way. At least you're known for something around town and it had a happy ending that makes a good story to tell. People always love good stories, especially the ones with happy endings. That's one reason I work in the library. I love stories and there are millions of them in here. Maybe one day, it will be a story that you will get to tell to a million people. Now wouldn't that be something?"

I replied in a short answer, "I guess so," without really understanding exactly what she meant by that but I thought it was an interesting comment.

She proceeded to help me find the section on agriculture. I thanked her and I kept looking until I found this book that looked to be all about cotton. My eyes began to scan through the pages and I found a section dealing with products made from cotton. I couldn't wait to get home and start on the assignment.

Later that day at home, as I began to see how many things came from cotton, I was simply amazed. I almost couldn't believe it. I read that out of only one single bale, they could make thousands of jeans, shirts, towels, diapers, socks; not to mention over three hundred thousand, one hundred dollar bills.

Who ever knew that cotton was put into dollar bills? I sure didn't. It puzzled me why the book mentioned the bills in the one hundred dollar denomination. One thing I knew for sure was that few folks around Little River had ever seen one of those bills that large. I sure doubted if I would see one myself anytime soon, not one that belonged to me anyway.

The irony of this newly found knowledge was that we were surrounded by cotton fields, growing millions of dollars' worth of hundred dollar bills, maybe even billions, but it didn't do me any good. Being the kid that I was, I wished I could get lucky, find and pick one single, hundred dollar bill out of our entire crop. I figured that would last me for years, especially since I was lucky to have a single quarter in my pocket if anything at all.

Back then I could do quite a bit though, with only one quarter. I was set for getting a lot of stuff I might want or do on any given day. I could go see a movie about a talking mule at the Grand Theater in town, and still have enough left to buy a coke for six cents and a five cent bag of popcorn.

Making money was a hard thing to do, especially if you were a kid. I could chop cotton early in the summer, when I got old enough for mama and daddy to trust me to not chop down half the cotton patch, and believed I could tell the difference between the weeds and the cotton. Then in the fall, kids could pick cotton on the days they were out of school. At two or three cents a pound, a person would only get paid two or three dollars and that's if you picked a hundred pounds. Most young kids like myself couldn't pick anywhere near that much, and picking would use up an entire Saturday. Plus, you had to get up at the break of dawn.

Dragging a heavy canvas sack down those never-ending, long rows of white cotton was the hottest, hard work I can ever remember doing in my life. The stalks were taller than me, and working my way through them felt like I was in a boxing match with kangaroos. By the end of the day, I looked like I had been beaten and it was all from the sharp, thorny bolls hitting and scratching me as I reached in and around those tall stalks, which resembled little trees to me.

My little brother Jack and I were not very good at picking cotton since we were so young and small. Dad would make us do it for a little bit at times, to learn about hard work, as he put it. Of course, being bad at it, partly by choice, we could weasel our way out of the chore most of the time. We were always so happy that we didn't have to do it very often, but of course daddy knew we were not grown into the job just yet. He would pay us our wages, maybe a dime, pat us on the head, and tell us, "job well done."

I eventually got my assignment on cotton finished, and I turned in my list of how many things were made from those little white picked bolls. When my teacher read my list, she turned to me and seemingly impressed, stated,

"Not bad for somebody that only knows about beans!"

CHAPTER FIVE
Real Zombies Don't Wear Clothes

There were two things Jack and I could usually be found doing, fishing or playing baseball. When we weren't playing ball ourselves, we would try to find the games on the radio of our favorite major league team, the Saint Louis Cardinals. We would listen to the Cardinals as much as we could find games broadcast on the radio, usually out of a Memphis radio station.

Decades later I could still remember the usual batting order of the Cardinals in the mid-sixties better than I knew the alphabet. Who could forget the great pitching they had and some who I figured might be in the Hall Of Fame one day. Then there was Harry Caray that every kid loved to hear call the games on the radio. I would pretend I was Caray and imitate his way of calling home runs over and over in my mind... "There she goes, way back, it might be, it could be, IT IS... A HOME RUN," as I visualized the ball sailing over the outfield fence and landing somewhere in the bleachers.

The Cardinals made it to the World Series two straight years in 1967 and 1968, after also having won it back in 1964 against none other than the New York Yankees. Back in those days, they played a lot of major league games during the day. I still can remember everyone walking around the school yard during those September months, with a radio on their shoulder, trying to catch the game during school breaks. It wasn't unheard of for some teachers to be playing the radio during class, with the World Series game on. It was that big of a deal.

At that time, the Cardinals were everything in sports to us, since they were the closest professional team to our little town. The Cardinals won it all in the '67 Series against the Boston Red Sox, but lost the Series to the Detroit Tigers the very next year in '68. Baseball was a big part of every kid's life, and if you asked any kid in our town what they hoped to be when they grew up, most would say they wanted to be a major league baseball player for the St. Louis Cardinals.

We could barely afford to buy baseballs and bats. The balls could get so bad and worn down to the core string inside, they sometimes looked like they would be more suited for knitting than for baseball. We would use broken bats all fixed with little nails and wrapped in tape until they fell apart. I remember using a bat that practically had no handle and all that was left was a little nub that I could hold in one hand.

There was nothing like getting hold of a spanking, new white baseball. You almost didn't want to mess up a new ball by playing with it. Anytime we could get a new one, we had a ritual we would go through. We would hold that beautiful, white thing in our hand, feeling how slick that brand new cowhide cover felt and admiring every single perfectly sewn stitch. We would hold it right up to our nose to get a whiff of that new ball smell. We would form a quiet, little circle and pass it around like the ball was holy water. We put the ceremony right up there with getting baptized in the church. We almost worshipped the ball for a bit before we could bring ourselves to put it to use. Then once we got down to business of playing baseball, we proceeded to beat the holy crap out of it, every time at bat.

At one point all our baseballs were getting in really bad shape and not very playable at all. I told my little brother that we needed to get a new one and scrounge up the money to buy one. We could get a brand new baseball from a couple of little stores in town for fifty cents. We had heard of some kids, going around collecting coke bottles to sell. So Jack knew what that meant. We would have to ride our bikes all the way to town, spending all day riding, looking for empty bottles.

My little brother Jack said he didn't feel like riding anymore, especially all the way to town and back. It was really hot and he had something else in mind to do.

"Beanie, don't you remember, they set up and turned on the irrigation in the cotton field a few days ago close to the house." Right then, I knew what he was getting at, as the water run-off from the cotton fields always made for a way to have some cool fun.

The irrigation pipes looked like something out of some space movie where aliens had these big walking machine weapons they were using to attack us earthlings, except the alien machines would shoot out lasers or maybe some electronic beam. The irrigation device had all these big pipes hooked together on these stands, with huge wheels that somehow would move around the fields spraying out big, long spouts of water for hundreds of feet. These contraptions could shoot out water that would outdo a fire truck. We knew we could count on having fun, playing in the irrigation ditches that watered the cotton fields. During long dry spells in early summer, it was a great way to cool off and have fun at the same time.

We always looked forward to the irrigation pipes being turned on. We would get muddy all over, slipping and sliding around the edge of the fields, but we had the most fun playing in the ditches along the roads and in between crops. It was our swimming pool. We could dive right in, swim as far as we wanted, as the ditches were long and seemed to never end. Of course, the water runoff was very dirty and muddy, but that didn't matter to us boys. Anything would be a relief from the hot, humid air. The times before when we played in the ditches, if we got tired, we just climbed out all muddy and filthy feeling like a million bucks and would head back home.

It didn't take long for Jack to talk me into joining him for having fun, playing around in the mud in the fields. Heck, we could go play baseball any old day. So off to the fields we went, jumping in and out of the ditches full of water, slipping and sliding in the mud all over the place. We were having a blast. A short time later, I suddenly got an idea for some more fun.

"Jack, I bet if I take some of this mud, put it all over myself with nothing but my underwear on, walk on out to the highway and stick my thumb out like hitching a ride, I bet folks will think I'm some kind of monster and drive off the road."

"Beanie, you're crazy! Besides, the mud will dry on your skin and cut off the air to your body and you might suffocate," Jack energetically exclaimed.

"Well maybe so, but it would be worth seeing the look on people's faces that drive by," I replied. I started stripping down to my underwear and got Jack to help pile the mud on my back where I couldn't reach, putting it on as thick as we could get it, until only the whites of my eyes were showing.

There was one thing I always understand about my little brother. He would take any dare and go even farther, and so he did with my proposal.

Jack said, "To do this right Beanie, you got to take off your underwear too and put mud over your butt and your you know what!"

"Now I know you're crazy," I emphatically answered. "I'm not taking my underwear off, especially in front of you."

Jack kept insisting the prank wouldn't go off as well if I didn't go all the way. After much chicken calling, I gave in and said, "Okay, I'll coat my whole body with mud on one condition!"

"What's that?" Jack asked.

"I'll do the whole thing naked if you will do it too," I replied.

Jack said no way at first but finally decided to go along with the fun. Of course, I knew Jack was one who would never back down from a challenge. I often used daring him in stuff, taking advantage of

Jack, getting him to do things I was too darn chicken to ever do myself.

With big extra, heaping coats of mud, as much as we could slap all over the both of us, we started heading toward the main highway which wasn't too far from where we were. As we slithered on our way, we were laughing so hard, we thought we were gonna shake the drying mud right off our skin. The dryer the mud got, the harder it got to walk, being wrapped up like a mummy. Also, the mud made it feel like we were carrying a hundred pounds on our bodies. As the mud dried, it pulled our skin so tight that it made us slump over with a hunch in our back. We could hardly bend our stiffened arms, so we had to hold them out, away from our bodies, causing us to walk funny. We didn't have to do much acting to walk like zombies. The heavy dried mud naturally had that effect on our bodies.

Finally, we got to the highway and with bent over bodies stiff from the mud, we were ready to give our prank a try. We were anxious to see what reaction we would get from folks driving by. We got right next to the road, sometimes sticking out our thumbs pretending we wanted a ride. Other times, reaching out to cars, we would hold our stiff arms straight out, waving 'em around like we figured zombies would do. We would make monster-like groaning noises, growling faces and zombie body gestures to any passing car.

Folks that came along, reacted in different ways. Some would go really slow with their jaws dropped wide open in dismay. They would almost come to a complete stop peering at us, trying to figure out what these silly kids were doing. Others would shake their heads, laughing a little, and we could hear them say, "Dang Crazy Kids." One car full of folks was laughing so hard they almost drove off the road, and we could hear 'em laughing until we couldn't see the car in the distance anymore.

This went on for about an hour or so, having so much fun, but we knew it was getting late and it was time to start heading back home. We were tired, thirsty, hungry, and not feeling very well. By now, the mud had gotten so stiff and hard on our skin it was really starting to get uncomfortable, and we figured we better start peeling it off. Well, the peeling wasn't so easy. The mud was stuck on our skin like some kind of dried paste. We could only scrape it off in little bits and pieces at a time with our fingernails.

We were slowly making our way down the road, scraping and peeling as we went. We finally got back to the ditch where the irrigation started and were so relieved to see that dirty water again. We jumped right in, and it didn't take very long to get the mud off. We never thought that a ditch full of muddy water could feel so clean and pure, but boy, it did! We had loads of fun and were finally 'clean' again at least by zombie standards and ready now to head on home. However, we had forgotten one little important thing.

"Beanie, where did we leave our clothes?" Jack asked in panic.

"Oh man, I don't remember, somewhere close to here, but the ditch all looks the same," I now nervously replied.

Real panic was starting to set in over both of us, so we took off running, totally naked, as fast as we could down the dirt road to get home. Every time we would get close to any house on the way, we would jump down into the ditch staying mostly immersed in the water, hoping not to draw much attention, until we got out of sight of that house.

We made it almost home, right to the bend in the dirt road in front of our house. That's when a truck with the Wilson boys, who lived on down the road, drove by and spotted us as we were trying to stay hidden, down low in the ditch. One of the Wilson boys was riding in the open back bed of the truck. He was leaning over the side, holding out our clothes with 'em flapping in the wind, proudly showing off what he knew belonged to us and shouted,

"We found these clothes up the road a little piece and figured they might belong to you boys, but we think we'll just keep 'em for a while." We could hear them laughing until they disappeared in the distance.

Once they were gone, in complete panic we ran to the back of the house and saw that there were some clothes mama had just put out on the clothesline drying in the sun. We didn't see mama and hoped she had gone inside for something. We thought this was our chance to not be spotted, so we grabbed up some clothes from the clothesline to wear. We put them on so fast we weren't sure whose clothes were whose.

About that time mama came back out. She stopped and stared at us in those clothes we had hurriedly put on. She knew the clothes weren't dry yet and also on the wrong person.

With a funny look on her face, she curiously asked, "Why in tarnation are y'all wearing each other's clothes and why are you both soaking wet like a couple of muskrats?"

We just smiled and innocently exclaimed, "We've just been playing down the road mama!"

Mama shook her head and sighed with a demonstrative, "Uh, huh, I bet!"

By supper time, Jack and I had changed into the proper clothes that belonged to each of us, but by now we were both starving to death. All that hard work, from our effort of having so much fun playing like zombies, had left us hungry.

Then, sitting down at the supper table, Jack for the second time asked mama to please pass the potatoes and he began to help himself to the biggest, heaping serving of those mashed potatoes I had ever seen him put on a plate.

Mama, with a little smirk remarked, "I didn't know zombies ate potatoes?"

Daddy heard what mama had called us and with the strangest look, peered over at her and calmly stated, "Belle, I've heard you call these boys lots of things before, but that's the first time I ever heard you call 'em zombies."

Jack and I innocently glanced at dad with a sideways look of our eyes and then looked back at each other, holding back subdued laughter with our mouths tightly closed. We leaned forward and tilted our head down to contain any outburst of laughter and simply grinned!

And, so did mama!

CHAPTER SIX
The House Of Potter

Dad was always on the go around the farm. I knew he didn't like having to sit in an office all day, which he never did anyway because his job required that he oversee every aspect of the farm. He hired field hands, managed the farm equipment, planted and harvested his own crops, and he accounted for every penny used to do those things. Every once in a while when his duties slowed down somewhat, he would let me ride with him in his truck around the fields. I loved the invigorating smell of the fresh overturned dirt in the springtime, seeing the black smoke of the tractor fumes, and especially noticing the smell of that smoke when you got close enough. The putt-putt sound of the tractor, echoing in the distance, sometimes would still be stuck in my head as I dozed off to sleep later at night. There are times when I think I can still hear that putt-putt sound today.

That Little Hand Of Mine

(a poem by the author)

When I was just a little lad
I remember all so well
The place of my beginnings
Of things that I will tell
I often rode with father
As we drove around the fields
We passed a tractor going slow
As we came around the hill
The cotton then grew tall like trees
It stood above my sight

Like clumps of snow upon a roof
In bowls so soft and white
He stopped the truck and we got out
The dirt it smelled so fine
He put a piece of cotton
In that little hand of mine
And dad would say we better leave
'Cause supper's on the stove
We climbed back in and headed home
Just ol dad and me
I know it now but didn't then
The love he had for me

I remember mama
Her apron always on
At home she stayed nowhere to go
Her work was never done
 She cleaned and cooked and sewed the clothes
And some she made by hand
When day was done and pa came home
I didn't understand
Not much we said, not much we did
I guess the day was done
I was put to bed as mama said
I'll see you in the morn
I fell asleep to quiet dreams
Of fields so white and fine
As I held onto that cotton
In that little hand of mine

Dad had this big cylinder fuel tank on the back of his truck with an attached pump, and he would often go out into the field delivering fuel to the various farm machinery. There was also a much bigger tank down at the barn, where tractors and machinery would fill up if they were working close by.

Sometimes Dad would have to leave the house during the night, as we would get word of someone trying to break the lock on the fuel tank down by the barn in order to steal the gas. Most farmers around us wouldn't steal other's equipment or necessary farming tools. That was considered like stealing a man's horse in the old days and it still held the same feelings today. Farming fuel was important and costly, just like a man's horse back then. The loss could mean a lot of money lost, that could go to other needed things.

One night, some kids from town snuck down to the barn and stole most of the fuel. The next day their dad found out about it. He made his boys come and apologize to my dad for stealing the fuel, and pay for the gas from their own pockets. Dad allowed them to do jobs around the farm to pay for any physical damages they may have caused while taking the fuel. Now I consider that a better method of restitution than a hanging, as would have been done over a horse in olden times.

Dad was the farm manager for C.J. Potter, who owned almost all the land around the town, and he oversaw the sharecroppers for Mr. Potter around where we lived. All of them, including us, leased several acres of land from Mr. Potter. A sharecropper would rent farm land, usually about forty acres, raise and sell the crops for money to live on and to make the lease payment to the landlord Mr. Potter. Most tenants would be allowed to live on the land in their own farmhouse, and some tenants might be provided with some of the equipment and tools to farm with. A contract for payment would have been worked out to settle things when harvest time came.

The more the landowner provided to the sharecropper, the bigger share of the ginned cotton he would get come picking time. The gin money that was paid for the baled cotton would go to the landlord first, and then in turn, he would pay the sharecropper according to the deal they had worked out together. It could be as much as half the money from the bales produced going to the landowner.

The landlord also got all the seed after ginning. The big risk for a sharecropping tenant family was that they might run up a lot of debt to the landowner for supplies and living expenses until harvest. Mr. Potter also owned the main grocery store, co-op and other stores in town, and would allow a certain amount of credit to the tenants. If a bad harvest came in the fall due to drought, flood, disease, or poor farming, there might be little profit. Consequently, very little money might be leftover for the tenant after paying the landlord money owed to him. The tenant might not see any money at all if things were bad enough. He would extend himself with more credit, hoping for a good harvest the next year if Mr. Potter allowed, and hopefully could catch up, and make enough money to live on.

Sometimes due to bad weather, or for being bad caretakers of the land, some tenants would never get out of debt. Consequently, the landowner would eventually be forced to evict them and start over with someone new. Sharecropping tenants took most of the risks when farming someone else's land. It was not an easy life. It consisted of long, drudging days in good and bad weather, three hundred sixty five days of a year. Few of these families were able to get out of debt or buy their own land, and during those years it seemed to be the way of life for most. It was just an accepted fact of living, if you were to live the life of a farmer.

I remember once when dad was called in to meet Mr. Potter at his office in town, he let me go with him. I was so proud anytime I would get to ride anywhere with dad. It was a most particularly hot, humid day as we headed into town. We rolled both truck windows all the way down, or else it would get too hot to breathe.

It was still so hot in the truck dad said, "Beanie, push open that little wing window to get more air flowing across here and point it this direction."

I pushed it open as far as it would go. I adjusted the angle just right, pointed it at me so the stiff wind would blow right across my face. I pushed my nose right up against the opening to feel the full force of the air flow. I was reveling in the gust of wind blowing so strongly right on me.

In the joy of the moment I opened my mouth to take in the air and as I began to make playful, yelping noises with the wind streaming across my lips and into my mouth, some bug went right into my mouth and down my throat. It must have been a big one. I coughed and coughed trying to spit it up, but to no avail. That darn bug wasn't coming up, and I was choking so badly that I couldn't talk and was having trouble breathing.

Dad was really getting concerned at my condition, so he pulled off to the side of the highway and began hitting me on the back between the shoulders, until finally the bug slid on down my throat.

A little concerned by now, dad asked, "Son, are you alright now? You had me worried there for a bit!"

Being relieved, I replied, "My throat is a little scratchy, but at least I can breathe now."

Dad exclaimed, "I was going to tell you not to open your mouth like that right into that window because of the bugs, but it's easier for you learning a lesson than me telling you!"

With a little chuckle, he continued, "Well now I guess you won't be needing to eat so much supper later."

I did think that was funny, but with my throat still hurting, I could only manage a quick, little smile and just nodded in agreement.

We finally arrived at Mr. Potter's office in town, and I felt like a "big wig" on an important secret mission with my dad. When we walked in, after being in the heat for so long, the sudden rush of cold air conditioning for a second gave me chills all over my body. Air conditioning was a luxury most farmers couldn't afford, so I wasn't quite accustomed to it. I had too many new things to observe and experience, however, to worry about being cold.

Sitting behind a large desk was a pretty young lady, who I assumed was Mr. Potter's secretary, busily typing away at some papers. Her name was on a little nameplate sitting at the edge of her desk. I peeked closer at the wooden nameplate and read aloud her name; "Jean Potter." I thought she was typing faster than I could speak the words, and I was truly amazed that someone could do that. She finished typing a little more, and quickly yanked a sheet of paper out of the typewriter and greeted us both in one, simultaneous motion. I could tell she had been doing this job for a while.

She pushed a button on her phone and in the sweetest, quiet voice spoke into the phone,

"Dad, Mr. Barnes is here to see you." Then pausing, listening to her dad respond on the phone, she said,

"Dad said he is expecting you and he will be out in just a minute."

As she hung up the phone, she looked directly at me with the deepest eyes of blue I had ever seen, and remarked,

"I've heard of the famous Bean, and now I finally get to meet him."

I was somewhat embarrassed, yet I chuckled with a little pride, knowing someone knew who I was without ever having met me, especially a beautiful girl. Acting sincerely interested she asked me,

"What's it like, being famous around town?"

Being smitten with such a pretty girl talking to me, I could barely get out an answer so I simply said,

"I guess it's kinda nice."

When she saw that I noticed a jar full of jelly beans on her desk, she asked if I wanted some and I politely refused, replying,

"No thanks." Yet on the inside I was hankering for a handful.

I was still coughing some, attempting to still clear my throat from the bug incident and didn't want to embarrass myself in front of her. Jean asked if I needed a drink of water, but I didn't want her to know I had swallowed a big bug, her being a lady and all. She pointed to this huge, glass bottle of water sitting upside down on a stand in the corner of her office. There were some paper cups in a slot beside it. She instructed me to hold the little handle up on the spigot every time I wanted to fill my cup. I couldn't believe folks had water in a container like that, and then would throw away each cup after only one drink of water. I thought it was such a waste of cups. We didn't waste things on the farm.

I drank at least eight cups of that cold water, until finally dad said, "Bean, don't drink their whole darn container dry, save some for other folks!" He looked at Jean and added, "I think the boy is a little thirsty."

"Oh, that's okay Mr. Barnes, there's lots more where that came from," she answered with a little quirky laugh.

I had drunk so much cold water so quickly, that now I had a headache, but at least the scratching in my throat was gone. I was so full of liquid that my stomach was all pooched out and the water sloshed around inside my stomach when I moved or walked. I couldn't hold one more sip. I thought to myself I was surely doing a great job of trying to embarrass myself in front of Jean. Learning that she was Mr. Potter's daughter made it all the worse.

I began to wonder how they filled that huge bottle of water when it got empty, without all the water running out of the bottom. I only knew it was refreshingly cold and tasted better than any soda at that moment, and it was helping to finally clear my throat of any bug parts that still remained. With my throat starting to feel better, I asked if I could still have some of those jelly beans.

Jean smiled and exclaimed, "Help yourself!"

As I inched closer to her desk, I could read a label on the jar that I assumed she had typed up that read, 'Jean's Jelly Beans'. I was impressed that she had thought of that name for the jar and how it rolled off your lips saying it. So I would say it to myself standing there, repeating that phrase a few times,

"Jean's Jelly Beans", "Jean's Jelly Beans" but I was thinking more of her than I was of that ol jar the whole time.

Then at the very moment I had taken the lid off the jar and about to reach in with my hand, I noticed this big long handle spoon that was sitting right next to the jar of jelly beans. I figured oops, I'm supposed to use that spoon to dish out the jelly beans. I was so glad I saw that spoon. The last thing I would have wanted was to come across as some ol dumb country kid and totally make a fool of myself.

Between having lots of cold water, enjoying cold air conditioning that I had become accustomed to by now, and devouring sweet, fruity jelly beans, I don't think I was ever so comfortable while enjoying new, modern conveniences away from the heat of outdoors. Sitting down on those slick, leather seats though was particularly cold to my skin, but that didn't stop me from wanting to get as close as I could to the cold air coming out of the vents. I thought I would be almost frozen by the time we left, but I wanted to just sit there and soak in that cold air, not wanting to ever forget how good it felt.

Finally, Mr. Potter came out and greeted dad with a big handshake. He looked at me and said,

"Looks like you brought your right hand man with ya today! How ya doin' Bean?" and he reached out to shake my hand. He shook my hand so hard, it shook my stomach too. It made all that water slosh around in there that I had drunk, and I was afraid everyone could hear the noise it was making.

As he and dad proceeded into the office, he looked back and said,

"Help yourself to some cold water over there Bean, you look kinda thirsty." Jean and I looked at each other and laughed.

As I sat waiting, Jean stepped into another open room in view, peeking over at me, occasionally smiling, while opening and closing some file drawers, sorting out papers and such. I was getting curious and wondered what could be discussed in such an important meeting between dad and Mr. Potter. I moved to the end of the couch, closer to the office door. I gradually nudged even closer to overhear most of their conversation through the door. I could hear dad pleading with Mr. Potter and I could make out dad saying,

"Can't we just give him a little more time? You know he has a family of five kids. Is there something else he can do to catch up, I mean, where else can he go C.J.? He has only been working the farm for a couple of years and maybe if I talk to him, he can start getting things straightened out."

"No Bill! He wastes any of the money he makes, stays in debt and he's constantly stirring up trouble with the other tenants about me and the way I run my business and I am just not going to put up with that."

Dad replied, "Let me talk to him, tell him how serious it is, and see if I can straighten this all out."

I could hear the resounding answer from Mr. Potter loud and clear,

"I've made up my mind Bill and that's the end of it."

I got up to get farther away from the office door when I knew the meeting was over and dad was about to come out of the office.

As we headed out the door, Jean emerged from the other room and in parting said, "It was so nice to meet you Bean, and I hope to see you again sometime."

In a dampened spirit I simply replied, "Me too and…thanks for the water and jelly beans."

Dad was stiff and quiet and didn't say much the entire way back home. Looking depressed and in a lowly demeanor put a damper on the good time I had enjoyed earlier riding with him to town and talking to Jean. I knew he didn't like what he was instructed to do, what he had to do! He had to inform some of his own neighbors, for whatever reason, it just wasn't working out, and they would have to be evicted from the farmland that they had worked and lived on for several years. They would be forced out if they didn't leave voluntarily.

The atmosphere in the truck was as cold as Mr. Potter's office from the air conditioning but in a different sorta way. Dad only made one statement on the way back. It was like he wasn't talking to me at all, but more to himself.

Staring straight ahead he said, "Sometimes I wish I was only tending my farm and not dealing with anybody else's bull. I have enough problems of my own, much less dealing with all these other people."

I think having to follow Mr. Potter's directive took a huge toll on dad. As far as I knew, that may not have been the only time he had to tell someone they were being evicted. It was just the only time that I happened to learn about it.

Now I began to understand what being the farm manager for Mr. Potter really meant. Dad's responsibility went way beyond trying to make good crops. He was dealing with the tenant problems, the equipment, hiring extra hands at harvest time and anything that came up between the sharecroppers and Mr. Potter. It was Dad's job to handle it; he was the in-between man. Good or bad, dad had to take care of it and with farming in those depressed years, there was always a lot of bad. However, this was his livelihood; our livelihood. It carried a lot of stress on him and ultimately on our family.

As days wore on, dad would come home more tired and worn out physically and mentally. I only wished that I were older and bigger to help relieve some of his burdens. I suppose every child feels that way at some time in hard times, but I felt this burden right up to the time we moved away from the farm and also afterward.

CHAPTER SEVEN
The Awakening

While you are very young, not even in your teens yet, you expect everything will remain exactly like it is at that time, always the same routine. It was like a list to be performed; to be checked off every day! For me it was school for us kids, dad working the farm all day; mama taking care of house and family; dad comes home; family supper; little relaxing; bedtime and repeat!

Life becomes this regular, unbroken pattern which also happens to offer up a way of welcomed security. You don't make a judgement about it. You are just living it. It's your life.

As long as you have all those necessary things, you don't think of a need to complain. So why worry about any of that at the moment for goodness sakes?

To me, daily life was great. On top of that, I had Christmas and Thanksgiving to look forward to every single year. During the holidays, I also loved getting my fill of my favorite thing to eat in the world, cherry pie, and I've been known to eat a whole one. Just ask Mrs. Wilson!

Then there is Jack, my little brother. It's something he can never escape. He will always be the "little" brother, no matter how old we get. Nothing will ever change that. For now, I always have him around to blame things on if I get into a little bit of trouble, or for doing something I know I shouldn't be doing.

So as far as I was concerned, things couldn't get any better. I always thought that way, every day, until that night. The night that seemed to change everything!

Nothing out of the ordinary had happened that week or that day. It was the end of the school and work week for most people. Kids were looking forward to being out of school and some folk at least, only having to work a half day on Saturday. Dad made it home for supper about the same time he always did. He was very tired like he often would be and said he was going to go get cleaned up before supper. After finishing eating, he did his usual routine of plopping down in his easy chair and grabbed a newspaper to read.

It was getting dark outside, so Jack and I had already come in from playing and thought maybe we could get dad to play with us for a bit. As we were approaching dad sitting in his easy chair, he put down the paper and said, "I need to go check on the barn… It looks like rain and gotta make sure the big doors are closed up. I shouldn't be too long." I wanted to go with him but he said, "I'll be back soon," and instructed me and Jack to be taking our baths and that maybe he would have a little time to play with us when he gets back before bedtime.

It got to be around ten o'clock and mama said, "He must have found something else to work on down there and you boys need to go on to bed. You can see dad in the morning and he will be better rested by then anyway." Jack had fallen asleep on the couch and I was getting sleepy too. Being a little disappointed, off to bed we went.

Later, while sound asleep, I was awakened by mama hovering right over me. I had no idea what time it was but I knew it had to be very late. Mama in a very quiet, almost whisper of a voice told me,

"Don't wake your little brother, put on some clothes and come into the living room."

In a hurried panic, I threw on some clothes, grabbed my shoes with no socks and nervously proceeded to meet mama to see why she got me up.

I asked her, "What's going on, did something happen?"
She told me that after dad said he was going down to the barn, he never did come back. She said, "I wasn't too concerned for a while…you know how there is always something he can find that

needs tending to down there and his job never goes exactly by the clock." But she nervously said it has been four hours since he left and it's already past midnight.

Mama with angst in her voice remarked, "I am now getting a little worried. He never stays gone this long…usually an hour or two at the most." She continued, "I know he didn't come back and leave in his truck as it is still parked out front, so I am a little concerned."

She had decided she wanted me to go with her to the barn to see if he was there and to make sure he was okay. Although I didn't like the sound of the circumstances, I was glad she thought I was old and responsible enough to be able to help out if needed.

Mama grabbed a flashlight that we kept handy and we quietly proceeded outside, down the road, toward the barn in the quiet of the night. I could hear what sounded like hundreds of frogs doing their repetitive croaking over and over from the ditches and fields nearby as we began to make our way down the road. I looked up and the moon was so full and bright, it hurt my eyes to stare at it. We ended up not really needing the flashlight, as you could see your own shadow from the moonlight as it followed us along on the ground. A strong shadow on a clear night with a bright full moon is an eerie thing. It's like someone else is following you the entire time, and your shadow seems to take on a life of its own. I was glad we weren't going toward the Black Veil that was in the opposite direction.

I was looking down as we walked, paying more attention to my ghostly shadow following me than to where I was walking on the road or what was ahead of me. Being distracted along the way, I was barely aware when we had arrived at the barn.

This was a really big barn that was on the side of the dirt road, about two hundred yards from the house. It could hold several trailers, tools of all kinds, lots of farm machinery and equipment, and always had some hay you could play around in. You had to be careful at night going in there as you could easily run into something that might end up getting your hurt, especially with very little light. The barn had these large doors, one on each end so a tractor could pull a cotton or bean trailer straight through and out the other side. Both those big doors were closed.

As we approached the barn to go in, my nervousness grew and grew and I began to worry if something bad may have happened to my dad. It was very quiet and dark, no lights anywhere. There was the small door just for walking through, to the side of the big large one for the tractors. This door appeared to be left halfway cracked open.

We slowly crept in, as mama flicked the switch by the door for the light but it didn't come on. The flashlight was so dim mama laid it to the side, as we were peeking through the dark musty eeriness. We could see a faint glow of a light way back in a dark corner of the barn. As we got closer, mama was calling out in a concerned voice, "William, are you in here, are you okay, William, are you in here?" No response!

We inched closer to the faint glow in the dark corner, being careful not to run into something and hurt ourselves and again mama was pleading, "William, we were worried about you, I know you're in here, William, please answer me?"

About that time, we heard some rustling noises as we were close to the very back corner where there was a dim light that appeared to only be hanging by a string, dangling down from the rafters. Yep, it was my dad and when he became aware we were there, he began saying demonstratively,

"Just get outta here, leave me alone, go on...go back home...let me be!" We could barely make him out, seeing only a hint of his face, being dark as it was, lying down, almost swallowed up in the big loose pile of hay.

Only the voice I heard didn't sound like dad at all. It was a ragged, tired, ugly voice that I had never heard him use before and I didn't like the sound of it. That wasn't my dad's voice! I knew something was terribly wrong. I thought... Is he hurt? Had he gotten into a fight with a tenant? As some time passed, I finally realized what was probably going on but I hoped it was actually something else. I was old enough by now to recognize that he had been drinking and this was the first time for me to witness it.

When we got all the way to where dad was, Mama kept one arm outstretched aimed back toward me to keep me behind her at this point. I peeked out to see dad lying there, and could make out what I thought was a mostly empty bottle of what I assumed was whiskey. Mama exclaimed,

"It's midnight and Lordy I didn't know what happened to you and was worried!"

"Well now you know I am okay. Just go back home and leave me alone," as he turned back away from us and rolled back over on his side in the hay.

With each repeated effort to try to get him up, dad would scream, "Let go of me, let me be!"

Mama and I looked at each other, shaking our heads, realizing it was a useless situation as we weren't sure he could make it back home anyway, with the condition he was in.

Finally, in frustration, apparently giving up, mama told dad, "Well, just stay here then and come back home when you sober up."

I could hear the helpless frustration in my mother's voice and wished there was something that I could do to help. She just stood there very still and somber, in a frozen state, staring into the darkness toward my dad. We both could hear his heavy breathing and it was like he had already forgotten we were there.

She continued to shake her head and in a defeated tone said, "We best just leave him be for now and get ourselves back to the house and check on Jack. We've been gone for quite a while. There's nothing else we can do. At least we know he isn't hurt."

When we got back to the house, mama sat down at the kitchen table and I just stood there next to her. She started sobbing and in a broken voice began telling me how she hated for me to see him in that condition, and was really worried about it getting worse and happening more often.

"There's been a time or two he would go into town and come back having drank a little too much and I just never said much to him about it," she explained. "He never drank too often during the week, just a little on the weekends I thought and it was just a thing to do with his buddies and no big concern." She calmly continued, "You know Benny, farming is a hard life and demands so much of a person. I never blamed him for having a drink once in a while but it is becoming more and more of a habit. If he keeps this up, he could end up losing his job for Mr. Potter. If we can't keep this farm, then what would we do?"

Being inquisitive like I am, I asked,

"Well, how long has he been drinking like this? When did it all start?"

She told me that before they got married, she stopped letting him come to see her over his drinking and told him he would have to quit for any chance of them ever being together.

"He stopped for a very long time and I thought that maybe that was the end of it but I guess I was either wrong or blind."

Now my mind got to working and I wondered how I never noticed something may have been going on with dad before now. How could I have never known? I got to thinking about it and told mama I remembered that time I was awakened by some commotion around the house late one night. I recounted how I saw her and the sheriff helping daddy get into the house. I asked what had happened and she told me that dad had gotten really sick with this bad stomach condition. I remembered the same thing happened again a couple of times later and asking why the sheriff was always bringing him home.

She went on and explained those were the times she was really aware of him drinking when Sheriff Mason had stopped him for driving drunk a few times. She explained how instead of arresting your dad, the sheriff would just bring him home to sleep it off. The sheriff would even have the deputy drop his truck back off at the house.

"After the last time it happened, a lot of time passed, so I thought maybe he quit drinking," she explained. "He kept promising me he would quit and I think he did at times but not for very long."

She said she hated for me to have to know about all this, but it was getting to the point that I was going to find out soon enough, as tonight proved.

By now, it was getting really late and mama said, "Just go on to bed son. Your dad will be better tomorrow morning, you'll see! We'll all be okay. We have to work through this. A lot of folks are having a hard time on the farm right now and it makes things difficult for them but for your dad especially."

Luckily, it was a Saturday night with no school the next day, so I could sleep late if I wanted to. I laid there in my bed thinking about what had happened and wanting to convince myself that it was only going to be some rare occurrence. But I think I knew better. I thought of that nervous walk with mama down the dirt road to the barn in the dark of the night, hoping it wasn't going to be a sign of anything to come.

I got my head as close to the open screened window as I could in my bed without disturbing Jack in the other twin bed. He stayed asleep the entire time. I could hear the peaceful sound of those frogs still croaking and crickets chirping coming through the open window in the soothing breeze. I wished life could be as calm as those night sounds, coming through my window. All I could think of was my dad being out there all alone, and me helpless to do anything, again!

CHAPTER EIGHT
A Picture In The Dirt

Jack and I were having fun playing on top of the little hill where our storm cellar was put in the ground. I always hated going down in that thing on the few occasions that we had to use it. That was enough for me, since it always gave me the creeps being totally closed in like that. Not to mention worrying what might have taken up residence in there, like spiders, snakes and other unwelcome critters.

It was musty, dark, with an irritating damp smell and downright uncomfortable. However, I guess anything would be better than sitting outside through a tornado inside the comfort of the house. Every house had a storm cellar. Funny thing is, I never saw anybody dig one or make one or however they did it. It was something that was just there, patiently waiting for the time it was needed.

The dirt over the cellar made just enough of a little hill in our yard to make it a favorite spot for Jack and me to play. It had provided enough slope to ride our bikes over extra fast or roll down in our beloved little red wagon without much of a push. Since it was one of our favorite places to play, especially running over it constantly with our bikes or wagon, we had worn out a slick track down the middle of it from top to bottom. The rest of our yard never had much grass either. I once commented to dad how people in town had such nice looking yards of plush green grass.

He once told me, "Yeah, those town folk waste all that good water on nothing but keeping their grass green... If it weren't for us farmers working out here on farms in the dust and dirt, they wouldn't have anything to eat but that nice grass."

That always gave me a little pride thinking about the important job of farmers. Without us, people not only wouldn't have clothes to wear, they wouldn't have any food to eat either.

Whenever we heard a vehicle coming down the gravel road in the distance, we always looked to see if we could tell that it was a white pickup. That meant it was a good chance it was dad coming home. With the sound made from a car on that gravel road leading to our house, you could hear one approaching from a half mile away, especially if the wind was blowing our direction. But along with the wind, it also meant a thick cloud of smothering dust would usually follow right behind, in a few delayed seconds after a vehicle stopped.

Jack and I would often make an out-loud counting game out of it.

"One...two...three... Close your eyes and mouth...dust bowl coming," and it would slowly and gently cover you in a smoky cloud, right on time.

Dust was something you lived with on a farm in one way or another and anything white, seemed to always stay covered in it. So, I always thought white was the worst color to have, living in the country with dusty roads like we had. Dad had told me he always drove a white truck. I remember him giving me a complete lesson once, why he always liked white for his truck.

Dad said, "The summer is way too hot to have anything but white and I'll take anything to help me stay cooler with the scorching sun blaring down... I sweat enough as it is. I sure don't need to add to it. I can't believe some people like black trucks. They're fine in the winter but a killer in the summertime."

There was one thing I always liked too, about his truck being white. With the dirt always on it, that would make it easy to write something with your finger and we loved writing things on the tailgate or sometimes on the side of his pickup truck. We would get creative and draw all sorts of pictures in that thick encrusted dirt on dad's truck.

Today, like eagle hawks, Jack and I had already spotted that white pickup coming and were anxiously ready to greet dad when he would get to the house. As he was pulling up in the yard, we had already started running down the little mound to meet him, and we barreled right up to his side of the truck, right up against his door and dad exclaimed, "Are you boys gonna let me get out of the truck or do I have to sit in here all day?"

On this day, dad had gotten home a little earlier than he usually would from the fields, so Jack and I saw a chance to spend a little more time than usual with him before we all had to go to bed. Most of the time, dad left the house for work long before Jack and I got up, and lots of days he would be late for supper which was usually ready around six. Sometimes he would be so late when he got home, it would be getting dark and mama would have to put his supper away and warm it up when he got there.

On most days, by the time he ate supper, got cleaned up and relaxed a little, there wasn't much time left to do anything with him. We would almost smother dad whenever he would have a little extra free time at home, just like today.

We went on in the house pulling and yanking all over dad like a couple of little monkeys. Mama saw us all over him and said, "Boys, give your daddy a chance to breathe and let him go get cleaned up first... I am just now starting on supper."

Dad responded, "Yeah Belle, these boys o' yours barely let me get out of my truck. They acted like they ain't seen me in ages. But, I want to rest just a bit... Let me sit down here for a minute," and he plopped right down in his big easy chair not far from the kitchen.

Mama was in the kitchen starting to get the flour out to make biscuits, grabbing some potatoes, and then she began to drain the brown beans she had been soaking overnight in water to get them ready to cook. I never had asked her what the reason was for soaking beans like that and my curiosity finally got to me, so I asked her.

"Mama, why do you have to soak the beans all night like that before you cook 'em?"

She was in the middle of draining the beans, leaned up and looked toward dad's direction, wanting him to hear what she was going to say and not at all looking at me remarked, "Well son, let's just put it this way. If I don't soak these beans, but instead just cook them right straight out of the bag, I would be kicking somebody out of the bed in the middle of the night. I could sleep with a clothespin on my nose all night long, but breathing out of my mouth would probably be worse."

I heard dad reply, "Hey! I heard that and it works both ways woman. I have to keep them clothes pins handy too."

They both just shook their head and giggled a little. About that time Jack let out a big poot, and then everybody just cracked up laughing.

Later when mama had finished cooking, Jack and I set the table with the plates and utensils. Dad had gotten all cleaned up, and we all sat down at the table.

Dad was more talkative than usual this evening. I think it was from not being quite as tired like most times when he got home from work. He began to tell us how he was glad they finally had come out and put down some fresh, new gravel on the dirt road coming up to the house. He went on saying how they had wasted so much time just grading the road over and over, and all that was doing was making it slicker.

Dad continued, "It's about time they got to doin' our road, and now I won't have to worry so much every time Belle has to go to town, wondering if she is going to slide off into the ditch like she did last week after that rain we had... Mr. Potter told me he was putting in a word to some people up at the county that it needed doin' and well... I reckon his word means something around here."

I thought to myself, Mr. Potter should have told 'em to pave it like the highway while he was at it and we would have had us a nice paved road coming in here.

We were having a good night and everybody was in a good mood. We were all finishing our supper and enjoying the family time when dad suddenly jumped up. He said he remembered he had promised to meet one of Mr. Potter's tenants down at the barn to discuss something about a tractor. I asked dad if I could go and he instructed, "Sure Bean you can go this time, but I don't want you jumping around no trailers."

Jack didn't want to go. His hero, Zorro, was about to come on television at its normal seven thirty time slot, and I knew he was not going to miss his favorite show. Dad told mama, "Belle, this shouldn't take very long so we'll be back shortly."

As we walked out past dad's truck, he pointed to a drawing in the dirt on his truck and asked, "What is that a picture of anyway?"

I said, "Oh, that's a picture of a 22-caliber rifle that I hope to get for Christmas."

Dad said, "Well, that sure looks more like a fishing pole than any rifle I ever seen."

"Well, it's been on there for a day or two and it's all smudged up some by now," I replied.

When we got to the barn, I saw Mr. Handley standing by his truck with his door swung open. I told dad I was going to go play in the hay for a bit since he didn't want me messing in the trailers. So I headed to the back corner where the hay was and dove in. I had my hands propped behind my head while relaxing in the hay, thinking to myself... This ain't such a bad life.

I could hear daddy and Mr. Handley in a serious conversation, but I couldn't make out many words. As their conversation continued, I could tell Mr. Handley was raising his voice more and dad's voice getting louder too.

I got up from the hay and cautiously began to creep closer. As I was making my way to the barn door, I plainly heard dad asking Mr. Handley to calm down and to talk this thing over.

I could hear Mr. Handley angrily saying, "What's there to talk over? I got thirty days to figure something out…thirty days, after two years of hard working for you and that greedy sumbitch Mr. Potter."

I heard my dad say he was sorry, but he didn't make the decision and was really a paid hand just like everybody else.

Dad said, "I'm just doing my job Harold, doing what I'm told or I lose my job."

I had crept close by to where they were, right outside the barn door. I saw Mr. Handley reach inside his truck seat and pull out a rifle of some sort, maybe a thirty-ought-six or something.

He pointed it at dad and said, "What does it feel like to have your whole life depending on what another man might do to you…That you have no control over? Don't feel very good does it?"

I stood frozen and didn't know what to do. Mr. Handley's hands were shaking and I was afraid the rifle might go off any minute, maybe unintentionally. I started praying… Please God, don't let him kill my daddy…don't let him hurt 'im… Please God, please! I never felt so helpless in all my life, but I knew there was nothing I could do.

Then dad started walking ever so slowly toward Harold saying,

"Harold, please put the gun down. You don't want to do something you'll regret. Think of your wife, your children. Don't do something you'll be sorry for the rest of your life."

"Stop right there Barnes… Don't come any closer," Handley replied.

Dad edged ever so slowly with one more step, only a few feet away and said, "Give me the gun Harold. You don't want to do this," and dad raised his open hand in a plea for him to hand over the rifle, within an inch or two of touching the barrel.

Mr. Handley turned and noticed me for the first time standing close by. At the same exact moment when Mr. Handley looked over at me, dad grabbed the barrel and the gun went off. The noise and shock that rang out from that blast sent chills up and down my spine. I was filled with deadly fear of my dad being shot. I was so close that the noise from the shot left a deafening ringing in my ears. I could barely hear anything for a minute or two. Dad looked at me to make sure I was okay. I thought the worst, but the bullet appeared to have passed in the few feet between dad and me, hitting neither one of us, at least I was hoping.

Everyone stood frozen for a minute; me, my dad, and Mr. Handley. No more words were spoken at all. Finally, with little expression, Mr. Handley walked in a normal way back to his truck, proceeded to get in and drove off in a cloud of dust.

I ran over to hug dad tightly and I nervously asked, "Dad, are you okay? I was so scared!"

He asked if I was alright and was so glad that no one had gotten hurt. He said, "Son, people do stupid things when they get desperate. This could have turned out really bad in so many different ways, but thank God it didn't."

We sat there for a while calming down from the shock of hearing that loud blast of a gun, so close to the both of us.

A few minutes later, mama came running up to the truck in a panic as she knew that something bad had happened. As we were all walking back toward the house, dad was explaining to mama what I already knew from overhearing him and his boss Mr. Potter, discussing Mr. Handley in town at his office. I didn't know at the time exactly who they were talking about evicting.

I surely knew now and was worried that Mr. Handley might try something again. He had a reputation for having a short, hot temper. I asked dad if we were going to call the Sheriff Mason. He said we should, but he wasn't going to press charges. He just wanted him to be aware of what had happened, since the sheriff would be the one to make sure Mr. Handley did leave the property, after being served an eviction notice.

Dad was still a little shook up of course, and mama told him to sit down while she got him a glass of water. Mama said she would make the call to Sheriff Mason. She was on the phone for a long time with the sheriff, explaining what had taken place.

Jack was in his pajamas and was going to bed when all this happened and I had to explain to him what had occurred. There was no way Jack could not have heard mom and dad discussing the event, while they were waiting on the sheriff to arrive.

I saw the lights of the sheriff's car finally pull up outside and mama said, "You boys go on to bed now."

Jack and I did go to our room but kept our ears pinned to the door. We could make out almost every word as we could still hear them discussing the whole incident.

Sheriff Mason kept repeating over and over, "Bill, are you absolutely sure you don't want to press charges? Belle, are you fine and agreeing with this? I think we all need to be on the same page here."

I heard the sheriff say he really couldn't do anything about it if dad didn't press charges.

I finally heard the sheriff say in parting, "Look, y'all think it over and if you change your mind, let me know. When Harold gets to drinking, there is no telling what he is capable of doing. I'll let him cool off tonight and then go see him in the morning. If you want my deputy to hang around here tonight, we can do that too."

Dad told him, "No, we will be fine Dean, don't worry about us. You go get some sleep."

The sheriff replied, "Y'all are the ones I'm worried about not getting any sleep tonight," and then he left to go on back to town.

Mama and dad came to check on us boys to tell us goodnight and how proud they were of how I handled the whole thing. Jack managed to go on to sleep in a little while but not being there when it all happened, didn't affect Jack the same as it did me. I thanked God he heard my prayer and for letting things turn out the way they did. That night could have been a night of tragedy but instead turned out okay in the end.

I lay there in bed, eyes wide open staring at the ceiling, playing the events of that night over and over in my head, hearing that deafening gunshot next to my face and a bullet go right by my dad. I was thinking how things could have turned out so differently. One event that could have changed all our lives forever but didn't. I hadn't cried the whole time during the incident, not after talking about it when we got home, and not one little tear all evening.

Then I remembered the picture of the rifle that I had drawn in the dirt on dad's white, dirty truck. Why of all times would I have drawn that picture on his truck and that of a rifle, like one that could have killed my daddy on this very night.

The emotion of events had built up in me by then, and in the silence of the night I pulled the sheet up to my face,

And I wept.

CHAPTER NINE
Stinky Business

When living in a small southern country town, a kid would play ball, ride bicycles, fish and sometimes hunt things like squirrels or rabbits with maybe a 22-caliber rifle, if you were lucky to have one. It just so happens that was mine and my brother's life, and when we did any of those things, we did them with all the gusto we could muster. We tried to keep the supplies needed to be successful in whichever venture in tip top shape, but finances more often than not, hindered us from doing so.

Our old fishing reels would become rusted, worn out, and difficult to use. We would repeatedly take 'em apart, clean 'em, straighten out the line, and they still wouldn't work very well. Something we couldn't have, as the expert fishermen we were, was mechanical failure to cause us to lose fish. We were back to using cane poles many times, but that kept us from getting our line out to the deeper good spots farther out in the river.

I had pleaded with dad several times how we badly needed some new reels, but each time, he would say something like, "Boys, all I ever used for fishing was cane poles, and we can't afford spending money on luxuries like them reels right now."

But Jack and I didn't regard them as luxuries. To us, reels in good working order were downright necessities. They were as important to us, as having a good-working farming tool was to dad. I knew Jack and I couldn't save enough money for new reels anytime soon. Every time we got a little money, fishing supplies alone would use up the money we had.

It was an early Sunday morning and I was trying to stay asleep in my bed, but Jack kept shaking me over and over again, saying, "Bean, get up! Get up, Bean...get up!"

I would tell him to leave me alone, roll back over, and I'd pull the covers right back over my head. He would keep yanking on the blanket to keep uncovering my head, exposing my eyes to the light to get me to wake me up.

Finally in desperation, Jack excitingly exclaimed, "Bean, look what I'm holding!" I cracked open my sleepy eyes just enough to get a glance of what it was he wanted to show me, without totally giving in to his pleading. I thought no way, I must still be dreaming. Jack, with the biggest smile, pushed right up to my face a spanking brand new rod and reel. He was so excited and was pushing the reel up so close to my nose, I could read the words Zebco 202 on the reel. I couldn't believe what I was seeing.

Jack continued, "Bean, guess what else? Look over there in the corner of the room!" I sat up with my mouth dropped half open in amazement from what I saw! There in the corner, was another new, identical rod and reel leaning against the wall. By now I'm getting excited too, and I jump out of bed to examine our new reels.

My thoughts ran back to what dad had said about spending money on luxuries, and guessed he must have changed his mind. With our new rods in hand, we ran to the kitchen where mama was pouring up a cup of black coffee, and dad was doing some figuring on paper.

We couldn't wait to show them our new found gifts. Mama was sitting down and was stirring some sugar into her coffee, and was raising her cup to take a sip, when Jack almost knocked the cup out of her hand. She exclaimed, "Jack, be careful son, this stuff is hot."

Jack couldn't wait, holding the rod and reel up close for mama to examine. Acting surprised, she said, "Wow, these things are really nice...bet y'all can do some real good fishing now."

I ran over to thank dad for our new fishing reels. He looked like he was in deep thought doing the figuring, looked up, and said, "Well boys, don't thank me, thank your mama! She gave up getting some new dishes she was wanting, just so y'all could get those reels. I told her if that was what she wanted to do with all those trade-in stamps she had saved up, then that was fine with me." He added, "We just got through spending a lot of money on that part for the tractor, so y'all are lucky your mama found a way to get those reels for ya."

Boy, were we ever thankful for what mama did and it wasn't even Christmas! I had wondered how mama had any money saved to spend on buying us new reels for fishing, so I shouted out, "Thank the Lord for those stamps."

Mama knew our dilemma with our old reels not working very well and how important fishing was to us. She had figured out another way to get us some new ones without exactly spending money. She said she was going through her stamp catalog, looking for some dishes she had been saving stamps for and came across the reels.

She would diligently save them up to trade in for things she would see in the catalog. Mama would receive stamps from the grocery store, according to the amount of money she spent. Stores often would have double stamp day, and she loved buying our groceries on that particular day. Each time she got some stamps, she would lick them and attach them on pages in the stamp books. With us kids to feed, she could run up a pretty good grocery bill and that meant a big wad of stamps to lick. The stamp catalog consisted of all sorts of things that she could trade them for. There was everything from dishes to sheets for the bed, or from jewelry to even fishing rods. When she had enough books of stamps to get a particular item, she would trade them in and have it shipped to us. We got all sorts of items by using stamps, but it was usually for things needed around the house. I think most of our dishes must have come that way.

Jack and I were so thankful that mama used them to get those rod and reels. She could have gotten something nice for herself or for the house, but instead she thought of me and Jack. When I asked, she told me it took around five thousand stamps, saved over a very long time, to get those reels. That was just like mama though, thinking of us boys, instead of herself.

We were heading out the door, to get things ready to try our new reels out down by the river, when dad said, "Boys, I need an extra hand or two with something that needs taken care of down by the barn. I know y'all want to go fishing real bad with your new reels. I don't think this will take very long, but I sure could use your help." We figured we could help dad get whatever he needed done, and still have plenty of time to go fishing.

We walked down to the barn, and he showed us this big hole where an old outhouse once was that the farmhands had used. He had moved the actual outhouse building itself, over to a different spot, but the old nasty hole was still there.

The hole that was left, although covered with a piece of wood, still stunk so badly you could hardly hold your face anywhere near that pit for the odor coming out. Daddy told us that we needed to get it covered up with something stronger than the plywood he had temporarily put down over the hole. He was telling us that until he could get that hole taken care of for good, at a later time, he needed to reinforce the plywood for now.

So we helped him round up some boards from the pile of wood and old boards from around the barn, and in approval, he said, "Yeah boys, those boards oughta do just fine."

He told Jack to go grab the shovel hanging inside by the barn door, and he first shoveled a little dirt into the pit. With a grimace look, trying to keep his head turned away from the odor, he said, "Whew...that is some bad smell; Some of this dirt on top ought to help keep down that stink a little!" He then laid out the boards over the hole and then put the plywood on top. "Each of y'all hold on to one end of a board, while I nail down the plywood. I don't want them boards to fall in the hole while I'm nailing, unless one of y'all want to go in to get 'em out," he said with a giggle!

So Jack and I held the boards steady, to keep them in place, one at a time, while daddy did the nailing. We put four big strong boards under the plywood, and were glad to be able to help daddy with a project around the farm, stinky as it was.

Daddy finished with the nailing, and then put the stakes back around the hole with some yellow ribbon, to keep people from walking over it. He said, "Hopefully I'll get a chance soon to come back and mound some dirt over it and be done with it."

We walked back toward the house, and were ready to gather our new reels, and head on down to the river. Mama was sitting on the front porch when we walked up. When we got close, she pinched her nose, and turned away from us like we had some contagious disease.

Mama, almost in pure agony, said in an emphatic voice, "What in the world is that terrible smell coming from y'all. That smell is so bad, it'd kill any rat that got a whiff of it!"

Daddy explained what we had been doing, but didn't think the odor would have carried over on us much. All three of us brought our arms up to our noses, like we didn't believe mama, to test for any odor. Yep, she was right. We stunk to high heaven. We had gotten used to working around the odor, so we couldn't smell it anymore. We didn't realize how badly we stunk.

Then dad chimed in and agreed, "Well, I guess we do stink a little Belle!"

Mama said, "A little ain't the word for it and y'all ain't sittin' foot in this house, before washing up some at the pump outside, to try to get some of that stink off first."

After washing up as much as we could at the pump by the house, mama made us further strip down to our underwear. She said, pretending not to watch, "I ain't looking now, so y'all get on in, and get cleaned up."

As we were heading in, we could hear her talking to herself, saying, "Lordy, I hope I can get this stink out of these clothes. Maybe I'd be better off just burning 'em! I best leave 'em out on the porch for tonight…maybe that'll help."

After having a bath and finally going to bed that night, those sheets never smelled so fresh and clean. Jack and I were so happy to be able to help dad do a chore like that and doing something that we figured was important around the farm. It made us feel like we had accomplished something alongside dad, as stinky as it was. We only hoped that was the last time we would have to mess with anything to do with an outhouse and were so thankful we ourselves had an indoor bathroom, even though we had to share it with everyone in the family. From that moment on, I never complained about having to share our bathroom again.

I was also hoping I would never have to wear those stinky clothes... Ever again!

CHAPTER TEN
Cousins Make A "Pit" Stop

The only waterways we might get to see that were clear water, would be creeks like the Fourche River up in the foothills of the Ozark Mountains. It was close to the Missouri state line where some of our relatives lived. We didn't see them very often, perhaps only once every couple of years. We preferred to go see them and do the visiting. That way, we could leave and go home, when we were good and ready. Jack and I did enjoy fishing and playing in that crystal, clear water there, but honestly didn't really care much about having to see our relatives, especially our cousins!

We didn't have enough, comfortable space at our house, for an entire visiting family to spend much time with us. Jack and I didn't care to have any visitors around at all. It meant we had to give up our beds, usually sleep on the floor, and be out of our room.

My Aunt and Uncle on my daddy's side lived up around those foothills on the Fourche River. Jack and I always hated it when they would come around. They had two boys who were older than us. These cousins were very mean, and would always mess with our toys, fishing reels or any of our stuff they could get their hands on. They would break your things, just for the fun of it.

On this particular day, Jack and I were having our usual sword fight in the yard, with our sticks we used for swords, when we heard a truck churning up that loose gravel.

We could see the dust cloud rising high above the electric poles, coming our way down the dry, dusty road. To our surprise, the old truck pulled right up in our front yard as it came to a screeching halt. Their brakes were so bad, they barely stopped within a foot of running into our house, making that horrible noise that hurt our ears. It was the kind of noise that sent this sharp, cringing, pain through your head. A sound like someone running their fingernails down a blackboard at school. It gave me and Jack, what we called the unpleasant willies, along with shivers up and down our spine.

Jack ran into the house announcing, "I think we are in for some company." That's when I realized, oh no, it was my worst nightmare conceivable. It was those menacing cousins from Fourche River. Trouble no doubt, has arrived!

Out jumped Aunt May and Uncle Remus, followed by those two least favorite cousins of ours. Aunt May was so happy to see us though. She wore these big, huge glasses that covered her whole face. The lenses were so thick, that when she looked at you, both eyes looked like the full moon was just winking back at you. It was adorable in a way and she was always very sweet with us boys.

Her hair was tied up in this tight bun on the top of her head, with this big looking needle thing stuck through it. I thought that hair needle resembled a weapon for sword fighting, more than it did for holding up hair. She had these strings of beads that were hanging way down from her neck. The beads would bang together, and make these noises that reminded me of a train going down a track, every time she moved her head...clack, clack, clackity, clack! She wore this perfume that was so strong, it would make me sneeze and my eyes water. Aunt May shouted out, "You kids have grown so much since I seen ya last... Y'all come here and give your Aunt May a big ol hug."

She was squeezing me so tight I thought my eyes were going to pop right out of my head that was buried in her chest, not to mention a little pain from those hard beads being pressed against the side of my face. I figured they were going to leave indentions in my face, after she got through hugging me.

Finally, after all the hugging and greeting, everybody began to make their way into the house. Aunt May plopped down on the couch, and told Uncle Remus to sit down. He took a seat by her side, and she was talking and going on, while nobody else was able to say anything. Uncle Remus would start to say something and Aunt May would quickly interject, "I'm still talking Remus, don't interrupt me."

Uncle Remus would let out a big exhale of frustration, look over at us boys, and with a long sigh, saying, "I can't ever get in a word edgewise with this woman."

Uncle Remus was a nice guy I suppose. He was never known to say a whole lot, but when he did, it was always to the point. Every time I had ever seen him, he had on what looked to be the same worn out overalls, and it prompted me to ask him if he ever just wore blue jeans or something different.

He said, "A real man only wears overalls or suspenders," and emphatically added, "Belts are for sissies!"

He always had quite the stomach, and I figured that's why he liked the overalls. Plus, he always liked hanging his thumbs around the straps at the top of his chest. I guess that was as good a place as any to put them. He had this long mustache that ran down both sides of his jaw and blended in with his long scruffy beard. I asked him if he ever shaved it. He said he couldn't remember the last time he didn't have a beard. His hair on top was almost all gone. All that was left was a couple of long strands of hair on top that he would pull over to one side. He treated those last two strands of hair like prized possessions. Those two lonely strands of hair on that bare head reminded me of a couple of spaghetti noodles left all alone on a bare plate, ready to be washed.

Aunt May had been going on and on talking for quite some time, but Uncle Remus finally had enough and burst in with this animated, enthusiastic expression on his face. He excitedly said, "I got some big news to tell y'all."

He explained how they were actually on their way to West Memphis and they couldn't stay but about an hour. They needed to get on their way before dark to see Aunt May's brother there.

He started telling how her brother had gone up north, got a good job at the car plant in Michigan, and was coming back next week to move their whole family up there. He wanted to talk to him to find out more about it. Uncle Remus went on saying he wanted to do the same thing, hoping to get hired there, and later come back to get Aunt May and the boys after getting settled in and saving enough money.

Daddy said, "That's a great idea Remus. I hear they pay real good money up there at those plants, and have lots of benefits they give their employees!"

Uncle Remus, nodding his head, continued, "Oh, they say you can go to a doctor practically free. Not only that, I've been told they also put money in a bank to build up for your retirement. They got these unions there too and the workers get together to make sure you have all these rights you don't get everywhere else."

Even though daddy acted happy for Remus, I could tell when he looked away, rolling his eyes, that he was thinking to himself something like… Yeah, if he doesn't get fired after the first month.

Daddy had told me once that Uncle Remus had tried to be a farmer. He said he simply never had it in him, wasn't cut out for it, and would never stick to one thing very long. He would take a job here and there, doing mainly odd jobs. Nevertheless, if he could get hired at a plant up there and stay with it, dad knew it would be good for his family.

I figured that we would stay farming and never go up north like that. Dad had told me before that he didn't like the cold weather there, and the little bit of snow we got here once or twice in the winter was enough for him.

Now the ladies were just yapping away while daddy leaned back just listening in. Uncle Remus reached into his side pocket of his overalls, pulled out this dark brown, square chunk of chewing tobacco, held it out to daddy, and offered him a piece. Daddy politely said, "No thanks Remus, my smoke will do me fine," and dad lit up a cigarette. He and mama both smoked cigarettes that had that unmistakable picture of a big camel on the front of the pack. I wondered what a camel had to do with cigarettes, but they sure did like them.

Dad explained to Remus, "I've mostly quit the chewing stuff since Belle doesn't like me doing it in the house, so I gave it up."

Uncle Remus replied, "Well, suit yourself, but I never let a woman decide what I can or can't do," and proceeded to tear off a nice size piece of chewing tobacco. With his finger and thumb, he grabbed the side of his jaw, pulled it open really wide, and stuffed it in.

Aunt May, after being quiet for a while, in a demonstrative voice says, "Ed... Ned, one of you boys go to the truck and get me my tobacco can."

Ned goes out for a minute, comes back and hands her the red can with the little flip top. Inside is her smoking tobacco. She takes this little white rectangular paper sleeve out of her pocket. She then takes the tobacco can, and carefully shakes out a precise, little row of tobacco on the paper. She starts to roll it up into a nice, little, pencil shape, and then licks down one side of the paper right before finishing the roll. She then continues rolling it up into a long, cylindrical shape, licking the entire thing, from end to end.

Finally, she folds it over one last time, pinching the ends together, to complete her masterpiece, and then asks Remus for a light. Once she started smoking it, she would have a few loose grains of tobacco to gently spit out, to complete the process.

She always spilled some tobacco on her lap and would swipe it off to the floor or the furniture. The whole ordeal to me was like tobacco art in motion. It was a fascinating ritual to watch, that I am sure she had repeated a thousand times. I wondered to myself why she didn't just buy cigarettes from a store all ready to smoke like my parents did. That sure seemed like it would be a whole lot less trouble.

I liked the smell of that tobacco a lot more than the tobacco Uncle Remus chews. That stuff would often make my stomach sick when he would start spitting out the juice. You could see some drool running down the corner of his mouth along his mustache.

Mama said, "Bean… Go grab that spittoon we got in the back room by the porch for your Uncle Remus."

I put down the spittoon close by, and although he was pretty good at hitting it, he would still miss sometimes. He always had this little, brown line of tobacco that was in one corner of his mouth. It was always stuck there and I couldn't keep myself from staring at it. Every time I looked at him when he would talk to me, all I could look at was that brown line down his jaw. It's like when somebody has a piece of food on their lip showing while eating, that just hangs there, and I want to do or say something about it, but I don't.

By now, mama, daddy and Aunt May are smoking up a storm, filling up the ashtrays and the room with smoke. I felt like I could barely breathe. Large, white grayish clouds filled the room, and would float in thick layers, hanging in a fixed position below the ceiling. I could hardly see the ceiling, because of all the smoke in the room. I would wave the smoke away from my face, watching it swirling around and then the cloud would circle right back in place. I never could get used to the pesky smoke, and I told myself that I would never smoke one cigarette when I grew up.

Finally, mama said, "Why don't you boys go on and play and let us adults talk now."

Jack and I really hated to hear those words, as we knew that surely was going to mean some trouble.

Cousins Ed and Ned are not the kind of cousins you just go and play with. They were big, physical boys, and meaner than dirt. They would bully you, and loved pinching you as hard as they could. They would do anything to make you mad or cry. They were about thirteen and fourteen years old, and especially loved picking on anybody younger and smaller than they were. They went running off to our rooms, and Jack and I know we are in for some trouble. When we got there, they were already messing with our toys, kicking and throwing 'em across the room.

Then Ed starts bending our construction set pieces, so we couldn't use them, and says, "Let's see ya build something out a' that!"

Now I'm getting mad and tell 'em, "Y'all quit doing that or you'll be sorry!"

Ed said, "Yeah, these things are for babies anyway."

Ned eyed my BB gun in the corner of the closet and exclaimed, "What have we here? Now this is more like it... I wonder how good this thing shoots!"

Ned cocked the handle and started firing shots at some little train cars we had on a track in the corner. He was counting the cars as he knocked them off the track. Jack told him to leave our stuff alone.

Ned said, "You want to do something about it, little baby." Jack finally had enough, grabbed a baseball, and hit Ned in the side of the head with it. Ned angrily said, "Now, you've done it boy," and pointing the BB gun right at Jack, shouted, "Y'all better run."

Jack replied, "We can outrun you fat boys any day. We'll run down to the river so fast... You won't be able to catch us."

So Jack and I took off running to get outside, and we could hear mama say as we darted by, "Boys, y'all quit your runnin' in the house."

I was following Jack, but instead of heading toward the river, I followed him to the back of the house, out of sight. We kept hidden until we saw them come out and start running toward the river, the opposite direction. Jack said, "I can't believe those big dummies believed me when I told 'em we were heading for the river."

I said, "Jack, that's a good idea telling 'em that. They will be looking for us down there for quite a while, thinking we're hiding somewhere down by the river bank."

We went on down to the barn, and Jack was by the stinky pit that we had helped daddy with earlier. Jack was kneeling there, staring at it, like he was deep in thought. I could see those wheels turning.

Jack said, "I got a great idea, if you want to have some real fun with those boys."

I wondered exactly what Jack had in mind. With a little devilish look on his face without speaking, he was pointing at the boards we had just put down to cover that nasty hole. I looked back at Jack and we began nodding in agreement without saying anything. It was like we were reading each other's mind, about what we were going to do.

I said, "Jack that is the best idea you have ever come up with."

So we started removing the stakes, the flagging around the hole, and the board cover we had only put down a little earlier with dad. We were already beginning to giggle, just thinking about our most glorious plot.

It took both of us with all our strength, to drag the contraption of wood we helped daddy build, and set it out of the way. Now we were wishing daddy hadn't used such big boards, because they made it very heavy to move. We were grunting and straining but managed to move the cover out of the way. With the surging odor rising out of that hole though, we knew we had to finish our little trap quickly.

Now there were some heaping piles of leaves all around, from the big trees close by. We could easily grab a big bunch of leaves all at once, as well as lots of various size sticks. With the longest, skinniest sticks we could find, we began our task of covering the hole. By the time we added all the sticks, leaves, and grass, we had the hole totally disguised. It didn't look a whole lot different from the ground around it.

There was this big pile of old lumber by the side of the barn on one side, and an old fence line that ran down the other side with little space between. It created this corridor that would lead right to our trap. There wasn't any way those boys would miss that hole, if we could get them to run through here. If we only got one of them to fall in it, the sight of that happening would be worth all our hard effort.

We waited until the boys realized we didn't go down toward the river. We knew they would head back toward the house looking for us, trying to find where we were. We were watching for them and would run around the barn in an obvious, loud manner, hoping they could see us in the distance.

When they spotted us, they ran in our direction, arrived at the barn, and started looking for us. We had hidden behind one of the big trees behind our ingenious trap.

We yelled out loudly, "Hey, you big, dumb nitwits... We're over here," and started throwing dirt clods at 'em.

Not to be out done, Ned yelled back, "Well, all y'all got is dirt clods... I got this here BB gun and I'm fixin' to do me some real target practice."

He started firing off shots, and we could hear the bb's pinging off the bark of the big oak tree. One shot managed to hit Jack in the back. He acted like it didn't bother him that much, but I know it had to hurt. We were bombarding 'em with dirt clods as fast and hard as we could throw 'em. They were jumping around, dodging most of them, but we did manage to land a few on our targets. Then one big clod hit Ned right square in the forehead, and now, they were really getting mad.

They had enough and came running our way as fast as they could, right straight toward the pit we covered up. It went just like we had planned. One of 'em fell right in, Ed first, then Ned followed right after.

They were wallowing around in that slimy, stinking mess of outhouse holdings, up to their chest, moaning and groaning, throwing a fit, and sounding like trapped varmints, screaming and hollering. They were cussing with words that I wasn't sure I had ever heard before. They would try to climb out and slip right back in a few times. They knew by now what they had fallen into.

Jack and I were just rolling in laughter, the kind of laugh that is so hard, it hurts your stomach but oh so enjoyable. We didn't want to hang around long enough to be there when they managed to get out. We ran back to the house but could barely contain ourselves laughing so hard. We didn't care what trouble we might get into for pulling that prank. It would be worth any punishment, even if it meant getting a few licks.

We finally got home still bursting with laughter, and stopped at the front porch, ready to run into the house when we spotted 'em coming. Mama heard us and came out on the porch. She knew something had to be up. She didn't see Ed or Ned anywhere.

In a manner like she knew we had done something, mama asked,

"What have you boys been up to? Where is Ed and Ned?"

I almost couldn't contain myself to answer. I tried to get control, but I kept interrupting my words with fits of laughter,

"I don't know...hehehe. They were down at the barn...hehehehe... Got...themselves...hehehe...in a stinking mess of...hehehe... something," as we continued laughing. Everybody else had come out on the porch to see what was going on.

Then Ed and Ned showed up looking like big, slimy snails. They were all covered in dirt, slime, old leaves, sticks and toilet holdings, stinking to high heaven and looking like a couple of zombies.

Everybody stood there not believing their eyes. Mama exclaimed in disbelief, "What in the world has happened to you boys?"

Those boys were so mad, their nostrils were going in and out like mad old bulls about to charge. They were glaring back and forth between Jack and me, staring at us with such intent of revenge, I thought their eyes were going to pop out of their sockets. We didn't think they could stink any worse than when they first showed up, but with a little help from us we managed to pull that off too.

Daddy looked at Jack and me with crossed arms and lowered his head toward us with a squint in his eyes, knowing we had everything to do with this. We pretty much knew he had figured out by now, what we somehow had done to those boys, knowing we had recently helped him cover up that nasty hole.

Ned and Ed went on to explain what had happened to them in no short order. Here, Jack and I are in some of the most serious trouble ever for something we did, but every time we glanced over at them in that stinking, slimy condition, we would burst out laughing all over again. We just couldn't help it. We were laughing so hard, we had to hold our hands down on our knees to keep standing up.

After everything settled down for a minute, mama made us apologize for what we did to the boys. Flustered with what we had done, she said, "You boys should be ashamed of yourselves, treating your cousins like that. Y'all go to your room, shut the door and don't come out, until your daddy and me sit down to figure this thing out, and what to do about it."

We happily went to our room just like mama told us to do but could still hear most of what was going on through our open window.

Ed and Ned got cleaned up the best they could at the water pump beside the house. Then mama went to get some of dad's old clothes that he didn't wear anymore, for the boys to have something clean to change into.

Finally, Aunt May said, "Time's a wastin', and we need to be getting on the road, to be sure to make it to West Memphis by dark."

They started loading up their truck, and mama gave them some food to eat along the way. She also gave them an apple pie she had just baked, to try to make up for what we had done. We could hear her again apologizing again for what we did. They were saying departing words, and daddy was telling them that he hoped things would work out for Uncle Remus concerning the job up north.

After they were gone, we heard mama say to daddy, "So what are you going to do to those boys now for pulling that prank?"

We heard daddy answer, "Today, they ain't mine, they're yours."

Then we heard 'em both start laughing almost as hard as Jack and I had! Jack and I watched the dust cloud from our window, rising high in the distance from their truck, heading down that same dusty road they had arrived on, just a short time earlier.

That rising dust could not begin to match how high our spirits had been lifted from our accomplishments, on that most glorious and wonderful day.

Cousins Make A Pit Stop (A poem by the author)

I heard their old truck comin' down the gravel road
Saw the dust cloud risin' 'bove the 'lectric poles
As their truck pulled up in a screeching halt
Their brakes so bad, they could barely stop
It was my Aunt, my Uncle and my cousins too
They said they'd stop for just an 'our or two
On their way to town, they was drivin' through
Now me and little brother gotta handle this crew

Out jumped Aunty May, hair stiff as a broom
 Could take her hair and sweep the room
 Strings of beads hanging down her neck
 That cling and clack like a train on a track
 Her glasses so big, 'bout covered her face
 Just add a handle and they'd make a rake
 Her eyes so big through her glasses it seemed
 Like seeing the moon winking back at me
 With perfume bought at the five and dime
 So strong it makes me dang near cry
 She gives a big hug and squeezes so tight
 I think my eyes might pop right out

 She takes a seat, plops down on the couch
 Then tells Uncle Remus to sit on down
 He takes a seat right by her side
 But can't get in a single word edgewise
 Now ol Uncle Remus, he's a nice enough guy
 Wears overalls purt near all the time
 Cause his stomach don't fit in regular pants
 Always scratching his butt like they's fire ants
 His mustache goes way down his jaw
 His beard so scruffy, feels sharp as a saw
 His hair on top is 'bout all gone
 'Cept a strand or two, 'bout a foot long
 Then cousins Ed and Ned, they come on in
 Bringin' their stuff like they movin' in
 So me and little brother gotta make us a plan
 How to deal with this rowdy unwelcome clan

Now Pa leans back, just listin' in
To the ladies yappin he's takin' in
Uncle Remus offers Pa a piece of his chew
Pa says no thanks, my pipe'll do
From his pocket Uncle Remus tears off a wad
Then sticks that chaw in the side o' his jaw
Soon a little drool comes runnin' down
And settles in a crack down the corner of his mouth
Sometimes he misses the spittoon when he spits
Gotta watch where you walk so's not to slip
Aunt May reaches for her tobacco can
Then rolls some smokes and licks 'em end to end
Now I can hardly breathe, clouds of smoke fill the room
Can't see the ceiling or across the room
I wave it away to keep it out of my face
But the smoke seems to stay right in place

Now cousins Ed and Ned are meaner that dirt
Ed pulled my hair, pinched little brother's butt
They'd do anything to make youngins cry
'Specially little folk 'bout half their size
They ran to our rooms fast as they could
Went to breakin' our toys like I knew they would
Then Ned shot brother with our BB gun
Took another aim and said, "Y'all better run"
So we went runnin' down the hill a bit
Past this place where Pa once dug a pit
Then we yelled out loud, "Y'all dumb nitwits"
Runnin' mad in a rage they fell down in the pit
It was the hole for the outhouse before Pa moved it

Now we ran back home laughin' all the way
Couldn't believe the fun we was havin' that day
Ma said, "Where's them boys at anyways"
I said, "Oh, they went on down the hill to play"
Ma said, "Well we're ready to eat"
Supper's on the stove, wash your hands, wipe your feet
Got beans and taters, cornbread too
Got sliced tomaters and a little stew
Then 'bout that time, them boys showed up
Sinking worse than they did when they first showed up
All covered in slime and lookin' like zombies
We went to laughin' so hard 'bout busted our tummies

When Ma found out just what we done
Said, "That's no way to treat your cousins
Y'all go to your room now and don't come out
Got to sit on down now and straighten this out"
She told the boys to go wash by the pump
They came back after still smelling like skunks
Uncle Remus said, "It's time to be leavin" then
As me and my brother watched with a grin
From our window we yelled out, "Y'all come back again"
'Cause me and little brother,
Sure enjoyed our kin

CHAPTER ELEVEN
Rising Waters

After months of cultivating, planting, and tending to the fields, it seemed like overnight they became one large white landscape. Those white canopies meant that harvest time was here, school would be starting, and sadly, that our summer was coming to an end.

There was the usual rush to get cotton into the gin as quickly as possible. The quiet countryside turned into a busy hubbub of activity. Tractors, trailers, and farm machinery was coming and going everywhere. So much cotton was strewn on the ground and on the dirt roads, even that black, cursed gumbo dirt had temporarily turned white. White cotton would accumulate and line each side of the country roads like little borders of white. Cotton was hanging on road signs, posts, fence lines and trees. It was up high on the electric power lines like hanging shredded white ropes. Strands of cotton were flying everywhere in the air, against the background of a beautiful, azure blue sky. With the massive white fields, the dangling whiteness decorating everything, everywhere, against that blue sky, the landscape was one gigantic, Norman Rockwell piece of art. But this one was drawn by nature, with the help of the unintentional work of all the cotton farmers at harvest time.

In only a few short weeks, however, all those beautiful, white fields would take on a metamorphosis. It was always astonishing, how the landscape could change at the end of harvest. Once all those fluffy white bowls were picked and hauled off to the gin, the fields would be left with only brown, bare stalks to be plowed under.

But this year Mother Nature would make the change happen more quickly, and much more dramatically. The entire year had been mostly dry with moderate rain, but combined with irrigation, it looked to be a decent enough harvest that the farmers could make a little money.

That's when things changed so quickly, almost in an instant. It suddenly began to rain and rain heavily for four miserable long days. The deep blue azure sky turned gray, then dark, and the white rows were trounced with a deluge from the heavens. The rain was relentless. Little River rose well over its banks, and because of the low, flat countryside, the water simply had no place to go, plus that same ol troublesome black gumbo dirt, didn't allow for very fast absorption of the water into the soil. The rising waters began to flood everywhere all around us. It kept rising, slowly creeping up to our house day by day, hour by hour. Dad shoved a stick in the ground, straight as he could get it, to keep an eye on how much and how quickly the water was coming up.

After the third day of non-stop rain, dad was getting more and more impatient with the situation and worriedly stated, "I have never seen this much water in the fields before. We've got too much cotton left in the field. This rain had better stop soon." I could hear the concern in his voice!

The rain seemed to never stop and water eventually covered the fields, the road to our house, and a good part of the highway going into town. The radio said our area had gotten twenty-five inches of rain. Dad said the water was a good two feet deep in some places.

It was such a prolonged, intensive downpour, pounding on the opened cotton bolls, and along with the flood itself, it would surely ruin much, if not all of the crops. Of course, all farming stopped, and all anyone could do was pray and wait. Because the water was so deep, farmers were using tractors to get around for food, supplies and to check on things.

Before the water had gotten very high, Jack, myself and mama, all helped dad move as many things outside and down at the barn to any higher position we could, to keep them away from the rising water. We were in the middle of the harvest, when all the heavy rain started. Now everyone was terrified with the fact of facing little or no harvest at all.

The flood water eventually made its way right up to the top of our doorstep but fortunately not into our house, but did get within inches. It kept rising for a while because of the runoff, even after the rain itself stopped. We were lucky that our house had been built somewhat off the ground, about three feet higher. Many others weren't that fortunate, as their house wasn't sitting quite as high as ours. The Wilsons had to leave, and go stay with some relatives in town.

One quirky thing about the flood, was that the water had brought with it fish out of the river, swimming and flopping around in our backyard. Once the rain let up enough to stand being out in it, we would jump around in the shallow water with a towel, or one of dad's biggest old work shirts, trying to snatch a fish. We actually managed to get a few carp that way. The high flood water also brought out many snakes, so we had to keep an eye out for those unwelcome visitors.

I was wading around in the water in the backyard, when I suddenly saw a water moccasin swim right past me. I shook up and down my spine for a minute. Snakes always gave me the willies anyway, but when I saw that one swim so close to me, I went trouncing through that water, running for my life in the opposite direction. I knew that snake was only interested in finding higher ground, but that didn't give me any comfort. The only higher ground available was inside our house, and I wasn't about to share it with a creepy snake. Living in the country, we were used to seeing snakes sometimes in the fields, and at the barn, but I certainly had no love lost for them.

Whenever I complained about them, dad always informed me, "Son, snakes are important for rodent control, and have a job to do like everything else."

I would respectively reply to him, "Well, as much as I hate rats, I'd take a rat any day over an ol creepy snake!"

We didn't enjoy all the negative effects from the flood waters, but it also caused school to close, as many roads around the farming community were impassable. So one nice benefit we did enjoy though, was not having to go to school for a few days, and we could spend much of the day playing in the safety of the shallow water around the house.

The radio said all the rain was a result of a hurricane that made landfall along the gulf coast of Mississippi and Alabama. What was left of it when it moved up to us, brought the torrential rain. The weather people thought it was going to miss us going further east,, but they were wrong. They had given it the name Camille. I don't think local folks had any idea that a hurricane could affect us in such a way, being so far from the gulf coast.

The rain finally stopped completely, the sun began to peek out from behind those dark clouds, and eventually, the water began to recede. It slowly crept away, just as it had inched its way toward us a few days earlier, and finally, one day, the water was gone.

The muddy gray landscape, along with unusually cold weather setting in, reflected the mood of the farmers, seeing the prospects of a good harvest vanish. Many tenants on the Potter farm had already dealt with a poor harvest for a few years before the flood happened. Some farmers would surely be in so much debt now, they would never be able to recover. I wondered if it meant more tenants would be forced to leave the Potter farm, knowing that dad would have to be the one to tell them. The future was looking very bleak for most farmers, and with some probably being forced into bankruptcy. I knew that would make my dad's job that much more of a strain on him.

After the water had subsided, the road coming to our house was still very muddy for several days. The bus couldn't make it down our road, so dad would drive us the short distance to the highway to meet the bus for school. Jack and I could tell dad was down in spirit after all the flooding, and we would try to cheer him up, but we didn't have much success. There wasn't much for dad to be happy about. I understood by now, that the prospect of future evictions he would have to handle, must have weighed heavily on his mind.

By the end of the next week, things dried out enough for the school bus to get all the way to our house. Since we didn't live very far from town, we were some of the last kids to be picked up in the morning, as the bus was making its way back to school. That meant also that we would be about the first to be dropped off in the afternoon. Usually, by the time the morning bus picked us up, dad already would be up and gone, but this day he was still home. The flood had upset everyone's schedule, and I knew things weren't normal like before the flood.

I wanted to say bye to dad, but mama told me he wasn't feeling well and that he was still asleep in bed. She asked us to not disturb him, so we went outside to wait on the bus. As I stood there waiting, I couldn't help peering back at dad's bedroom window, feeling badly, not being able to see dad before leaving, but I honored mama's wishes.

This particular cold morning, the heater on the bus wasn't working, which made for a very cold ride to school. I was sitting all the way on the inside corner of the seat against the window, trying to nuzzle my body in a way to keep myself as warm as possible. I had my head lowered into my chest, hands stuffed under my jacket sleeves all the way under my armpits, all pressed against my own body to fight off as much of the cold as I could. As the bus seemed to ever so slowly make its way down the familiar trek to school, I had my head leaned up against the window. Without turning my head, I shifted my eyes toward the now silent devastated fields along the way, watching the former glorious white rows quickly pass by in the window, row after row, appearing as slumping, defeated soldiers from some horrendous battle. Only this battle was one lost to Mother Nature.

I began to sadly reminisce about all the fun Jack and I had during the warm summer months, playing in those same fields that were once thriving and alive. But now I couldn't help but think about the devastating effect that was certainly to come from the recent unfortunate turn of events for all the farmers. A spiritual coldness began to descend on me, one far worse than the physical chill I was feeling from that cold bus ride. I was old enough now to understand that there might be a lot of pain coming very soon for so many of my neighbors and friends.

As I closed my eyes, I saw their familiar faces I had grown to know and was worried for their future, including my own family, but I especially worried;

For my dad!

CHAPTER TWELVE
Force and Resistance

When our bus arrived at school, we jumped off at the usual spot beside the elementary building where it always stopped to let us out. Jack, who was not so happy for school to start back, depressingly remarked, "I'll see ya later Bean," and sluggishly went on his way, straight into the elementary building. I continued on the long sidewalk, making my way to the middle school building, that was a few more yards away.

This was the first year for me to have a different teacher in each subject. That was the biggest change in middle school, but I sure did love it. Plus, I wasn't bunched up with all those pesky little kids in the first and second grade anymore. One thing I had always looked forward to, being in middle school, was relief from not being stuck in the same classroom all day, every day, with the same teacher. When I had a teacher in elementary school I didn't particularly like, that was it. I would have to wait another entire year to get a new teacher. That could surely make for a very long year.

It was so refreshing to change classrooms and teachers throughout the day but one bad thing about having so many teachers now, was the homework they gave. It was like every teacher thought they weren't doing their job, if they didn't assign tons of homework most nights. Then they would give assignments over the weekends sometimes too, and I really hated that. I think their goal at times was to make a kid's life miserable.

My favorite teacher was Mr. Huggins. He taught science, and had a way to keep me really interested in the subject. He didn't always teach exactly out of the book. He would do outrageous things at times, in order to teach a principle of science he was trying to get the class to understand. He would teach us to question not only how things worked, but why they worked, and he would often demonstrate it.

I will never forget the time he was teaching us about force and resistance. Mr. Huggins was using a big heavy anvil, a big thick board and a sledge hammer for the demonstration. He had two strong high school boys to assist in the demonstration. He laid down on his back on a table and he grabbed the board himself to lay over his chest. Then with one boy each holding one end of the anvil, they gently and ever so slowly placed that heavy anvil in position of resting on his chest. They stayed close by in case they needed to re-balance the anvil to keep it from falling to one side or the other. I thought all that weight alone might crush his ribs. While lying there, he instructed another assistant to hit the anvil, as hard as he could with a big hammer several times. The entire classroom, including myself, cringed in disbelief and near horror as we watched, but somehow were totally intrigued at the same time. As his assistant holding the hammer pounded down onto the metal on his chest, Mr. Huggins maintained a calm smile during the entire exercise. He said it was to demonstrate that he would feel none of the force of the hammer on his body, and that the anvil would absorb all the energy from his assistant's pounding with the sledge hammer. It was the most amazing thing I think I had ever seen in my life, and certainly in school. Somehow I figured all future education, for the rest of my life, might prove to be boring after this class. Mr. Huggins later got reprimanded by the school principal for doing that force and resistance exercise, with that anvil and hammer.

Today however, he was teaching us about gravity, using a tall ladder and some simple props. He told the class to push the desks together out of the way, to where everyone could stand in a circle to get a good view of the results of the experiment. The ladder was so tall, it scraped some paint off the ceiling when he went to stand the ladder up. Staring up at the dent he made in the ceiling, He remarked, "Oops... I think I can fix that with a little paint?"

He then took the baseball that always sat on his desk and also this pillow he kept for back support from his desk chair and laid the pillow at the bottom of the ladder on the floor. Surrounded by the class in a circle, he proceeded climbing to the top of the ladder holding the baseball. When he got to the top, he took a ping pong ball out of his shirt pocket, while still holding the baseball in the other hand.

He asked the class to guess which one would hit the floor first if he dropped them at the same time; the larger heavier baseball or the smaller, lighter ping pong ball? Of course, most of the class was shouting, "The baseball, the baseball." He held both objects out and carefully dropped both at the same moment. The two objects appeared to hit the floor at the same time. He said, "This in simple terms class, is the law of gravity, and that by demonstrating it, I hope to get the point across much better than just talking about it. Regardless of the weight of any two objects I drop, both will hit the floor at the exact same time when dropped."

He went on to repeat the experiment several times, with all kinds of objects, but always with something heavy in one hand, and something much lighter in the other. After using various shapes and sizes of objects to illustrate his point, to our amazement, he went to his desk, and this time he reached underneath and rolled out a heavy bowling ball. I thought if he keeps this up, next thing you know, he will be pulling out a rabbit from under that desk. He held the bowling bowl up high for everyone to see and then showed us a little marble he had in his pocket. He held both up together, side by side, to instill in the class the immensity and weight of the bowling ball, compared to the tiny marble. The students all looked back and forth at each other with puzzled looks on their faces, figuring the bowling ball will surely damage the floor if dropped from that height, even with a pillow to soften the blow.

He began to make his way up the ladder, appearing to hold on for dear life to the heavy bowling ball. He would stop at each step, to get a breath, really making a show of it. Climbing with the heavy ball was truly difficult but with the exaggerated acting to engage the class even more, it was quite the entertainment. He wanted to make sure he had every student's complete attention but by now he had certainly accomplished that easily.

Mr. Huggins finally got to the last step of the ladder, propped the bowling ball on the top of the ladder to rest and out of breath exclaimed, "Whew! Now I know why I don't go bowling very often," and the class responded with somewhat of a cautious laugh! He proceeded to precariously hold the bowling ball with one arm propped over the top of the ladder, while easily holding the little marble in the other hand. He would pause, looking back and forth at the two obviously different objects, with one last comparative look, as if ready now to begin the experiment. Every student gazed in awe with their mouths dropped open, and the room got deathly quiet, anticipating the moment he would let go of that bowling ball and marble.

He then instructed, "Okay everybody... Stand back...don't be too close. I don't want to smash anyone's foot!" He began to slowly and demonstratively count down; "Five... Four... Three... Two... One..." and just as he appeared that he was going to drop the heavy ball and marble, he calmly exclaimed, "I'm only joking about dropping the bowling ball," and the entire class burst out laughing this time. He then continued, "Did y'all really think I was going to drop that bowling ball? Well, I hope I got the point of the lesson across, and besides, I can't afford to pay the school to fix a hole in the floor either."

The whole class was still laughing as he descended down the ladder. Mr. Huggins had an unusual but very effective way of teaching, but he certainly was never boring, and we always learned something. Who could ever forget such a demonstration?

The principal would come in the room unannounced at times, to see what crazy experiment Mr. Huggins might be doing in class on that particular day. Mr. Huggins warned us to never try his demonstrations at home, except harmless ones he assigned. We would sometimes overhear other teachers making fun of his quirky ways, but he was the most loved by all the students and the other teachers. They knew he was amusingly eccentric and was one thing I think they adored about him. They all regarded him as a genius.

Still, as much as I loved Mr. Huggins science class, I couldn't wait to get home after school. Jack would always have a handful of pages he had colored with crayons, or some writing he did, learning his letters. He did a lot of coloring and drawing in the third grade.

On the way home on the bus, I was telling Jack about the fascinating experiment we did with gravity in Mr. Huggins science class, with the tall ladder, and different objects he dropped from the top of the ladder. I was really wanting to get to the funny part about the bowling ball, but Jack didn't act very interested in what I was saying. I could tell he could care less in learning about gravity. Still, his disinterest didn't stop me from talking about it. As an educated "man of science", I felt it was my obligation to teach Jack these important scientific principles that he should learn as I was sure they would come in handy later in life.

I couldn't wait to get home, and tell mama about the experiment in science class. I also thought it might be a way to cheer her up due to all the recent events. I think she had learned a lot about science too, from me always telling her about what we did in class, whether she really wanted to hear it or not. She usually would listen patiently, while sometimes busily doing other things. She might make a half-hearted comment, and in an almost dismissive way say something like,

"Well, that is very interestin', Bean."

When we arrived home, and got off the bus, I could see daddy's truck, parked in his usual spot out front. Mama's blue station wagon was there also, so I knew dad had to be there. I thought that he still must not be feeling well since he was still at the house, but I would be glad to get to see him so soon right after school.

Jack and I hurried in to see dad, in hopes to find him feeling better than when we had left for school that morning. As we were making our way through the living room, I could see mama and dad in the kitchen.

As I approached them, I began exclaiming, "Guess what we did in science class today? Mr. Huggins was up on a tall ladder, holding a heavy bowling ball in one hand, and a little marble in another when he...," and I stopped in the middle of my sentence!

Mama and dad were very quiet, in the most glum mood. I could tell they were distraught and not listening to me at all. It was like they didn't know Jack and I were there. Dad had his elbow propped up on the table, with one hand under his chin, sadly glaring toward the wall. Mama was standing quietly at the sink, with arms crossed, staring out the window.

Jack ran over to dad, repeatedly pulling on his shirt sleeve, and pushing a drawing he had done at school, close to dad's face. Jack was desperately trying to get his attention, pleading, "Dad, look what I drew, doesn't this look just like our barn, look dad, look!"

Jack persisted, not giving up on getting dad's attention to his drawing. In a quiet voice, sounding very tired, dad finally answered, "That's nice son," as he was getting up. He lightly rubbed the top of Jack's head as he was walking away, barely acknowledging us. Never looking at us, saying only a few simple words, he added, "I'll be back later."

He went out the front door, and jumped in his truck, without saying anything more as Jack quickly followed behind. Jack stopped at the doorway and stood there silently still, sadly observing the trail of dust rising from his pickup truck, as dad drove away.

Jack, in an apologetic, timid voice, assuming he had done something wrong, asked mama if dad was mad at him for bothering him with the drawing. She assured him, "Goodness no son, you didn't do anything wrong, your dad has something very heavy on his mind right now, and he just needs some time to himself." After pausing a bit, she continued, "Y'all sit down here for a minute."

I had no idea what she was about to say, but by the somber tone in her voice, I wasn't sure I wanted to find out. Mama said she would rather dad tell us himself, but she knew we wouldn't be satisfied, until we were told what was going on.

She told us how the farms weren't producing in recent years like they were before, and also, how the new combines and picking machines had been replacing much of the need for farmhands. Now with the recent flood, things had gotten worse all around for everyone.

Then she told us the most devastating news of all. She went on to say that things had gotten so bad, that Mr. Potter was having to let dad go as his farm manager. She hesitantly added, "We are going to have to leave the farm, and move into town soon." She said that Mr. Potter hated letting dad go, but he had no choice under the circumstances.

At this point, Jack and I didn't know how to respond to this news. It was much to take in all at once. Jack and I sat quietly looking back at each other, not sure of what all this would mean for us. I asked mama, "What would dad do anyway if we moved into town?"

She told us that dad had an idea about a new business to try, but in the meantime, she also had applied for a job at the new garment factory that had recently opened up. She said if she got that job that would help us get by, until we could get back on our feet. She said they had a little money saved up, and plus, Mr. Potter was giving dad what she called some severance pay. They were thinking it would be enough money for us to move to Little River and start over in town.

Jack, not understanding entirely what was happening, was excited about the prospects of moving into town. I was worried how our entire life, perhaps was about to change. I thought back how dad had told me many times, "Farming's the only thing I know how to do well son, and I don't think I could ever see myself doing anything else." Those words kept playing over and over in my head.

I wasn't quite sure I was being told about everything that was happening, but I couldn't question mama. Even though I suspected there might be more to it all than what I was being told, I also knew I couldn't do anything about it. I thought I might as well try to make the best of the situation and remain positive. One thing for sure, we were at least not moving far away. It would still be the same town, the same school, and maybe not such a big deal after all. I mostly felt concern for dad, giving up the life he had always loved, to try something different.

By bedtime, dad wasn't back yet, but mama told us we needed to get to sleep soon, reminding us that the bus always showed up at 7:20 in the morning. My mind was going in a thousand directions, and there was no way I could go to sleep. Not now, not tonight!

Being the comforter mama was, she remarked, "No need to worry, things will work out, and besides, we might come to like living in town." She then gave us both an especially long hug and sent us off to bed.

In spite of all the gloominess, Jack was excited about the prospects of living in town. He said he was beginning to think of all the advantages of living there. He began to spout out a seemingly well thought out list, as if he had been studying the situation coming for a long time.

First, he talked about being close to the bridges that went over the river in town. Those spots under the bridges always made for good fishing and there were three places a bridge went over Little River. Jack then brought up how we could ride our bikes close to the drive-in theater by the highway, and watch movies for free. We rarely got to see a movie in town. Although we would not be able to hear what was being said on the huge drive-in movie screen, Jack kept reminding me how it wouldn't cost anything, and still be some fun. I told him I heard a lot of teenagers like Donny Hobson that had cars would sneak a bunch of their friends in, by hiding them in the trunk, and only the driver had to pay to get in. I wasn't old enough to drive yet but I considered that doing something like that was wrong and was the same as stealing. I would never do such a thing anyway as Dad always taught us it was wrong to steal, cheat or not earn what you get.

Jack continued talking about how it would be easier to find empty coke bottles in town to sell. He added that the stores were right there close by, to trade them in and we might have more money to spend. He finally added that we might end up moving close to where some of our school buddies lived too.

That boy's mind was going ninety to nothing. It may have been the most I had ever heard him talk without stopping. I don't think he took one breath!

Nonetheless, he almost had me in a total positive frame of mind about the whole thing of moving, and he was making some very good points, but I was tired of hearing him talk non-stop and exclaimed, "Jack, please? Go on to sleep!"

Still, in a tired, sleepy voice, while yawning in between words, he continued, "Maybe, we will move into a house...close to that...nice baseball...field...too... I think it may be..."

Finally, in one last desperate attempt to get him to shut up, I sternly pleaded, "Jack... Pu...leasseee! Go on to sleep!"

As he continued mumbling, seemingly half-awake, half-asleep, I shook my head, rolled over, and buried my head under the covers. Jack was looking on the bright side of things, but I wasn't totally convinced! I lay in bed, rolling over and over, not being able to sleep.

Then I remembered the experiment Mr. Huggins did in class, teaching the principle about force and resistance. I would have never dreamed how symbolic it would be of what I would learn when I got home that evening, learning of a new heavy burden placed on our family.

I thought of how that experiment mirrored what we would now have to endure, a forced action to move, not by our choosing, but as a result of something unexpectedly being pressed upon us. I wondered if we could somehow come out smiling, like Mr. Huggins did, while lying there on that table with that heavy weight upon him.

Our teacher suffered no harm and was totally fine in the end. But this was no science experiment. This was real life. I could not help but worry what the future might have in-store for our family.

But I mostly thought of dad!

Part Two

CHAPTER THIRTEEN
New Horizons

The day had finally arrived. I had spent my last night in the only house I had ever known. We had already moved all the big stuff to our new house in town, leaving only a few small things to hold us over that last night in our soon to be former, old house. Finally, we had loaded every last thing, and we were getting ready to head up the dirt road to the highway, for the very last time.

As we were all about to leave, Jack, myself, mama, and dad stopped, and paused beside mama's blue station wagon. We turned to face the old homestead, as we all stood in solemn silence. Not one of us said a word. We remained standing there, as if trying to freeze that moment of time in our memory. I would never want to forget what that place had meant to me. I wanted the picture of the house, the barn, and surrounding fields, to be stuck in my mind forever. I wanted to always be able to close my eyes and recall that picture, while remembering everything; the smells, the sky, the colors, the fields, the moment. This little house that was only a tiny blip in the middle of an endless horizon of farmland, was about to disappear from my life forever, but hopefully not from my memory.

Jack was riding with dad, as they slowly pulled out first. Mama, getting in the car with some quiet tears, streaming down her face, said something I will never forget.

She leaned across the seat, looked straight at me, and very softly said, "Benny, leaving things behind will never be as hard as leaving those you love." She went on explaining that things will come and go, and sometimes people may leave, but the ones you really love will always be part of you. She then asked, "Do you understand what I am saying to you?"

I responded, "I think I understand. Things might come and go in my life, but I'm always stuck with my family, even Jack."

Mama quipped, "That's right, even Jack."

As we took the slow ride up the old dirt road, I thought about the dark trail of dust, rising from our vehicles in a way that I never had before. That familiar dusty cloud in the past, had always been a sign that we were close to home. The same cloud that welcomed me home so many times before, now meant we were leaving something behind. That long trail of dust, seemed to be hanging in the air a little longer than usual. It was as if the farm that we had come to know for so long, was raising a lonely, weary dusty hand, waving to say goodbye.

The move to our new place in town was not that far away, but I thought it might as well be a million miles. It wasn't the distance so much, but rather how I feared what the change in our way of life might mean in the future.

We arrived in town, and after crossing over the main bridge, we slowly made the turn onto Main Street where the city hall and police station were. As we were coming around the curve, we saw Sheriff Mason standing outside, opening his car door and about to get in. He turned and spotted dad's truck and motioned us on over. Dad pulled in, followed by mama, and dad parked right beside the sheriff's car. Happy to see us, the sheriff smiled and propped one arm on top of dad's truck above the window as they began to talk. I heard him tell dad if we needed any help getting settled in, to let him know.

The sheriff suddenly quipped, "Are you boys thirsty? Why don't y'all come on in the office and I'll tell Deputy Tillis to get you a cold coke out of the machine before y'all head on, that is, if it's alright with your daddy. It won't take but a second."

Dad told us that would be okay, but he and mama didn't get out while Jack and I got our cokes and hurried back out. Dad and the sheriff kept talking a little longer, and by that time, Jack and I had just finished the last drop of our refreshing cokes.

I told the sheriff, "Thanks for the drink Sir. It was so good and cold, I could sure drink another one."

Acting a little embarrassed, mama exclaimed, "Bean, where are your manners son?"

Sheriff Mason chuckled, "Oh, that's okay Belle. I heard-tell that Bean can consume a lot of liquid. I heard he once killed off the entire five-gallon water container at Mr. Potter's office."

I couldn't believe he knew about the time I swallowed a bug on the way to Mr. Potter's office, while riding with dad in his truck. When we got to Mr. Potter's office, I almost emptied out their entire water jar, trying to wash that bug down. I suppose I was lucky I didn't wind up with the nickname Bug. Bean sure sounded like a whole lot cooler name.

Finally, the adults finally stopped talking, and we proceeded to get back on our way. As we pulled out, I saw the advertisement for movies on the front of the sign of The Grand Theater, which was a short distance from city hall. I had been to see a movie there a time or two, and figured I might get to go to the movie theater more often now, living in town. Girls were always swooning over movie stars at school, and I thought maybe I would get to see Jean Potter there sometime. Now if any cowboy movie was playing, I would definitely be interested in seeing one of those.

As we made our way down Main Street, I was noticing all the business names on the buildings in a way I hadn't noticed before, when I came to town with my parents. Now they would all be very close and in only a few minutes, I could be here on my bicycle I supposed. I saw the Little River Record Newspaper office, Henson Appliance & Repair, River Café, but what stood out was Holmes Drugs. It had a big picture on the window of an ice cream float with soda and ice cream running down its sides, with a big long spoon stuck in the cold glass and a happy girl holding and smiling down at her refreshing looking treat. Boy, I knew I couldn't wait to get a little money and to try one of those out soon.

As we proceeded toward the end of Main Street, about to turn by Coleman Bothers gas station, we saw Mrs. Harrison walking by, and she gave mama a big wave. She was a friend of mama and dad, and she owned the department store in town. She would come and visit mama once in a while at the farm. I was glad mama and dad already had close friends in town. I suppose she already knew about us moving into town.

In just a few blocks, we made another turn by the railroad tracks and I noticed they came to a dead end. I asked mama about that and she told me our little train that came to town had to back its way out somehow, as the tracks stopped right there. I couldn't wait to catch seeing a train come in town one day and see exactly how they managed doing that.

We progressed on, making a right turn just past a church, as mama exclaimed, "This is our street…just a little farther now."

I noticed the faded, green, slightly crooked street sign, with the pole bent at an angle and I read the name of the street out loud; "Elm Street." For some reason, I was happy that was going to be the name of the street that we would be living on. It sounded like a great name and good as any, if I were picking out the name. I was impressed driving on all smooth, paved streets with names, after living around rough gravel and dusty dirt roads for so long in the country.

After crossing a few more streets, trying to read their names as we passed by, we arrived at our new house. Jack was so excited he almost didn't wait for dad to stop, before he was trying to jump out of dad's truck.

Mama pulled up right behind dad, and he said, "Well, here it is; our nice, new home. Pretty ain't it; what do you think?" I sat there with the car door open, halfway in the car and halfway out with one foot on the ground, almost hesitant to get out. I began examining the house, the yard, the huge trees blowing in the wind, and I told myself to be positive, and I thought maybe this won't be so bad.

What really stood out were the bright, white walls of the outside of the house, compared to houses around the farm, including ours. Our old house on the farm had hardly ever seen a can of paint. The fact is, most farmers we knew, never bothered with painting their house. They figured it would be a waste of money, when there was always something else pressing that the money needed to be spent on.

I remarked to dad, "They must have just painted it, right before we were to move in."

"No, I think Mr. Coleman told me it had been a couple of years since it was last painted, but it still looks good," replied dad.

"Who is Mr. Coleman?"

He told me he was an old friend who owned that service station in town we passed and sold him the house. Then I knew he was talking about the Coleman gas station, which was not far from this old wooden bridge over Little River, that I had been over a time or two.

Dad showing the glimpse of a little smile, for the first time in a while, told us that Mr. Coleman made him a great deal on the house to help us get back on our feet. I was glad to finally see dad happy about something, and if I ever saw Mr. Coleman in person, I was going to be sure and thank him!

Our new house was much bigger than the one on the farm. It actually had a carport attached to the side of the house, with a nice smooth, concrete surface, and big enough for one vehicle to park under the roof. The carport had these impressive, large, red brick pillars along the side.

I could tell Mama really loved that carport. With excitement in her voice, she was telling us that when she got back from the store now, she could get out of bad weather easily, especially if it was raining. She could keep her shoes clean, and go straight into the house through the porch with the groceries.

The neighbors next door, across the side alley happened to pull up, and I watched as they and their car disappeared through a huge door that was going up. They had a garage with a gigantic door that could be raised and lowered by a motor, and they could park their car inside. Now that was really something! It was big enough inside they could park two vehicles side by side. Nobody out where we had lived had a garage like that. I thought what a waste of space, only to park vehicles in, but did think it was awfully nice. The thought ran through my mind that I'm not back on the farm anymore and we got rich folk for neighbors. But soon my thoughts turned back to our own new house.

More important to us than the inside of the house, was what was outside. Jack and I were so accustomed to open fields, and not being hemmed in, it was important to have a big yard. Before we even thought of seeing what the inside looked like, we ran around to the back of the house to check out the yard. I think dad, knowing what we were thinking, followed us, and pointed out, saying, "Shoot, this lot is big enough you could build another house here. You boys will have plenty of room to play around in back here."

It indeed, was a surprisingly large backyard, especially compared to most of the other houses in town. There was enough room to hit baseballs in, especially with all a lot of trees and bushes, acting like fences, to knock the ball down. There were huge oak and maple trees that formed a kind of border along the back, and also, along the front of the house just off the street. In between them, it was mostly clear space except for this one really, gigantic, old oak tree that stood like a giant in the back corner of the lot.

Dad, pointing toward that huge tree remarked, "That would be a great tree to build a treehouse in one day. If I get time, maybe I can help you get started on it sometime?"

I replied, "Would you dad? That would be great," and I gave him the biggest hug.

Dad said, "Sure Bean, once everything settles down, and I get some free time."

About that time, I heard mama from the back door of the house, shouting in a pleading tone, "Bill, I need you in here to help me."

Dad reassuringly proclaimed, "I'm coming Belle, hold your horses, just showing the boys something", and turning to go inside, he added, "I better go help your mama tend to stuff inside before she gets herself into a hissy."

I stood there, staring at that giant oak tree, with its massive trunk, and outstretched arms of limbs and branches. I thought, if we build a treehouse, we might as well build something extra nice and really big. I would want it to be the envy of all the kids in the entire neighborhood.

I began to envision what this magnificent treehouse would look like. It would have a ladder in front built into the tree; a front door that could be closed; a deck area to be able to walk all around it; a good roof so we could stay up there when it rained; a rope and pulley system to get big, heavy stuff up to the treehouse, and a big swinging rope hanging down from one of the huge branches to swing down on.

My imagination went on and on, like a chief engineer drawing up the plans in my head, as I stood there thinking of the possibilities. I pictured myself being there, high up in the air, sleeping all snuggled up to the sound of raindrops, dancing on a tin roof.

The only drawback about the tree was its proximity to a neighbor on that side of our lot. It was just a few feet from this metal fence separating our house from the Suttons, an older couple, that dad said lived on that side of the house. They had a big dog in their backyard that had the biggest, fancy dog house I had ever seen. Whenever we would get close to the fence, he would come out of the dog house and stick his nose through the fence, growling and barking constantly while we were there. It looked like a German Shepard, but I wasn't sure what kind of dog it was.

A long alleyway ran right beside our house going one way, and it continued across the street, going the other direction. There was another alleyway that ran behind our house that we learned the city would use to come through with the garbage trucks.

Our new house was pretty much located in the middle of town, so that would make it easy to go anywhere in just a few minutes on our bikes. The alleys made it nice too, as they cut across town in any direction, and that would allow us to take short cuts, avoiding people and cars when we wanted too. We could ride our bikes easily all around town, since all the roads were paved, a big plus of living in town. In just a very short distance, I could be at school or any store on Main Street, maybe trying out one of Holmes Drugs ice cream floats. I could easily get to any of the fishing spots on Little River that would be close to home now. I couldn't wait to try out the spot around the old wooden bridge that was just past Mr. Coleman's service station.

On the farm, the fields were our backyard, but here, they would be replaced with an entire town to play in. Here the houses were all bunched up, new neighbors to meet, and an almost endless maze of streets and places to check out. Jack and I couldn't wait to get on our bikes and ride around town and check out all the streets.

Jack and I decided to peek a little ways down the alley beside our house, and saw a huge empty space in between houses. What a sight it was! It was a flat, big, green field that ran a couple of hundred feet in every direction. It extended all the way to the alley that ran beside our house. We knew it would be a great place to play baseball and had trees blocking most of the houses. We could have a nice infield with all the bases, and make use of thick, tall bushes behind the home plate area to serve as a backstop. It had a line of trees down both sides that could serve as foul lines. We could make the alleyway in the outfield be an automatic home run, that is, if anyone hit a ball that far.

This place was perfect. I already knew what to name it, so I said to Jack, "Let's call this place, The Greenfield." We might be able to round up enough kids to choose and have teams living in town.

Across from The Greenfield, on the other side of the alley, we saw neighbors that had apple, plum, and other fruit trees in their backyards. I had never seen so many fruit trees in one place. I knew there wasn't any way that one family alone could eat all those apples or plums by themselves. I visualized playing baseball, getting hungry, and taking part in some of the fruit off those trees. I was thinking those folks wouldn't mind sharing a little.

We had been outside for a while, and we began to make our way back to the house. That's when we could hear mama calling loudly, "Jack... Bean, what on earth are y'all doing? Y'all get in here and help unpack stuff."

Jack and I both realized we had not yet seen the inside of the house. We shouted back so we knew mama could hear us, almost in unison, "We're coming mama!"

We were close to the back porch, so we went inside through the back door of the house. The back door led straight into a nice, size utility room, where dad was tinkering with some hoses going to a new washing machine. On one side of the room was another door, and I wondered what was in there. It was a very small room, with a few shelves and a small window to the outside. I envisioned using it for something just for myself, if mama or dad didn't claim it for anything in particular. That utility room in the back of the house, led right into the kitchen where I saw mama busily sorting out dishes.

Mama said, "I can't believe you boys haven't wanted to see your room yet. Your dad has already set up your beds in your rooms, but y'all can start unpacking the boxes we put in your rooms, and put your stuff up."

I heard mama say rooms, and to our disbelief, Jack and I had our own separate bedrooms, right next to each other. We couldn't believe it. Now I could keep my room organized the way I like it, especially me being so much neater than Jack. I wouldn't have to put up with him messing up my room anymore.

I was putting up the last of my clothes in my dresser, when I heard a knock on the front door, which was right by my room. I wondered who could be coming by already? I rushed to open the door, and what a surprise, to both myself and our first visitor. We stood there with our mouths dropped open in disbelief. It was my new friend I had made at school that year, Bobby Jansen. Neither one of us could believe it.

Bobby shaking his head in total surprise, said, "I saw y'all moving in, and some kids looking around outside, but had no idea it was you Bean moving in this house. I live down at the end of the alley."

I couldn't believe my new, best friend lived close by me. I had no idea before where he lived in town, but now it made things just that much better.

I asked Bobby, "Is yours that long, green house, the last one just past that open, green field, before the alley comes out onto the next street?"

"Yep, that's it. We have been there for only a couple of months ourselves. Now we can play together anytime we want to, since we are so close to each other."

I told him about my idea about playing baseball in that spot I had named The Greenfield, and he said he liked that name.

I introduced Bobby to mama, dad, and Jack, and how he lived right down the alley. Bobby said he thought he had seen Jack around school but they never really talked.

After introducing Bobby as my friend, Dad said, "That's nice son. You have a friend right by to play with anytime you want too."

It didn't take long for Jack to ask Bobby, "Have you got any younger brothers?"

"No…just a couple of nagging sisters that hog our bathroom all the time. You're lucky you don't have any!" Jack appeared disappointed, and I assured him that some of his friends must live around here somewhere too.

Dad heard us talking, and hearing his last name, asked Bobby if his dad was the same Mr. Jansen that worked on TV's down at Henson Appliance & Repair on Main Street.

Bobby answered, "Yes sir, that's him. He works on televisions, radios and other electronic stuff for Mr. Henson the store owner. My dad's an electronic genius."

My dad replied, "Well Bobby, I'll have to be seeing him before long, as our television has been acting funny lately, and maybe he can fix it…can't afford to buy a new right now."

Bobby replied, "Oh, he'll be glad to take a look at it and tell you what it would cost to fix it."

I was glad dad got to meet my new friend whom I had met at school, but I think Jack might have been a little jealous. Living out in the country, Jack had only me to play with, and now my closest friend lived practically next door. I think Jack felt like he might get left out, being so much younger.

I had mostly finished putting all my stuff up in my room, and I asked, "Can I go see Bobby's house down the alley."

Dad said, "Sure, if your mama doesn't have anything else you need to do right now."

Mama said, "You boys go on, we're about done here for today anyway. I'm tired, and anything else will have to wait 'till tomorrow… Just be back in time for supper before seven."

"Okay mama."

Bobby and I excitedly begin walking together down the alley when Jack came out and was leaning out of the screened door of the back porch. He was sadly peering in our direction with this depressed look on his face. I think it wasn't so much for me finding a new friend, but that he was feeling left alone for the first time.

As Jack sadly gazed our way while leaving him behind, I yelled assuredly, "I'll be back in a little while Jack!"

As we approached Bobby's house, the aroma of something good cooking was almost more than I could take. We proceeded to the kitchen where his mama was frying some chicken, had corn on the cob boiling in a pot and some biscuits baking in the oven.

Bobby couldn't wait to tell somebody; anybody his good news. "Mama, this is Bean that I told you about at school."

"You mean this is the famous Bean…a lot of people have heard about you," of course referring to the bean trailer incident when I was younger. I felt a little embarrassed but also surprised that she knew about that event.

Then Bobby continued, "Where's dad? I want him to meet Bean too."

She responded, "He's staying being a little late at work, finishing fixin' some appliance, but will be home soon, as supper is almost ready." She looked at me and said, "Bean, you're welcome to eat with us too if you like."

I was getting awfully hungry, and the food smelled enticing, but I answered, "No thanks Mrs. Jansen, Mama's cooking too, and I better not spoil my supper!"

Bobby told me the only good thing about having a couple of sisters, was that he got to have his own bedroom, while they had to share one. In his room I saw a baseball bat that looked brand new, a BB gun sitting in the corner, and some toy trucks that he told me he had outgrown. He asked, "You think Jack might like to have those trucks? I don't play with them anymore."

I told him, "Yeah, that really might help cheer Jack up, if you're sure you don't want them anymore."

While grabbing the BB gun Bobby said, "This is one of my favorite things to do. I practice with it all the time in my backyard. You want to go try it out Bean?"

I replied, "Well I need the practice… I gotta couple of really mean cousins I would love to use it on!"

Bobby said, "Oh yeah, I remember you telling me about 'em, when those boys from up at Fourche Creek came to visit you and Jack back on the farm. You sure did get more than even with 'em if you asked me. I would have rather got shot with the BB rifle than winding up in that stinky toilet mess y'all got them boys into." Bobby continued, "Let's go outside and see how good a shot you are?"

He said his dad told him he could shoot it, but only in one direction toward this one line of big trees and bushes, that would stop the bbs from going anywhere. We went out back, set up some tin cans in front of the trees, and started shooting. I managed to hit my target pretty regularly, once I got my aim down. There were lots of tin cans lying there with holes in them, so I could tell Bobby practiced a lot. He never missed a shot, and I was really impressed at how accurate he was.

We were stacking the cans back up when we heard Mr. Jansen pull up in the front. Bobby took off running to the front of the house to greet his dad, and I followed right behind.

Bobby proudly exclaimed, "Dad, this is my new friend Bean from school. His family just moved into the house at the end of the alley. We were shooting the BB gun a little bit in the backyard."

Mr. Jansen replied, "Nice to finally meet you Bean. I heard someone was moving into that house, but I didn't know who it was."

I told Mr. Jansen about our old TV acting up, and how it would be nice to get it fixed for good, once and for all.

He said, "I'll be glad to take a look at it, and maybe it would be something easy to fix. You never know…could be something real simple. Tell your dad to bring it by the store."

"Okay, I'll be sure and tell him."

We followed him into the house, and again I was asked if I wanted to stay for supper. I told them no thanks, and that I had better be getting back, since we were just getting settled into our new house. I told them all goodbye, and headed back down the alley, but that good smelling fried chicken had made me starving by now.

When I got back home, dad was setting up the TV and trying to get a picture to come in, but it kept cutting out. He would go over to it, and bang on the side a couple of times to get it to stay on. It would work okay for a second, and then cut out again.

In frustration, dad remarked, "I'm going to have to get this dang thing to Mr. Jansen pretty soon, before it quits working altogether."

I told dad how I had met Mr. Jansen, and he said to bring the TV by anytime to the Henson Appliance store, where he worked.

Dad then remarked, "Bean, you're just a regular ol socialite," and added, "Hey, you boys want to go with me tomorrow into town? I have something I want to show you that I'm doing that I'm excited about too. I don't want to tell you about it now, but you'll find out tomorrow!" Though Jack and I begged dad to tell us what he was talking about, he said, "Let's save that surprise for tomorrow."

We were eating a late supper with all the things mama had to do that day. She said she was sorry that we were only having bologna sandwiches tonight. With the busy day of moving, she told us she was too tired to cook a regular good supper. It was only bologna, but on this day, it tasted like the best darn sandwich I had eaten in a very long time.

Later that night, I lay in bed, thinking how today had turned out so differently than what I had expected. What a turn of events. I had a great, new house, my own room, and had discovered my new best friend lived close by, right down the alley. On top of all that, dad had this big, new surprise waiting to show us in town tomorrow.

Like the sadness I had felt only a few hours earlier in leaving the farm behind, I was now beginning to feel excitement and anticipation, in these new but welcome horizons.

What a marvelous day, indeed!

CHAPTER FOURTEEN
Dad's Big Surprise

I almost couldn't sleep that first night in our new house. The excitement for all that had happened, kept my mind thinking of all the new possibilities from living in town now. It seemed like a very long night as I couldn't wait to see what the next day would bring. How could it be any better than the day I had just experienced? Finally my tired eyes gave in and I felt like I must have gone to sleep with a smile on my face.

I awoke to the morning sunlight shining through my window on that much anticipated Sunday morning. It seemed just a little brighter than recent mornings. It's funny how colors of nature seem so much more vibrant when your own outlook is a happy one. I was indeed happy and could not imagine things being any better. In addition, dad had this surprise in town he promised to show me and Jack. I couldn't wait to find out what that was.

I could hear mama and dad scurrying around in the kitchen when Jack came running in my room. "Don't you know how to knock Jack?" I exclaimed emphatically.

Jack said he was sorry and he would have to get used to us having our own rooms now and would try not go barreling into my room anymore whenever he felt like it. I was accustomed to our old bedroom back at the farmhouse not having a door lock while also having to share the room with Jack. I would now have to remind myself that I can lock my door whenever I wanted privacy. Jack, like relaying a stern command from a general, said, "Mama told me to tell you breakfast is ready!"

About the same time I heard her calling out, "You boys get yourselves in here to eat right now before stuff gets cold!"

We both, in almost unison, shouted back, "We'll be right there mama!"

On his way to the kitchen, Jack turned on the television hoping to find his favorite cartoon about a flying squirrel named Rocky and his moose pal called Bullwinkle, like we watched on Sunday mornings back on the farm. Our favorite episodes had a Canadian policeman named Dudley Do-right that was always saving people on the show.

Jack was determined to find the cartoon, but Dad realized what we were doing and reiterated what mama said, "Boys, we don't have time to waste this morning. Get yourselves on in the kitchen like your mama told you."

Somehow Jack managed to quickly get the TV on the station the cartoon was on and we could faintly hear the characters talking when we got to the kitchen. Jack begged mama to let us eat in the living room and watch the show while we ate. She told both of us to sit down and eat, and it wasn't going to kill us to miss watching one episode.

She was making mine and Jack's favorite, pancakes and had fried up some bacon too. Jack and I ate like it was a contest to see who could eat the most pancakes. Jack would put so much syrup on his, dad said, "Why don't you save a little room on your plate for the pancakes Jack?"

Jack just looked at dad and smiled without saying a word or missing a bite. I blurted out to everybody, "Jack is smaller than me but I think he can eat twice as much."

Mama replied, "Yeah, he has always had a big appetite; I never know where he puts all that food he eats."

Jack responded, "Well bigger brains require more eating," and we all chuckled a little.

Dad glanced at his watch and told us we needed to hurry and finish up, as it was almost time to head into town. He said he had agreed to meet someone at 9 o'clock and he didn't want to be late. Dad and I quickly got ready to go, waiting only for Jack to wash his sticky fingers from eating breakfast. I swear he had syrup all over his arms too and some in his hair. Mama was going with us to town and we were happy we were all going together.

Mama was reminding us how she never left dirty dishes in the sink but knowing we were almost running late, dad said, "Belle, worry about them dishes later. They ain't going nowhere, and they'll still be there when we get back."

We finally got out the door and as we were all loading up in daddy's truck, he said, "You boys can ride in the back, but stay sitting down until we get there." Jack and I were so excited to see what the big surprise was in town. Dad was in a great mood also. I could tell he was eager to show us what he was keeping secret up until now.

We headed straight to Main Street. It was the one street that really defined our town. It was straight as an arrow and about a football field in length. The bank was on one end across from city hall and Harrison's Department Store was on the opposite end where we pulled up in dad's truck. I was already thinking about one of those ice cream floats you could get at the drug store.

Dad parked right in front, where the very last shop would be, next to the department store. Dad and mama jumped out and dad let down the tailgate for me and Jack to hop out. I noticed that most of the stores were closed. It was Sunday after all. So there was very little traffic on the street and it was like having the town all to ourselves. It was so quiet, it reminded me for a moment, of being back out in the country, on a calm Sunday afternoon on the farm. But here we were, all four of us standing in front of a big glass window in town, on Main Street, in front of what was once a business but was now empty.

Dad stood in front of the big glass front, stretched out his opened arms like an embracement of the building and proudly exclaimed,

"Well, here she is?" Jack and I with a puzzled look glanced at each other and then back at dad.

I surprisingly said, "Are you saying this building is ours?"

Dad demonstratively replied, "That's what I'm saying! What do you think boys? Let's go have ourselves a look."

Dad wrestled in his pocket for the keys and I couldn't wait to get inside and see what it looked like. About the same time as dad was unlocking the door and pushing it open, Jack hurriedly slid under dad's arms and beat everyone inside to get the first look.

Dad held the door open and told me, "Well go ahead on son. Your Ma and me have already seen it and we know you're excited to see the place."

It was one long rectangular room with two smaller rooms in the back. Jack asked dad, "What are you going to do with this place?"

He explained, "Well, I'm going to rent this space to put in a new business I'm starting. Belle's always been telling me how I'm good with people and would probably make a good salesman, so I'm trying something different."

He went on to tell us how he had worked out a deal to rent the building and could have everything up and running in a matter of days. As he was talking, Mr. Coleman from whom dad had bought our house in town walked in.

Mr. Coleman remarked, "Well I see you brought the whole family. What do you boys think of your dad's new place, right here on Main Street? Can't beat the location!"

Jack and I were excited for dad, without knowing what business dad was starting. We didn't care. We were happy for dad that things might finally be looking up after we had to leave the farm and dad lost his job for Mr. Potter. Dad, mama and Mr. Coleman talked for some time and in parting he said, "I'll check back in a few days to see how things are going. Be sure and call if you have any questions."

Dad said, "Thanks for everything Mr. Coleman and I'll be in touch after I get settled in."

Dad explained that he had saved some money and together with the severance pay from Mr. Potter, had enough to put a down payment on the house and to get started in the new business. He also told us how Mr. Coleman owed him a favor and he had agreed to let him rent the space the first month free, to help him get back on his feet.

So by now, we were yanking all over dad to tell us what was going on exactly. I saw a lot of boxes with some markings, naming various things in them, mostly in the back room.

I asked, "What's in those boxes dad? What kind of store is this going to be?"

Dad thought for a minute, scratching his head and remarked, "Well let me see if I can explain it? I've obtained what's called in business a franchise and I would be like what they call the franchisee."

I had no idea what he was talking about but he went on to explain a little further. He said he has this company that supplies him with various products with their name on it that he can sell at his store and if he wants to, can go on the road and sell to people door to door.

In more detail, he continued, "I only have to pay a small percentage of what the product costs... Then, I turn around and sell it with a higher markup to make my profit. All I have to do is order the stuff and then sell it. The company is called Watleys Products and they have stuff everybody can use."

I said, "That sure sounds like a good plan, plus we get to use the stuff for free."

Dad quickly answered, "Not exactly son! I still have to pay for it, but it'll be at a big discount. That'll save us some money and make your mama happy."

Mama told us she had thought about helping to run the store but they had decided it was better for her to take the job at the clothes factory, at least until they got the store going well. She said the factory told her she could start a week from Monday on her new job there.

Leaning against the wall was this big sign that read, "Watleys Products Sold Here." Dad said he could hang that sign in the big front window so everyone would know what kind of store it was. He showed us those boxes that had already come in that he had ordered and was showing us some of the things he would be selling. I could read various names of what type of products were in the boxes. I saw there were a lot of liniments, salves, camphors, soaps and other assorted names of items I figured to be used mostly in the home.

There were lots of unassembled shelves stacked, lying on the floor against the wall. Dad, in an asking sort of way stated, "I could use you boys to help me assemble those shelves. The sooner I get them up, the sooner we can get everything displayed and get the store open...but I need to get our sign up this weekend too... I want to be open by Monday, the first of the week... If we don't have a sign out, people won't know you're here."

About that time, with the front door halfway open, Sheriff Mason popped his head in saying, "Can I come in?"

Dad replied, "Hey Dean, come on in and have a look at my new place!"

The sheriff remarked, "Hello Belle! How's it going Bill? This place should work out great for y'all, right here on Main Street. People can't miss it! You ought to do great here!"

Belle, in a somewhat sarcastic and somber tone, replied, "Well I hope so. Can't ask for a better location. If it doesn't make it here, I don't think the business would make it anywhere!"

Dad was a little taken back and answered, "Belle, I hope you don't have a lot of doubt about doing this. You know I am good with townsfolk and you always told me how I would make a good salesman. Well here's my chance to prove myself, you just wait and see what I..."

"I don't think Belle is doubting this whole enterprise Bill...You know the ladies are always the cautious type anyway! Y'all are having to make so many big changes lately all at once. It can get a little unnerving for anybody, especially for the women folk!"

Now I thought, huh oh. This is getting interesting. The Sheriff is digging himself a big hole he ain't gonna be able to get out of this time.

In a strong tone, mama remarked, "What does that supposed to mean? If you men had to do half of what we women are expected to do, you would..."

Dad interrupted, "Belle, what's got into you? Dean is only trying to help," and pausing, looking at the sheriff continued, "Dean, you have to excuse Belle. With all the tension lately, she's kinda high strung about things lately!"

With that mama realized she was outnumbered as she closed her eyes, showing a bit of a frown in frustration. At the same time, slowly shaking her head with an exhausted look, mama finally said, "Men! What's the use?"

Sheriff Mason, feeling a little embarrassed and wanting to squirm his way out of there by now said, "Well I best be going and leave everything with you folks before I stir up any more trouble. I need to get back to the station anyway."

Dad walked with him out the front door and they stood on the sidewalk and talked for quite a little bit longer. Finally, the sheriff waved goodbye to the rest of us as he departed on his way. We spent the next few hours, helping dad begin assembling some shelves for displaying his products and to finish unpacking the boxes he had already received. He also had some stuff in his office in the back room that we helped organize to get it all straight.

Although it was a perfect day for Jack and I to try out some new fishing spots, or check out playing baseball on our newly discovered field by our house, we loved the opportunity to be with dad and mama, all of us together, excited about a new venture for dad.

I didn't care about doing anything else that day. I was so excited for the prospect of dad finding something new to do, I didn't want to leave.

I remarked, "I think I could just sleep up here and help look out after the store."

"Bean you will probably get sick of coming around here, especially if it interfered with playing baseball or stuff you like doing on weekends. It might get to be too much like a job."

I enthusiastically replied, "No dad. I'm old enough now to help out. I am willing and able and you could count on me anytime."

Jack exclaimed, "Me too dad! I am willing and able."

Dad remarked, "Well, looks like I got my first two employees but not sure what I can afford to pay 'em right off the bat. Maybe we can figure something out?"

Jack and I both looked at each other and then looked at dad, with big proud grins on both our faces! I think with that, mama managed a slight grin too!

CHAPTER FIFTEEN
The Grand Opening

Dad had the store up and running for a couple of weeks and told us it was time to have what folks call a grand opening, not without of course mama's help, and what little Jack and I could contribute. I think mama was even busier than dad. She had started her own job at the clothes factory, was still taking care of the house, preparing meals for everyone and handling most of the stuff that would come up having to do with school for Jack and myself. She never complained however, even though I knew she had to be very tired most of the time, especially toward the end of a long, hard week at work. I wondered how she ever managed to have any time to herself, without worrying about me, Jack and dad.

Well the time had finally arrived. It was the Saturday that dad had planned to have his grand opening. It really looked to be a fun time and we were so happy to have helped dad with getting the store ready for the celebration. We hung colorful stuff all over the place, inside and out. We had streaming ribbons and big balloons for everyone to see that drove or walked by. Dad had the front door propped open with this big thing he called a "stanchion" everyone could see. It was mounted on this heavy base, so it wouldn't be blown around in the wind. It was in the shape of a large brown bottle, about as tall as the door with the Watleys Products logo plainly to be read. Jack had a big bag of different flavored suckers and little candy treats that dad had bought for the kids, if any came with their parents. Jack would pass them out to any kids that came by or that would pass by on Main Street. All the other store owners came by and as well as lots of regular townsfolk.

Dad had hundreds of flyers made a couple weeks before. He had ordered them from a print shop in the nearby town of Marked Tree, a town a little bigger than ours but it did have a printing shop. Jack and I had spent our afternoons all week, passing out the flyers all over town; to every house, business and car window we could find.

One particular day, I was on my bike, dropping off flyers and came to a little store called Louis Grocery, not far from our house that was far away from the other stores on Main Street. I was hoping they might hang it in the window for customers to see. I handed the flyer to Mr. Louis, the owner who was there, informed him we had recently moved to town and were starting the business on the flyer. He commented how he also passes out advertisements like that every so often and he pays kids like me a little money to pass them out around town. Mr. Louis pointed to the last flyer he printed, that was hanging by his register. I saw in big letters; "Pickled Pigs' Feet Special, 19 cents." I couldn't believe who in this world would want to eat pigs' feet that were pickled. Now some tasty fried bacon, I could go for; but pigs' feet, no way. I thought if a store can make money selling pigs' feet, dad could surely make money selling all those products for the home. I told Mr. Louis thanks for hanging up our flyer and to be sure and come see us at our grand opening. He said he hope he could be there.

Dad had taken out an ad advertising the grand opening with special prices for the event in the local newspaper called, 'The Little River Record'. It was run by a lady we had met at the store previously. Her name was Esther Bentley. She had run the newspaper for years and was for the most part, its sole writer, photographer, editor and publisher. The paper came out only twice a week and most folks couldn't wait to read it. Usually, nothing big or important really happened in our town. Most of the news in the paper was about things happening at school, a whole lot of farming news and just downright local stuff, like relatives visiting someone from out of town. But it was our local paper and we were proud to have it. Heck, if a crime ever happened, that would be big news and definitely front page headlines.

About the biggest crime committed was usually some theft or an occasional break-in at a business by a local resident. Our town was so small, that usually someone would know the perpetrator and they would get caught fairly quickly. You sure didn't want to get on Sheriff Mason's bad side either. In our small city, you might run into our sheriff several times in one day somewhere around town. He knew all the locals and sometimes if a kid did something wrong, even a teenager, he was known to take them home, tell their parents and let them handle it. Many times that worked out a lot better in the long run in taking care of the problem.

Mrs. Bentley of course, getting any news for our newspaper, was at our grand opening running around taking pictures inside and outside the store. She took some pictures of dad proudly behind the cash register taking money from a sale, handing the customer their purchase with a big smile on their face as instructed by Mrs. Bentley. I could tell she knew her job and how to make the best pictures for the paper.

She at one point got our family all together in front of the store to take a photo. She told dad, "Squeeze over a little so I can get that Watleys bottle stanchion in the photo…that'll look good in the picture." She said, "You guys all give me a big smile. I am giving you a half page in my newspaper for free and I want this photo to look great." After a few poses and pictures, she then turned to me and said,

"Bean, this will be a much happier article in the paper than the one I wrote about you almost suffocating in that soybean trailer on the farm. But you were okay in the end, so I guess it was a happy article too when you think about it. It could have been a tragedy if we had lost you."

I was taken back with a bit of a shocked look on my face when she told me that. Now I know why everybody in town had heard of the bean trailer incident. For some reason I never saw her newspaper article about it and I told her I didn't know anything about that article.

"Well, if you want to read it, come by the office sometime and I'll see if I can't dig up a copy of it."

"I will surely do that Mrs. Bentley. I would love to read something written about me in the paper, however embarrassing it might be!"

"Don't worry Bean. It's all good. You'll like it."

The day went on as more of the townsfolk dropped in. We had two doctors in our little town. One was Doctor Holmes that had a small office a little farther down the street and owned the drug store. The other was Doctor Thombs that lived out on the edge of town, close to one branch of the river where we would often fish. He actually had an office with a small clinic. His wife was the nurse. Dr. Thombs was usually the one we would see if we needed a doctor. Both of the doctors came by that day.

Dr. Holmes told dad he had a very special present for his opening. He presented dad with a prettily wrapped bottle of wine with a label that read Boones Farm.

Dad accepted the gift, while promptly stating, "Thanks Doc, this looks like something medicinal and I am sure to put this to good use."

Mama saw that exchange and exclaimed, "I might have to have some of that before this day is over," and they all chuckled.

Doctor Thombs the other doctor in town had dropped by with his wife, Nurse Thombs, as most folks referred to her. She was a petite sweet lady by all measure, well-loved in the community and also known as a great baker of things.

She was holding the most delicious looking dessert I think I had ever seen. She happily held it up, almost right up to my nose and proclaimed, "Well here is a homemade cheesecake I made myself. A slice of this should go perfect with that glass of Boones Farm."

Dad thanked her while mama said she can't remember the last time she had a piece of cheesecake, if ever. I know I had never tasted one and couldn't wait to devour a piece of something that looked and smelled that good. I was getting excited, thinking about all the good eating we would have at home after all this was over.

Mrs. Harrison from the department store next door hung around for almost the entire day. She was a very social type and loved greeting and talking to people. She was a tiny woman and always wore this funny little straw hat but it also made her look adorable. She was good friends with mama and was someone mama could count on when she needed a friend.

To everyone's surprise, Mr. Potter came by for a visit. I heard him tell dad, "Bill, I just wanted to come by and sincerely wish you good luck. I hate the way things ended up between us, but I hope we can still be friends. I just don't want us to feel like we have to avoid each other when we see one another around town."

Dad replied, "Sure C.J... I completely agree... I feel the same way and thanks for coming by." Mr. Potter extended his arm for a handshake with dad, and started to depart.

Halfway out the door, while looking at me, he stated, "Bean, I always got plenty of those jelly beans at the office... Anytime you want to, drop on by and grab some. You could say hi to Jean too. I think she likes you."

I couldn't believe those words Mr. Potter spoke. Now I was lost in deep thought, only thinking about what he said. His daughter Jean likes me; the most beautiful girl in the world likes me. So here among all this excitement, I find my mind drifting to a vision in another place; thinking about her flowing, sleek blonde hair, those beautiful eyes like an ocean of deep blue; the most appealing soft voice.

Next thing I know, Bobby Jansen is shaking me exclaiming,

"Bean, are you okay? You look like you are in a trance of some sort."

"Nah, I was lost in deep thought about something!"

"Well I sure hope it was something nice!"

"Oh yeah, it was nice Bobby, believe me!" I had never told him about meeting Jean Potter at her dad's office awhile back. I thought he might poke fun of me if I did. Besides, that was one beautiful vision I didn't want to share with anyone, not even my best friend.

Mr. Coleman the landlord came by and remarked how well the store looked. He bought some of the liniment that was supposed to help with a back ache.

He remarked, "I'm not sure whether to drink this stuff or get Wanda to rub it on my back. Either way it should help I suppose, and laughed."

The Jansens dropped by and Bobby's mama brought a chocolate cake she had baked. She had writing on the top that said, "Congratulations, All The Best."

Bobby was already there on his bike and he reminded me how our dads would now be working close by each other since his dad worked at Henson Appliance, just down the street.

Bobby said, "Mr. Henson doesn't mind me hanging around the shop with my dad and I would love to show you all the gadgets he has back there to work on televisions. My dad also lets me help sometimes. I've learned a lot about electricity and electronic devices from him! I even know what an ohmmeter is."

I had no idea what the heck he was talking about but it sure sounded interesting. Bobby's dad heard him and added, "Sure Bean, drop by with Bobby sometime and I would be glad to show you around the shop for a little bit. I might have time to show you what that ohmmeter does if I'm not too busy. As a matter of fact, I have to get on back there now and finish up on something I was working on today as we close at one o'clock on Saturdays."

Bobby stayed with me as we both told his parents goodbye, but all I could think about was eating a piece of that chocolate cake and what the heck an ohmmeter looked like!

Everything had gone great with everyone having been in a great mood with lots of laughter and folks being just happy to have an excuse to get together. That day was one of the happiest times I remember as a family and just a fun day all the way around. We were all there together, having a great time, celebrating a new event in our lives with so many friends, new people and welcome gifts. Then there was so much great food, especially desserts that we usually didn't get that often.

At the end of the busy day, we started loading all the gifts people brought into mama's blue station wagon to take them home, as well as all the leftover food. We still had so many pies and cakes, they filled up the car pretty quickly.

Mama said, "Shoot, we will have to make a couple of trips to get all this food and stuff to the house... Looks like I won't have to do any baking for a quite some time."

I happily knew I was in for some good eating for days. I had drank so many sodas and eaten so many desserts, I couldn't hold one more bite or drink of anything. Well... At least until I got home, I thought.

I think the feeling of that day and all the celebration helped go a long way in leaving the old life behind on the farm and getting started on a new adventure. It seemed to be a great start for dad's new enterprise and for our future.

At least I hoped so!

CHAPTER SIXTEEN
The Final Straw

Dad was so proud of his new store and he started working much longer hours. In bad weather, sometimes he would drop Jack and me off at school in his truck and then be at the store from eight in the morning until eight in the evening. Many stores closed at six p.m. but dad told us he needed to stretch the hours out a little, until he got himself established. Being that most stores closed earlier, it did get him a little more business traffic. For nothing else, out of curiosity or boredom I suppose, people walking around Main Street would come in and browse, even though they might not purchase anything at all. Plus, getting to know most folks, now that we were living in town, dad loved to just talk to people dropping by anyway.

So often, when I came by after school, I would hear him discussing farming more than anything else, and sometimes politics, which never interested me very much. I'd hear them talk about the price of cotton or beans, how the weather was going to affect the crops or how the harvest was looking. Sometimes, knowing dad with all his farming knowledge, they would ask about a problem with a tractor or some farm machinery, and what dad might think it would take to fix it. I began to think sometimes he should have started a consulting business for all the farmers around, still asking his advice about farming. But I guess a person couldn't make very much money doing that, as they wouldn't be willing to probably pay much money for only some information.

One afternoon I happened to be hanging around the store with dad and Bobby Jansen had come over from his pop's place. Bobby was holding onto one of the poles out in front of the store, swinging in circles making me dizzy just watching. We saw an old red dirty pick-up stop right on Main Street, in front of the store. The truck door opened and barreling into the store went a man walking hurriedly with some intent. Bobby commented, "That man sure doesn't look very happy. He must have a gripe about something." We followed right behind into the store.

But I recognized him immediately. It was Harold Handley, the tenant farmer that dad had that run in with, back on the farm, after dad told him that he was being evicted. I will never forget the angry look on that man's face, or the terror that I experienced when the gun went off while that man was shoving a rifle into my dad's face in the barn. I never wanted to have to ever feel that kind of horror again, as long as I live. I also hoped I would never see that man again, but here he was, face to face again with my dad. Thankfully, I didn't see him holding a gun this time but I was still very worried.

Without pausing or noticing anything else at all, he went straight to dad behind the counter and said, "See Barnes, you ain't no better than me. Looks like you finally got what you deserve too from Potter. I can't believe he put up with you as long as he did. From what I hear, you will never make it with running this place either…what a joke! This place is a dump. Nobody wants to buy this crap. I'll see you in hell!"

Then, not waiting for any response from my dad, he turned around and in the same hurried purposeful manner, walked right back out, mumbling some cuss words the entire way out. He kicked over the stanchion sign out front that dad had left there from the grand opening and I heard him say, "What a dam stupid sign!" Almost as fast as he had arrived, he hopped back into his truck and sped away.

Bobby asked me, "Gosh Bean, what was that all about? Who was that angry man?"

"I'll tell you later about it Bobby, but right now, I don't feel like talking about it."

Bobby nodded and put his hand on my shoulder in a jest of comfort as he understood whatever it was about, that it wasn't pleasant and it had affected me in some awful way.

At home that evening, dad decided to tell mama about the unwelcome visit from Mr. Handley at the store. She asked dad if that was the first time he had seen Mr. Handley since the farm incident. Dad said that Sheriff Dean had told him that Handley had moved out toward Dyess somewhere, but that was all he knew.

As far as I was concerned, Dyess wasn't far enough. I had hoped he moved out of the county, maybe to West Memphis or even farther. I only hoped this time that it would be the last visit from him.

Many times, I would drop by the store and dad would have a sign on the front door saying he was out making deliveries and what time he expected to return, if at all. He would take orders for products not in stock, or something someone would want from the Watleys Products book and personally deliver the product straight to their house when it came in. He thought it was really important to make the business more personal this way and get repeat customers. He told me that once you get people to like something and if you hand delivered it to them, they might re-order more often. He said that always added this extra little touch that most businesses just wouldn't do.

He also would try to get a down payment on what a customer would order, so if they refused to take it later, he would at least maybe cover his cost of goods. He told me, "Bean, this is a totally different way of making money than farming." He went on explaining. "It's a lot easier in many ways but then you count on people paying for it when the product comes in. Sometimes they just say they don't have enough money to pay for it and for me to keep it." He said that would happen a lot and often he did let them keep it, while still owing him money. Besides, what could he do with an opened or used bottle of some item?

They would promise dad they would pay what they owed at the end of the week or maybe the next week or the next. He started extending credit to more and more customers for longer periods of time for purchases. Dad began to spend more time trying to collect what customers owed, than actually making sales.

This went on for months and it got to be quite often I would hear mama and dad discussing the store and how sales were just not bringing in much money. By now, mama was making more at the factory than dad was with the store. They didn't pay her very well either. She told me when she started working there, they paid her around a dollar & thirty-five cents an hour. It was still more than what dad was making from the store. Business was slow enough at the store that dad closed it by six p.m. most days now and he could be home in time for supper most nights. The usual topic then became how slow business was and how the store was not living up to what they expected or hoped that it would be.

Mama kept reiterating, "If we don't start bringing in more money, we are not going to be able to pay for this house and all the other bills we have."

Dad responded, "Don't you think I know that. I am doing all that I can do. I can't force people to buy my stuff or pay what they owe. You know I spend some days out on the road all day, all around the county trying to get people to buy my product. They tell me…it's too expensive…times are hard… Or they have gotten it on credit and I can't get them to pay what they owe."

One night I heard mama tell dad he might have to find a job somewhere, even if it meant driving to West Memphis or Jonesboro if things got any worse. That didn't go over very well with dad and they would fuss back and forth.

I heard dad finally say, "The holidays are coming up soon. Maybe people will start shopping and sales will come up then."

"Bill, they are not going to have any more money by then... They will probably have less as they will be spending it on Christmas presents for their kids, and not on liniments, soaps, and the types of things we sell to older people," she sarcastically responded.

Dad finally promised mama, "Okay, if things don't turn around by spring...say March... I'll start looking for a job."

Mama exhaustingly replied, "One thing for sure... By then...the situation will take care of itself...one way or the other."

I suppose dad, not being sure what to infer from that, simply replied, "Okay... Whatever." That ended their discussing the store for quite a while as I think it was becoming the same old pointless argument, over and over.

More time passed and business wasn't getting any better. Their arguments became frequent and heated again. I would hear him and mama talking about debt piling up and unless something happened, mama would tell dad she didn't see any way out of it unless he also got a regular job. Dad started getting home later in the evening and would rarely be there to eat supper with us anymore. Mama was working hard herself by this time.

She would work all day, grinding away at the factory and come home taking care of the house, the laundry and often making a trip to the grocery store and then come back and start cooking supper. She would expect Jack and me to be there at supper time but dad was rarely there. She would put a plate aside for him for when he got home and sometimes he would say he wasn't hungry when he got there. This would upset mama as hard as she worked to help with the finances by working all day and then putting in so much effort to make sure we all had something good to eat at night.

One particular night, it wasn't that late and right after supper time. Sheriff Mason pulled up driving dad's truck and was helping dad get out of the other side of the truck. The Sheriff drove his truck home and dad was slouched over on the passenger side.

Mama and I rushed out to the truck as Sheriff Dean was helping dad walk into the house. Dad was in a bad way and his words were not making a lot of sense. I could make out he said he had this terrible episode of his stomach killing him, that he had been throwing up over and over. It was so bad that Dean said dad had called him to come drive him home. Dad was so weak, the sheriff helped him all the way to his bed and he plopped down without trying to speak anymore.

Mama told Jack and me to go to our rooms. I could hear mama telling Sheriff Dean she didn't know what she was going to do. She said this was exactly what happened back on the farm, like the times the sheriff brought dad home back then, after dad had been drinking and driving.

She said, "He needs help Dean but I think he is to the point he has to help himself, as no one can do it for him." I was hearing words I didn't want to hear but I knew they were the truth.

Then I heard Sheriff Mason tell her, "I might as well tell you Belle... and I hate doing it as it's not my place to do so... Mr. Coleman gave Bill an eviction notice. Evidently, he hasn't paid rent in months and is giving Bill 'till the end of the month to get everything moved out... Mr. Coleman had told me he tried working with him as long as he could but it just wasn't working out."

The sheriff reached into his pocket, took out a piece of paper and hesitantly handed it to mama. As she looked down at the paper, clutching it in her hand, slowly opening and glancing at it, the sheriff continued, "That is the eviction notice that fell out of Bill's pocket when I picked him up. I am so sorry to tell you all this but I felt obligated to do so."

The sheriff finally said, "I think I hear Deputy Tillis out front, here to pick me up. I wish I could do more Belle, you know I care for you, your boys…it's just a really bad situation all the way around. Let him get some sleep and we will talk more later on if you need me. I gotta go…the Deputy is waiting." The sheriff left without him or mama saying anything more.

In the past on the farm when this sort of thing happened, I remember mama crying about it but now it was different. I saw mama only sit down dejected, staring out toward the wall like she was giving up. I think she had cried all the tears she had to give and now she was totally calm, at least on the outside about the whole thing. I only wished that I could help. My dad will be back without any income again for sure now, and my mama was doing all she could do.

I went to my room and began to think back on how many times I would hear dad complain when he got home that his stomach hurt and he couldn't eat anything or was always feeling sick.

Mama would often say, "Bill if your stomach is hurting that much where you can't eat, you probably need to go see Doctor Thombs or Dr. Holmes, and get it looked at."

Dad usually replied, "We can't afford any unnecessary doctor bills right now. I'll be alright. Just give me some time."

Weeks went by and I could tell mama was starting to get more impatient with dad. He would go for a while and appear to be totally okay, nothing happening at all, but then other times he would go right back to the same old bad pattern.

One night it was getting around 9:30 p.m., when Jack and I usually had to go to bed on a weeknight. We had asked where dad was and mama said she didn't know but don't worry and go on to bed. I could not fall asleep and it was getting late by now. My bedroom was close not far from the front door and I heard dad storm through the house, straight into their bedroom.

By then it was about 10:30 p.m. I heard mama follow dad into the bedroom and I could hear them arguing. Part of me didn't want to listen but another part was wanting to know what they were saying. I am sure they would be mad if they had known that I was eavesdropping. I quietly came out of my room and got close enough to hear some of what they were saying.

I heard mama say, "Bill, I've had it... This drinking has got to stop. You promised me you would stop when we moved to town. I know that's why so many nights you come home late. The night the sheriff had to drive you home and help you into the house was totally embarrassing. All our neighbors are beginning to talk. We can't live like this. You need some serious help." She went on to say, "Drinking doesn't solve any problems we have. It only makes them worse."

Back and forth they went, and of course, I knew mama was right but dad would keep saying he only drank every now and then and only on occasion would he get carried away like the few times she mentioned. I had already had my own suspicions early on but I didn't want to admit it to myself. I had gone by the store several times when his truck was there parked in the back and the front and back door both were locked with the closed sign put out front.

I made excuses in my mind that he must be visiting with someone down the street for a bit or some other reason for the store being locked up and closed. But now, I was beginning to acknowledge the truth... The ugly truth! Dad had lapsed back into drinking like he did on the farm when mama and I found him in the back of the barn, curled up in the hay like a helpless hurt child. The more I thought about all the events up to now, they all started to make more sense.

I made the decision that it was time that I finally faced it... Dad was an alcoholic. I hated having to acknowledge that reality and to stop denying what I had really already known. What added to the hurt was that there was absolutely nothing a twelve-year-old boy like me could do about it.

I went to bed both dejected and fearful as I lay there thinking how our new life in town had at first seemed to shine with such new promise. But now, those last dark days on the farm had followed us, like the long dust trails on the dirt roads we had left behind.

In the still, dark quiet of the night, with soft tears streaming down onto my pillow, I began praying. "God, please heal my daddy... Please take away this terrible curse that is upon my dad and our family. Please God... I'll never ask for anything more... Please God!"

I was determined to keep praying that night as long as I could, and I did, until I finally fell asleep.

CHAPTER SEVENTEEN
Against The Light

We usually either walked or rode our bikes to school, but this day was very cold & rainy. Dad was still asleep in bed, so mama had dropped us off at school in her old blue station wagon. I was glad the heat worked well in that old car as I held my hands as close to the heat vents as I could get them, all the way to school. The old radiator heaters in all the classrooms were working pretty well that day, so I at least was comfortable for most of the school day.

I finally got to my third class period, Ms. Lacy's sixth grade English. I liked her well enough as a teacher, but the subject was about as boring and depressing as those gray fields from the flood, we left behind on the farm. I did my schoolwork okay, and I didn't hate school, but I could only sit in class, thinking of how the return of the warm springtime could not come soon enough and maybe help brighten things up at home somehow.

Ms. Lacy was a petite, pretty lady and quite young, maybe not even thirty years old yet. She had lovely, flowing blonde hair that freely fell down both sides of her face. She was constantly giving her head a little shake, just enough to keep her soft glowing hair out of her eyes. She had milky white skin and the prettiest green eyes that made me think of all those huge green fields in springtime, back on the farm before the harvest.

I think all the boys in class had a crush on her and she used it to her advantage. Not in a bad way, but it enabled her to maintain everyone's attention in class, even with the most boring of subjects. Her voice was soft and appealing and seemed to command your attention.

After she took the roll call, she proceeded to open the lesson book, and instructed, "We need to get to our lesson for today... Please turn to page fifteen in your workbook." A slight grumbling could be heard as the classroom suddenly gave way to the shuffling noise of all the students, in unison, flipping vigorously through the pages of our workbooks.

After spending class time, working on the proper use of adverbs in sentences nearing the last part of class, she told us to put the book away.

She said, with a little excitement in her voice, "We have just enough time to get to the poem for the day!"

Ms. Lacy loved poetry. Near the end of class, a few minutes before the bell rang, she had a ritual of reading a poem to the class on Wednesdays, so we might have more time to discuss it the rest of the school week. She told us that poetry was a way for us to express our frail condition as humans. No matter what we had to study in class that week, she always took the time to read a poem she selected. On rare occasions when she would miss a Wednesday class, she would leave specific instructions for the substitute teacher, on what poem was to be read.

Today, she told all the students she was going to read a famous poem by the Welsh poet Dylan Thomas. Most kids in the sixth grade, certainly never heard of him, and wouldn't know what being Welsh meant. As she began to read the poem, John Torry, who never passed up a chance to raise his hand, interrupted her with a question.

John asked, "Where is the country of Welsh?" He knew that if he could get her talking about something, and off the subject, the class time would be over before she would realize it.

Ms. Lacy, finally able to continue, explained that Wales wasn't exactly the name of a country itself.

"Welsh is what they call the people that live in this place called Wales, which is part of Great Britain."

"Well, what's the difference between England and Great Britain?" John almost seemed sincere in his question but I knew better, although I thought that was an excellent question. I surely didn't know the difference and wouldn't mind knowing the answer to that myself.

By now, many others had their hands up and Ms. Lacy answered, "Well John, you see Great Britain is the…" and interrupting her own sentence while raising her voice slightly, she exhaustingly remarked, "Okay class, no more questions… Y'all please put your hands down and I don't want to hear any more questions unless it is an emergency. We only have a few minutes left before the bell!"

Everyone immediately obeyed, except for one hand going right back up high in the air, waving it back and forth, in some sort of desperation. Of course, it was John's.

"John… What could possibly be an emergency now?" Ms. Lacy asked in frustration.

"I kinda got an emergency… I need to go to the bathroom bad."

"First, that's badly, you have to go badly. We just finished studying adjectives and adverbs. Don't you ever listen to anything I teach you? Anyway, you can go after I read our poem for today. You're a big boy and you will just have to tough it out for a bit."

The rest of the class gave a little giggle aimed at John, knowing Ms. Lacy got the better of him this time around. Being a little embarrassed, John lowered his head giving the class a now humbled, sideways glance.

Ms. Lacy was glad to finally get to the reciting of the poem. As she was about to read the first line, she hesitated, looked up straight at me and said, "I have a better idea… Bean…why don't you come up here and read this poem for us today! I think you have enough time before class lets out!"

Being taken back a little and hoping that bell would ring soon to get me out of it, I responded, "Are you sure you want me to read it? You always make any poem sound great when you do it."

"Oh you'll do fine Bean... Come on up here!"

I left my seat in terrified trepidation, being thrust unexpectedly in front of the class, especially to read some old poem. I really liked her as a teacher, so I was not about to disappoint her. I took my place in front of the entire class as she handed me the sheet with the poem on it. I was hoping it wasn't one of those old poems that repeated big ancient words that you could barely pronounce.

I looked down intently at the words, glanced back up at the class and then back at the poem again without speaking any words yet. The words I was seeing had enthralled me and I wanted to read some of them for myself, before I read them out loud.

"We're waiting Bean…you can begin anytime now!"

Lost in thought, I replied, "Yes mam, I'm sorry, I was looking at some of the words, making sure I could pronounce them correctly."

As I proceeded to the reading, I knew this was the kind of poem of which I had never read or heard before. It actually garnered my interest and had me thinking about the words. I slowly, methodically made my way through the verses, finally reciting the last few lines;

> And you, my father, there on the sad height,
> Curse, bless me now with your fierce tears, I pray.
> Do not go gentle into that good night,
> Rage, rage against the dying of the light.

As I was taking my seat, Bobby gave me a little poke, elbow to elbow, and quietly whispered, "Good job Bean, didn't know you had that in you."

All the while, as the class remained unusually quiet, they looked at me like in some new found way while taking my seat.

"Wow Bean… That was an incredible rendering of that poem. I don't know that I have ever seen the class so still or interested. I guess I need to let you do that more often," Ms. Lacy proudly stated.

Of course, I swelled with pride myself and I could not believe how well I had delivered those words. It was as though someone else was speaking them through me. The class could have been mistaken for a church congregation, listening attentively to a commanding sermon. It was the strangest of feelings that I have never felt before. Everyone in the class, including John Torry, was intrigued with the words of the poem and very curious about its meaning.

Of course hands went up again all over the room with questions. It was like those words had sparked a sudden interest into poetry, like never before shown by the class. She asked John Torry to quickly pass out a copy to each student, unless he was still having that emergency.

"No mam, I'm fine now."

She told the class we would wait to discuss the poem on Monday. She wanted us spending proper time on it, since that would give us the rest of the school week and the entire weekend to read it over and think about the meaning of the poem. She also told everyone to feel free to share it with their parents, a relative or a friend.

All the students were staring at the clock, as it was only a couple of minutes until the time for the bell to ring. At that time, we got a glimpse of the principal, Mr. Hayes, pecking on the little window in the classroom door. He was summoning our teacher to come into the hall. She told the class to excuse her for a second, and that she would be right back. I could see a concerned look on both their faces through the glass, with whatever they were discussing. I could tell that whatever it was, it looked to be very serious.

Finally, Ms. Lacy gently and hesitantly, slowly pushed the door open. It was like the door had become super heavy and she barely had the strength to push it open. I could tell she was crying, silently looking up toward the ceiling, with one hand over her mouth trying to contain her emotion. Principal Hayes walked in slowly right behind her, stopped for a second and then he turned to my desk. Looking directly at me, in a solemn, almost apologetic sounding voice that I had never heard from him before, said, "Benny, I need you to come with me for a minute."

Ms. Lacy gestured to the class in such a way that they understood to respectfully remain silent. As she put her arm gently around my shoulder, she then asked them to be on their best behavior until she returned. All the students gave me this definite inquisitive stare as I gathered my books, while being escorted out of the room.

We made our way through the corridors, and I knew by everyone's behavior around the office, something was very wrong. By this time, Ms. Lacy was crying profusely, and now I thought for certain that something really bad had happened to Jack.

I was pleading, "What's wrong, what's happened? Is Jack okay?"

Then in relief, I saw Jack sitting on the bench seat, in front of the principal's office. They had already gotten him from his third grade class, and he appeared to be patiently sitting there. Jack said they told him to sit there for a minute, and that they assured him that he wasn't in trouble of any kind.

Jack and I both were asking questions, wanting to know what was going on, but no one would say anything.

Mr. Hayes simply said, "Don't be afraid boys...you've done nothing wrong... Deputy Tillis is waiting outside to take you home."

Now my thoughts were beginning to run wild. Has something happened to mama or dad? I kept my thoughts to myself, as I didn't want to upset Jack any more than necessary but I was very worried.

Ms. Lacy and the principal walked with us out to the car where Deputy Tillis was waiting. With tears streaming down her face, Mrs. Lacy reached out, and put her arms around us both, saying, "God bless you sweet boys," as we got into the car. I heard the bell ring and could see the scurry of classes changing.

We looked back, as we made our way down the street, watching her and the principal peering toward us in the distance, as if to get the last glimpse of us possible, before we would disappear from their sight.

As I watched their concerned faces become smaller and smaller through the back of the car window, it was like they knew we were leaving a place of safety, and now headed to someplace they didn't want us to go.

Deputy Tillis didn't speak a word for a while but finally spoke and only stated that he would have us home in just a couple of minutes. He avoided looking at us, or saying anything else as Jack and I sat in confused silence and fear the entire way home.

He pulled up in front of our house, and we saw several people including Sheriff Mason, the Jansens, and other friends of the family, coming in and out of the house. John's mother, Mrs. Torry, who had become a good friend of mama's, came up to us first. She was visibly crying also. She didn't say anything either, and while shakily holding onto Jack and me, began escorting us into the living room.

By now, I didn't want to go in. I knew this couldn't be good, especially having seen enough near tragedies and other bad ordeals up to now. Judging by the terrible atmosphere, I knew this was going to be worse than any I had experienced before. I reluctantly, along with Jack, made it into the living room.

There I saw mama was sitting on the bench, with her head down sobbing. She would not look up at us for quite some time, knowing we were right in front of her. When she finally recognized our being there, she remained seated and grabbed onto both of us, hugging us ever so tightly. Jack and I still haven't said a word since arriving, and remained silent. We were too scared to speak or ask anything. Mama still would not look directly at us, keeping her head buried in our chests. She finally, slowly tilted her head up toward our face with immense tears streaming down her cheeks, and gently pushed us back, with one arm resting on my shoulder and one arm on Jack. She then took a deep breath and after pausing with barely breathing, she would utter the words that would change all of our lives forever.

In broken speech, she said, "I'm so sorry boys, I don't know how to gently tell you this, but your daddy...your daddy...he...he's gone! I don't know any other way to say it, but he's gone!"

In total denial of what I was hearing, I stood there frozen like a statue.

"Well where is dad? Where did he go? I want to see him. Did he leave?" Jack confusingly asked.

"Son, please don't make me say it again, but your father is dead!"

Jack sat there squinching his eyes with a look of unbelief, as if questioning mama's words. He tilted back his head like a boxer in a fight to deflect a glancing blow and demonstratively replied, "Dad's not dead, he can't be... He's not old enough to die! Dad's not sick!"

It was something that Jack could not accept as a possibility. He of course knew what death was, but like me or any other kid, figured it was something that always happened to someone else; maybe a soldier and usually someone you didn't know, but certainly not his dad.

I remained standing there in a trance-like state, not moving at all. I was hearing those words and understood unequivocally what they meant. I couldn't believe I wasn't breaking down in some way. I was displaying no real outward emotion but a deepened inner sadness came over my spirit like an ominous black cloud. My stomach felt like a great rope, tied in one huge knot. But I could not cry for some reason. I didn't understand my own reaction or the lack of it, and wondered what was wrong with me? I just heard my dad has died, everyone in the room is sobbing, including Jack by now, but I'm standing here with no outburst of emotion.

I began to take deep heavy breaths and could feel a state of helplessness overtake me. This was something that was totally out of my control. No wishing, no praying, nothing I could do this time would change any of what I just heard. It was a hopeless and lost feeling, like being in the bottom of the deepest pit with no way out.

Jack was clutching onto mama while she was gently stroking her fingers through his blonde hair in some way for comfort, as if she was assuring him that things would still be okay. But I wanted to only be left alone. I had the overwhelming urge to get away from people, from everyone.

Without saying anything or speaking to anyone, I ran out of the room, through the back of the house to the backyard.

I stopped at the big oak tree in the back corner of the yard where we had started building our treehouse about two weeks ago. I looked up and I saw my sanctuary. We had only built the floor, the frame for the walls and some of the rafters for the roof. I climbed the ladder and made my way to the bosom of that rickety, shaky structure of a house with no walls yet to help sturdy it. Although it was only the shell of a house so far, and had only a start for a floor, it felt more like a strong palace of stone up on a hill, secure from any outside invading army. This enemy however, was my own world collapsing around me, and this was the one place of all places that offered refuge in that moment, as I lay there in silence.

It wasn't long before I heard a gentle voice calling from below. It wasn't mama, or Jack, or any of the adults. No, it was my best friend. The voice seemed to echo up the tree.

"Bean, it's me, Bobby. Are you up there? My dad came and picked me up from school in case you needed me. I got here as fast as I could. If anything happened to you, I would be lost in this world. You are my one true friend! You're the only one I can talk to!"

I didn't respond in any way and Bobby didn't say anything else for quite some time.

After about five minutes of silence, he quietly said, "I'm just gonna sit down here by this tree, and if you need me, I'll be right here. I'm not gonna say anything more or go anywhere, unless you tell me too!"

I still didn't respond but at the same time, I didn't want him to leave either. I felt like he was sharing my pain without us having to be exactly in each other's presence. It was like he knew what I needed at that moment without speaking.

I remained silent in the treehouse, lying there wrapped securely and warm in the old blankets we had left there, although they were still somewhat damp from the humid night. I was going over and over in my head, all the close calls my dad had with so many bad things that had happened to him. Some brought about by others by no fault of his own and then some, which I knew was the result of having to live a hard life.

I guess I had to think through some things. I had reason things out a little before I could talk to or face anyone, including my friend Bobby. I finally had the courage to peek my head out and I said, "Come on up Bobby if you still want to."

"Well of course I do you knucklehead, if you're sure that's okay."

He was the only one in the world that could call me by that name, in a time like this, and be able to take it as a way of comfort, which I did! He had often called me that in jest.

He said, "They all know I am out here with you and you're not alone, so they are not worried about you right now."

I asked where Jack was and he told me he was staying right beside mama in the house.

He remarked "I know all those people are here because they care but I have to get away from big crowds myself most of the time. I can only handle being around so many people at one time. Big crowds always get to me."

I began to talk a little more and relayed to him some of things that had happened to dad and my family. I told him about the incident in the barn back on the farm when Harold Handley almost killed him for only doing his job; about the time mama and I would find dad in the dark, drunken and all alone not coming home or being brought home by the sheriff on several occasions. I went on and on, as Bobby sat and listened, with one arm lightly over on my shoulder and tears in his eyes.

Then suddenly, I remembered the poem I read in front of the class, not more than an hour ago. Some of the words from the poem that spoke about raging against the dying of the light kept ringing through my head. I remembered I had stuffed into my back pocket, the copy of the poem John handed out, right before I was pulled out of class. I gingerly pulled it out of my pocket like it was the most delicate and valuable of things.

I remembered something in the last verse of the poem mentioning, "My father". At the time, I had been pondering what those words meant and what they referred to. I knew it wasn't any ordinary poem but understood it had to do with life and death.

As I held the wadded up sheet of paper in my hand, I slowly began unfolding it, searching for the now wrinkled up words to come into view. With my eyes glued to that sheet of paper, I silently read the verses this time, noticing my own lips moving in silent unison with the words, until I got to the last verse.

There I hesitated, sitting and staring intently at that final verse for a time. I looked up at Bobby and then back down to the paper. I proceeded to read out loud for the second time today, in a totally different understanding now, the words:

> And you, my father, there on the sad height,
> Curse, bless me now with your fierce tears, I pray
> Do not go gentle into that good night,
> Rage, rage against the dying of the light.

I finished reading that verse and it was like those words had been written for me...to me, on this very day, like a message from my own father.

Bobby, after hearing them, started crying like I had never heard him cry before. I knew his tears were for me and for my pain. In broken words, he assured me, "Well, I'll always be here for ya Bean...whenever you need me...no matter what or wherever we go... I'll always be here!"

Then as he hugged me, I broke into vehement sobbing and a groaning of agony, the likes of which I had never known!

CHAPTER EIGHTEEN
The Last Verse

After I finally came down from the treehouse Bobby stayed by my side so I wouldn't feel alone. While on one hand my insides were bursting with wanting mama to tell me what happened to dad, on the other I knew it would be some painful words for her to utter. I suppose one might say that it would take courage for a twelve-year-old to have to ask about something so devastating and traumatic, or was I just playing the coward?

I finally sat in a corner most of the time, while Jack held onto mama. I sat there staring down at the floor, lost in my own thoughts. At the same time, I was also holding my head down to avoid seeing the looks on their faces. Whenever I did it was like every person was staring right at me, struggling to communicate something but forbidden to say it out loud. It's the same feeling when someone believes you've done something wrong and everyone is talking about it. They give you this certain look as if they know you are the guilty one. Of course, I knew I hadn't done anything wrong but that didn't make the feeling go away.

Evening approached after being full of mumblings, whispers and quiet conversations. People were holding their hand next to their mouth, trying to shield their words. But as the mumblings continued on for quite some time, I finally overheard the one word I didn't think existed in my vocabulary. That cutting word was… Suicide.

I heard that word and my body shook all over. Surely this couldn't be. I had reasoned it had to have been an accident, a heart attack, anything else but not suicide. No way would dad do that. Why would he? How could he? But now the reality of it began to sink in and my spirit sank even lower. Now I knew. There was no more guessing. I knew how my dad died but not any details. Becoming evident that a father has taken his own life is one thing that no young boy should ever have to learn from overhearing others talking. Not only that, but I also heard something about a 38 pistol.

But I knew now for certain. It wasn't hard to figure out. My dad had taken his own life with a gun but I figured the details at that point didn't really matter. Knowing he was responsible for his own death was as devastating as his death itself, if not more. It could have been prevented. It didn't have to be…but it was.

Finally, everyone had left except the Jansens, Mrs. Torry and Sheriff Mason. Mrs. Torry offered to stay the night to help with us boys or be there if she needed something. She almost insisted but mama wouldn't hear it. She would only thank Loretta Torry and say that she thought it would be better for only her to be there with us boys that night.

Bobby also had offered to spend the night too if I wanted but his parents didn't think that was a good idea. They said they really needed to go home to give us our privacy. Bobby told me his parents said he could come back tomorrow if I needed him. I simply told him thanks for being there and I would see him later. I was thankful he was there for most of the day.

After everyone had gone, the last person to leave that fateful day was Sheriff Mason. I heard him tell mama, "Belle, look if you need anything at all, anything, call down to the police station and I'll take care of it, okay!" Mama only nodded in agreement and didn't say anything as he left.

By now mama's tears had mostly subsided and understanding that I had heard all the talk, she said, "Benny I think you already know what happened. That will have to be all you need to know for now… I am not prepared to discuss it right now and I really don't know much else to say about it anyway."

I listened and then in almost a whisper, I only said, "Okay mama."

As we sat in the silence of the late evening with a now empty house, mama sat there hugging me and Jack for quite a while. Neither of us had anything to say. At this point, there wasn't much point to talking about it. Trying to accept the reality that dad was gone was enough to deal with for now. Mama was exhausted from not only having to deal with the tragedy herself but also hearing folks whispering about it, though they meant well.

It was going to be three days before I would get to see my dad again and although I was surrounded by people, I never felt so alone in all my life. Ironically at the same time, I wanted it that way. How could I accept any comfort at all while there would be none for my dad? It was like a necessary punishment of isolation to deal with a tragedy. In death there is always pain and that pain cannot be magically removed by someone else. It was something only I could deal with. No one else could understand, no matter how sympathetic, or how hard they tried to console me. It was between me and my dad. I didn't want a lot of people in-between or in the way. It was something I knew I would have to wrestle with, not only now but for the rest of my life... Alone!

What made Saturday even worse, if that was possible, was that was always the day the local newspaper came out. The Little River Record I was told would publish what they called dad's obituary. Under the circumstances of my dad's death, I knew it would get more attention in the paper than only a statement about the funeral, and I was painfully right. The local paper already had news about the incident. I found the paper and seeing the headlines for the first time, I read the following article:

GUNSHOT WOUND WAS FATAL
FOR WILLIAM C. BARNES, 53

William C. (Bill) Barnes, operator of a concession store on north main street Little River and area representative for Watleys Products was found dead around 9:40 a.m. Wednesday, March 29 at his home. He was 53. Services will be held at 2:30 p.m. Saturday, in First Baptist Church with Rev. Jeff Chamblis pastor, officiating. Burial will follow in Riverside Memorial Cemetery with Rivercrest Funeral Service in charge. County Coroner Paul Robinson of Truman and Little River City Marshall Dean Mason said that death was due to self-inflicted gunshot wounds from a .38 caliber revolver. The bullet was fired directly into the heart and death was instantaneous. A coroner's inquest was not held due to that fact that Mr. Barnes had left a suicide note absolving everyone from blame.

Mrs. Barnes told investigating officers that her husband had arose at 6:30 a.m. and awakened her, and that she had prepared breakfast for the family. She took the children to school and went back by the house before intending to leave for work at the local clothes factory. When she arrived back home, Mr. Barnes came out of the bedroom and told her he was going back to bed, that he felt so badly he wasn't going to work. Mrs. Barnes said she then decided to stay home out of concern for her husband being so sick. Sometime later, she was working in the kitchen when Mr. Barnes emerged from his bedroom and handed her his billfold. He told her to keep it. He went back into the bedroom and the pistol shot was heard.

Investigating officers said the contents of the note revealed Mr. Barnes had taken his own life due to ill health. The suicide note dated March 29, was in the billfold.

Mr. Barnes was practically a lifelong resident of the Little River farming area, moving to neighboring West Ridge vicinity when he was about 13 years old. He served as farm manager for C.J. Potter for a number of years, until he opened his business on Main Street last summer.

I read those words over and over. I envisioned it, seeing those events of that day happening in my mind. I imagined my dad taking his last breath before putting that pistol right next to his heart and then pulling the trigger. I wondered what was the last thing he was thinking about? What was that very last thought that ran through his mind? Was he thinking of finally being rid of the pain he was carrying or was he thinking of me, Jack and mama? Questions, to which of course, no one would ever be able to know the answers to.

For many things that happened back on the farm, we always knew the reason. We could always point to something as the cause. Bad weather, bad economic times, or whatever but it was never a mystery. But a thing like this, without explanation or reason, without anyone or anything to blame is the worst. What possible explanation could there be for my dad to do something so drastic, something so final!

Then I remembered the news article said dad had left a note and I wanted to see it. I had to see it. I wanted to know what dad said in that note, written in his own hand in the last few seconds of his life. Maybe I could learn a reason or some justification or a closure of some kind.

I told mama that I learned dad had left a note when I read the newspaper article that I found.

"I know dad left a note and I have to see it... I need to know what he said. I am old enough to know these things and Jack doesn't have to know anything about this." I said.

"Son, we are about to head to the funeral in a short while. This is not the best time for this."

But I insisted, and she finally gave in. She went to her bedroom and came back, handing me a neatly folded sheet of paper with no envelope. She told me to go to my room, lock the door, and to give it back before Jack gets out of the bathtub.

As I sat on my bed, I did nothing but hold that note in my hand for the longest time. It was like it had an invisible lock. Did I want to unlock it or should I leave it secure and stow it away? I knew once I read it that it would be the end, the last vestige of my dad. I figured it would be like the last conversation I would ever hear from him. I thought perhaps I should save it and preserve his words for some future time when I'm older. But I knew that wasn't being true. It would be like lying to myself and refusing to talk to dad this last time. Then I stopped, only to stare at it as my mind drifted back to a moment, not unlike this one, only a few days earlier.

I was thinking back to the treehouse and taking that folded-up note with the poem out of my back pocket. I thought no words would ever be harder in my life than reading the last verse of that poem on that terrible day. But I knew I was wrong. I knew this was going to be far more difficult.

I continued to carefully and slowly unfold my dad's note, knowing I would not be reading a famous verse from a Welsh poet like before in class. Perhaps, in a not so different way, I would be reading another last verse. But this time, this verse would be written by my own father in his own writing.

He had written on a light green colored paper that had perforations on one side. The single sheet had been torn from a book and at the top I saw the heading; "T. R. Watleys Return For Credit."

There were lines with some columns headed by item number, quantity, description, price, etc. but there were no entries for work items, only dad's handwritten words.

I began to read slowly and deliberately, almost like a first grader learning to read, purposefully pausing over every single word, to delay as long as possible getting to the end. I didn't want to get to the end. But I proceeded to read the following words:

I am leaving this note as proof that no one is to blame for this action I have taken today. I'm absolving anyone of any blame whatsoever. This was my decision and mine alone. My boys, when and if you read this one day, I hope you can somehow forgive me. You are good boys and I know will grow up to be strong men of courage. I can no longer stand the pain I'm having inside and out and this is the only way I saw to have relief. Belle, I am sorry I failed you all.

I love you.

March 29, William C. Barnes

I sat sobbing, wondering about the pain he referred to. I thought about all the ways he probably considered he had failed us as the provider for the family; losing his job on the farm and starting another failed business; then mama also having to get a job at the clothes factory. I knew he was having some bad health problems, perhaps caused by his drinking and the pain which it had caused to the family. Dad saw one way out and he took it.

I wanted to be so angry at him for doing what he did, but I couldn't. I had every right to be mad at him making such a life changing decision for three other people, for the entire family made by him alone. That wasn't in the least fair.

But dad was always telling me, "Son, life is never fair and if you expect it to be, you will live a disappointed life. You have to learn to take the good with the bad!"

This was the furthest thing from fair I thought I would ever have to accept and certainly the worst I hoped to ever have to endure.

I handed the note back to mama and asked what she was going to do with it. She told me she had to get it back to the sheriff to keep for their records for a period of time. She said he wasn't supposed to let her have possession of the note, as it was part of the investigation. But he figured it wouldn't hurt to let her keep it for a couple of days.

I looked at the clock and it was almost 2 p.m. when Mrs. Jansen softly opened the front door, and in a quiet somber tone said, "Belle, we're here to pick you up if y'all are ready to go…it's almost 2?"

Bobby pushed his head inside the door underneath his mom and said, "My dad said we can all fit in his car." I was happy that Bobby was riding with me to the church and it made me feel more at ease.

"Okay... We're ready," mama replied, while combing Jack's hair as we proceeded out the door.

As we were getting in the car mama said, "I forgot my purse. My mind is in a million places right now, I'll be right back."

While we waited for a minute, Mr. Jansen in a complimentary tone exclaimed, "Bean you look real nice all dressed up… You too Jack!"

Both Jack and I responded, "Thank you sir!"

Having a bit of a reticent look after giving that compliment, I think he realized the reality of the circumstances and thought maybe it wasn't the best thing he could have said. I figured it was far better than ignoring us and we knew Mr. Jansen always meant well.

We hardly spoke as we slowly made our way to the church. Everything about a death and a funeral seems to put things into a kind of quiet, deliberate motion. It is as though time itself slows down, affecting everything around you with people walking, people talking and their motions too. Everything slows down! It is as if time becomes cold and frozen. Perhaps it does in some way, pausing to acknowledge one of its departing passengers.

As we arrived at the church, the thought of getting to see dad for the first time after three days and knowing this day would also be the last time I would ever see him, made me wish that I could actually make time stop. For this was it. This would be forever, the last time I would see him.

There was his body, lying in an open casket in the back corner of the church. He looked completely normal and totally at peace. The three of us stood there with mama in the middle holding Jack's hand on one side and me on her other side.

Mama turned to me and said, "I'll leave you alone with him for a couple of minutes Benny," as she and Jack stepped to the side.

I stood there keeping him alive in my mind I suppose by recounting some of our better times. It was like a movie I began to play in my mind.

I envisioned the time I was riding to town and I swallowed that huge bug with the truck window open, and thought I was choking to death. I replayed Jack and me building that outhouse trap back on the farm for our terrible cousins to fall into and how it impressed dad of our devilish ingenuity. I thought of all the times I saw him proudly stand by a finished, big white bale of cotton or happily riding around those same cotton fields in his old white truck, both of us content not having to speak one single word.

Eventually, everyone began to take their seats and I heard some songs sung by a couple of members of the church, followed by a quite lengthy talk by the pastor speaking about redemption and resurrection. I only hoped he was right, if I was to ever have the possibility of seeing my dad again.

Finally, everyone was asked to leave except mama, Jack and me. We could view dad one last time before they closed the casket and we would have to get in the procession heading to Riverside Cemetery.

I could not stop thinking about the newspaper article or dad's note, as my mind was still racing with questions. But I realized right then, nothing was ever going to change this day, this moment. As strange as it sounds, I wanted this last picture of my dad stored in my head forever, so I wouldn't forget this last glimpse. I needed to focus.

I reached down to dad's hands that were folded neatly on his chest and I held onto his cold hands for a moment. I knew it would be the last time to touch him and leaning over, giving him a kiss on his head, while trying to control my erupting emotions, I simply said, "Goodbye dad, I hope I get to see you again one day!"

An usher then led us into a room to sit for a bit until they had closed the casket and loaded it into the hearse. After a few minutes, we were escorted to the car that would follow right behind dad in the procession to the cemetery. Sitting there in that car, with not a word being spoken by anyone as the seconds ticked by, was a sad, deep communal silence that I had never experienced before.

Then I thought of the words long ago that mama told me, while standing in front of the old farmhouse, getting that last glimpse of the farm before leaving it behind. I will never forget her parting words, now ingrained in my memory forever, as they resounded over and over in my head, on that seemingly long and silent drive. "Benny, leaving things behind will never be as hard as leaving those you love!"

After we returned home from the funeral, I did not want to sleep in my room by myself and neither did Jack. I would always be reminded of what happened to my dad in that house and being alone at night brought about the worst feelings and downright nightmares. I was going to have to learn to cope with them somehow. There was certainly no way I was going to say anything to mama. I figured she had it worse than me, so how could I ask for or look for any consolation. After all, she would still have to go to work and do all the things she did before and now the family more than ever would depend on her support for everything now. So I kept all my thoughts to myself. At times I would talk about it with Bobby and he would sit and listen like a good friend but I didn't want to over burden him with it either.

Mama told me that Jack and I were going to have to share my room for a while, as it might be some time before she could sleep again in her bedroom alone. I certainly didn't blame her and I understood. All our friends offered to put us up in their house, even though none of them had any room for us. The Torrys; the Jansens; Mrs. Harrison and others all offered, but mama said she didn't want to be a burden on anyone else.

For many evenings at the supper table, it was completely silent. No one hardly spoke a word. It was like a thick curtain of gloom that couldn't be shaken had enveloped the house. It was a house filled with sadness. I asked mama if we were going to move, but she said we couldn't afford to.

I wondered how could I ever be happy again? How can I face the other kids at school? How will I be able to handle the constant stares and talking behind my back, like something was wrong with me? I felt less than a whole person and didn't know if I would ever feel right again but I knew I couldn't go on forever feeling like that.

Bobby was always doing his best to try to cheer me up somehow. He came over one Friday evening and said, "Bean, you know what we need to do? We need to finish that treehouse. It's been awhile since we worked on it. How about let's get back to it tomorrow? What do you think?"

I was in my usual sad state of mind and sat there for a minute without responding, but suddenly the thought of getting back to work on that treehouse raised my spirits and in defining agreement I said, "Yeah! It's time... We need to finish what we started."

All of a sudden, I felt some burden lifted with the thought of getting busy doing something positive by building something. It was as though the rain had stopped falling, gray clouds were parting and a few rays of light were beginning to eke through.

I couldn't wait for tomorrow to get started!

Part Three

CHAPTER NINETEEN
The House Up In The Air

A House We Built Up In The Air
(A poem by the author)

With cracked old boards and rusty nails
A house we built up in the air
On bough and limbs like outstretched arms
This giant stood in our backyard
A tree it was that most would see
But to us it was our revelry
A palace others did not see
Only stare they did so dreadfully

The world was simple, yet confused
Searching for a path to use
A 'King', a President the world all knew
Had fallen by the way too soon
By drifting souls longing for
A way to have their mark restored
By bullets slung they to assail
As voices screamed, "Over there"
If only they had built their world
With cracked old boards and rusty nails

Then brothers old enough to serve
Were called to duty in the war
Some returned with limbs not there
Some came back to breathe no air

The powers both used guns and bombs
To kill each other in alarm

Now it's the same, though times have changed
With years gone by these still remain
If only they could learn to build
With cracked old boards and rusty nails
And how I wish I could still be there
Up in the house built in the air

The work of building a magnificent treehouse in our backyard was some feat, built by only some young kids' old's architectural ingenuity. Bobby and I had sketched up some basic plans, along with all the supplies, materials and tools we figured we would need to do the job. Sam Torry heard about our project and volunteered his expertise if we needed it. He was older, would be graduating soon and was known as some kind of math genius. He liked drawing up plans for things and loved any kind of challenge. He could do anything with numbers, measurements and calculations. So it was easy to get him on board to help.

Once he knew our basic design, he specifically drew out the entire schematics of all the dimensions and measurements for the materials we needed. From experience, I knew how slow and tedious sawing every board by hand was. Sam could keep us from making mistakes and sawing stuff right the first time. He had every board measured for the walls, the roof and the entire project. We even took off the old floor we had started with as it wasn't very straight or sturdy and followed Sam's new and better design.

We had time guidelines and a construction schedule to have a certain phase of the project completed each week, in order to mark our progress so we would stay on schedule. We built into our plan, nonwork days each week to allow for rain or some unforeseen delay. We meticulously had every detail on paper. We even had a couple of hard hats to wear once in a while, to really feel the part. Bobby had found them lying around in the old shed outside his house. We had thought of everything. Of course, the dates for the timeline had gotten way off track with the recent events but we simply moved the schedule back a few weeks. We had a list of kids we could possibly entice as a labor force to help in the construction, by promising to let them have some access to the treehouse, once we finished. We would assign certain jobs to who we thought could handle different tasks.

I followed our laid out plans but the biggest obstacle was having enough boards needed as the house progressed. We would often run out of them and end up spending days, going through the neighborhood, scouting for more and hauling them back on our little red wagon we had. It was amazing how many boards we could stack on that thing. We even built sides for the wagon to hold more boards.

We would ask anyone we could find, if we could have old boards that were lying around and they were usually glad to get rid of them. We would take them all, pick out only the good strong boards and discard the bad ones. We always had to be careful with old nails sticking out of some of the boards but we needed those nails too. We couldn't afford to buy new ones at the Little River Lumber Company, and it was a lot of work pulling out the old bent ones from the used boards. Bobby and I both had half our fingers taped up from scrapes and cuts while getting those stubborn nails out.

One morning, I met Bobby to get started working on the treehouse and he was excited to show me what he was holding. It was not one but two brand new big boxes of nails. He said his dad knew how hard we were working and thought he would contribute the nails to help out a little. What a relief it was to get those new nails and it certainly sped our progress way up.

The hardest part was getting the heavy boards up the tree. Bobby and I put our heads together and derived a plan to do just that. We searched and found several old pulleys and along with some ropes, we built a system to get the heaviest boards up there. It was quite an impressive contraption. Once we got the solid floor built with a place for us to stand and sit the boards on, the job got easier. The younger Torry brothers would help sometimes and we didn't turn them down. John and Barry would help often but would only work so long before having to leave . Sam being responsible as our head architect was there most of the time. Being a few years older, he had more experience in building things and he carried the notepad with all our construction notes. Being known as the math wizard at school, we were glad to have him draw up the scale and measurements for what we wanted to build. You never would see Sam without that notepad and a special, long triangular shaped ruler he always carried. He said it was given to him by a relative who was an architect and he called it an architect ruler. Plus, being taller, older and stronger, whenever we needed some extra muscle, we were glad he was around.

So we had designated Sam as our architect and Bobby as our engineer. Bobby could build about anything and tell us what parts we needed. He said his dad told him once he would make a great mechanical engineer, although I didn't understand at the time what that was.

I told Bobby, "Well, I believe your dad was exactly right. You're that mechanical engineer your dad was talking about, in getting this amazing treehouse built."

So that left only me. I called myself, the foreman. I was the one person that had to make everything work smoothly toward the one goal we were wanting to achieve. I was the guy who had to keep it all going and make sure we had all our supplies and tools. Also at times I suppose, it made me come across a little bossy trying to get things done, though not intentional.

With the activity of kids running around getting supplies and all the noise of hammering and sawing going on in that backyard, it reminded me of building the pyramids in Egypt, in the movie about Moses and his people being slaves in Egypt.

Most kids had gotten to see it at the Grand Theater not long ago. Several classes at a time would load up on a school bus and be driven to the theater on a certain day. I couldn't believe we would get out of school to go see a movie about Moses and his people in the land of Egypt. Under Egypt's king they called a Pharaoh, Moses and his people were made as slaves and forced to hard labor. They would be laboring below their taskmasters, moving heavy stones and making bricks and mortar for construction.

I once made the mistake of mentioning the scene of Moses parting the waters of the sea in that movie. What kid could forget what looked like a mile high wall of water on each side of the Israelites, as they safely walked across on dry land. Then to watch the wall of water come crashing down and drowning thousands of Pharaoh's soldiers, all their chariots and horses along with them. It was something I would never forget, as the Pharaoh stood on the edge of the sea, helplessly watching the demise of his army.

Jack, along with John and Barry Torry who were helping down below on one particular day heard me talking about that movie, and Barry remarked, "Yeah, you, Bobby and our own brother Sam with your fancy titles are just like the taskmasters in that movie, treating us like slaves, getting us to do all this hard work, while y'all are up there staying cool in the breeze."

"Well, we are the brains and y'all are the brawn and Sam is too good at math calculations, to leave him to menial tasks. He can recite Pi out to about twenty-five digits," I replied.

I couldn't believe I said it like that but it was just the way it came out. Barry paused, as he squinched his eyes in some confusion looking off to the side, as if thinking about the meaning of what I said. I'm not sure if Barry had any idea of what Pi referred to except something to eat. But after getting the gist of the meaning, and not knowing how to reply to such a statement, Barry only shook his head and grabbed the next board needed.

Jack also had enough of my orders. When I broke my pencil and I told him I needed another one from the house, he told me to get down and go get it myself.

Hearing that, Bobby said, "I think we are about to have us a labor strike."

I told Jack he could wear my hard hat and that did the trick. He went and got my pencil. I let him wear it from then on but the hat was so big he would be pushing it up out of his eyes constantly. He looked so funny with that hat tilting down over his face but he was proud of it regardless.

I was fortunate to have Bobby there. He was great at doing things that most kids our age had no idea about. He was the most talented kid around with knowledge about so many things that some adults didn't know. I was always learning stuff from him.

Once, being only eleven years old, he showed me how he repaired the light switch in his own bedroom. After making sure the circuit was turned off, he went to his closet and pulled out this little plastic box with a dial and wires hanging out. He said he would use it to test the circuit. Wanting to impress him trying to remember what the thing was called, I exclaimed, "Oh yeah, that's a, uh...uh...I got it...an...uh...uh...ohm...an... Ohmmeter, like the one you showed me at your dad's shop when I first moved to town!"

"That's good Bean," as Bobby's face lit up with the biggest smile, realizing I remembered that. "You were really paying attention that day. Now you see how this thing can come in handy…don't ya?"

He proceeded to show me exactly how to use it to test the wires and it did give me a little pride not only knowing what an ohmmeter was, but then on top of that, learning how to use one.

He then continued yanking and pulling until he got the switch out of the wall. "See that black wire where it's burned off at that screw on that one side. I bet if I redo it where it's broken off, that might fix it." He went on to explain how the black wire carried the current through the switch to the light bulb and when you flipped the switch off, it was the same as having a break in the wire to stop the flow of electricity. He repaired the wire, got the switch back in the wall, turned on the circuit and flipped that switch. Sure enough, the light came on and I was simply amazed.

Bobby had a way of explaining things so you can readily learn what he was talking about. I always thought he would make a great teacher and I often told him that. The last time I mentioned it, he responded, "Yeah, I could do that but its lots more fun to be creating and making things. I wouldn't want to be stuck in a classroom all day, but who knows, that might be where I end up. I guess it wouldn't be too bad of a job."

Then he continued. "You know what I really want to be when I grow up Bean?"

"What's that?"

"I want to be a land surveyor. It only requires knowing a little math and using a couple of simple instruments like they had in ancient days. The best part is you get to be outside in nature, in the forests and mountains, and not bothered by tons of people. It usually only takes you and one or two other people to do the job."

Sam heard him talking about it and remarked, "That sure sounds like a neat job, but I know what I want to be... I'm either gonna be a riverboat captain or a gourmet chef. Heck, on the boat, I might be able to do both. I don't like big crowds either and there is nothing like being on the water and away from the hustle and bustle of the city. It'd be just you, a few deck hands and the river and eating all the good food I would want, especially if I cooked it." Sam Torry had a reputation of being a fine cook at such a young age and actually did a lot of it at his home.

Sam was doing some figuring but suddenly stopped and said, "Shoot! That reminds me. I told mom I would be home to start supper tonight. She's had a hard week at work at the clothes factory and I have this special pork chops meal in mind that I told her I was making tonight. Guess I better get going. Ain't nobody really had pork chops, until they've had my pork chops."

Sam quickly wrote something quite long on a sheet in the notepad, ripped it out and hurriedly climbed down the ladder. He met Barry at the bottom and handed him the sheet.

"What's this?" Barry asked. Sam smiled but didn't answer him and told us goodbye as he went running down the alley toward home.

Bobby yelled down to Barry, "What does the note say?"

"It doesn't make any sense. It's just a page with a whole long string of numbers." Barry answered.

"Well, what are the numbers?" Bobby inquired.

"It's the number three with a decimal and followed by the biggest bunch of numbers I ever seen. You mean you want me to read all of 'em?"

"Yeah, we want to hear 'em... All of 'em." Bobby said.

So Barry proceeded to methodically and carefully rap off that long list of numbers that came after the three, one at a time,

"141592653589793238462643383279", exactly as Sam had written them down.

I asked Barry to count how many numbers that was. He didn't want to do that but I told him it was a secret code, knowing how many numbers were on that page. I told him we had devised it so nobody would go to the trouble of trying to figure it out. That way, only a few of us with the treehouse would know.

Sure enough, he gave a frustrated sigh, went back to counting again, only to himself this time, though we could hear him slowly reciting, "One, two, three, four, five, six, seven... Thirty! That's thirty numbers Sam wrote down after the decimal point, all after the number three. What do they mean?" Bobby and I shockingly looked at each other.

I remarked to Bobby, "Sam sure is one humble fella. He told me he only knew twenty-five digits of Pi, which is unbelievable, but he wrote down thirty numbers... Thirty numbers in a flash. Heck, I hardly know any digits past the decimal."

"Who the heck does?" Bobby emphatically said, and then shouted down, "Barry, that there is your number for Pi and actually, it's a mathematical expression you will be expected to memorize in school next year too."

Barry retorted, "Well, I'm skipping as much math then as they will let me. I could never memorize that many numbers." Bobby and I cracked up laughing but I think Barry knew we weren't being exactly straightforward with the Pi explanation.

After about another half hour, John and Barry had piled up the last of the boards needed for the day. John said, "We better get going too. We don't want to miss out on any of Sam's special pork chops."

Barry added, "We never say anything to mama but Sam cooks better than her or any fancy restaurant you could ever eat at! I know one thing! When I get home, I'm going to ask Sam about all those dang thirty numbers having to do with Pi... Whatever that is?"

So now the Torry boys left us and it was back to only me and Bobby and one other kid who lived on the other side of the alley, Ricky Louis. I yelled down, "Ricky, you might as well go home too. I think we'll just call it a day as its getting kinda late anyway."

He said, "Okay, I'll see you guys later." Ricky was a nice kid and always easy to get along with.

By now with the work stopping, Bobby and I laid down on the floor of the treehouse, hands propped behind our heads to take in our progress so far. But my mind, being the active one it is, visualized being far away, on Captain Sam's riverboat, with the name The PI inscribed on the side, floating down a lazy river with nothing but mountains and forest on each side and only stopping to let Bobby off to do the surveying of some primitive land.

Bobby asked me what I was thinking about. As I told him my vision, he said, "That sure sounds nice Bean, the way you always have of describing things. You are surely a dreamer but maybe one day, it might not be a dream. My pa is always telling me that's why he likes fixing things or making something with your own hands. He says it's nice to dream but you have to go after that dream, and build the life you desire. It's never just handed to you. It's up to you. Dad calls it, your own handiwork to make your dream come true."

I said, "Yep, that's exactly what we'd be doing too with our project of the treehouse! Building something we knew we would be proud of, with our own hands. For now, this treehouse would be our own handiwork."

Thinking ahead though, I said, "One day Bobby, when we are older, me and you are going to use our smarts together to build that riverboat and maybe Sam could be the captain... That is, as long as I ain't playing for the Cardinals and you or Sam ain't working for NASA."

Days and weeks went by as we continued working on that treehouse every chance we got. The revelry of staying busy and seeing our project come to fruition, helped me push back all the pain from the tragic, recent events below. It was as if being high up in the air, the pain was too heavy to reach up to me, though it often tried.

After several months, we eventually got through building it, with only a few bruises here and there and no major accidents. That house would become the envy of all the kids in our entire little town. No kid had ever seen anything like it.

It was not little either, by any means. Bobby and I had designed it to be big enough for four kids to sleep in. It was a marvel to behold. We took pride in the fact that we had built it ourselves, high up in that giant oak, with our own two hands. It was indeed, our own handiwork.

The oak tree itself was like a gentle giant and the defender of the gate, wrapping its protecting arms around us, fending off any attempts by evil forces to enter. Whenever something bad would happen to me, anyone close to me, that treehouse was always there to offer comfort. We often slept up there, and felt safe and protected in our house. The treehouse was our sanctuary, our place to get away from all the troubles of the outside world.

There was always something special about being up there when it rained too, listening to the soft, sleepy, constant tapping of raindrops, falling on the tin roof. During the worst storms, we felt nothing but calm and protected in our treehouse. In the dead of night, in the most quiet of times, it was like a religious assurance of some kind, like being close to God with angels playing a heavenly symphony. Being so far up in the air, hearing the rushing of the breeze, rustling through the leaves and the branches, with the birds singing along for the music and then the tree itself swaying in a rhythmic ritual of a slow dance with the wind, what else could it be?

Although it was a sanctuary, far above the troubles of the world below, it was also a place where we had so much fun, in a house we built up in the air. We decided to give our house a name and painted it in two huge, white letters on the door.

We named it "P I."

CHAPTER TWENTY
It's All In The Head

Jack was up in the treehouse, swinging down to the ground. We had attached a long rope on one of the big, strong branches. We could use the rope to avoid having to climb down and it was much more fun. I watched Jack for a while as he would still be at a running pace when he finally let go of the rope. He would do it at just the right moment, to be going as fast as he could, when his feet hit the ground. He would climb right back up to the treehouse, doing it over and over, scraping the ground with his feet, dragging and landing in the same worn out spot we had made over time. No wonder he wore out shoes so fast. I was sure that the department store, the main store in town that sold shoes, loved that treehouse more than we did. We went through a lot of shoes.

The only person who didn't like that rope was the next door neighbor Mr. Sutton. The tree we built the house in, was only about ten feet from the fence he put up to separate his yard from ours. With that same big swinging rope, we could get up some good momentum, swing over the fence into his yard, and then swing back to our side. He didn't like that at all, and it would make him angry if he caught us doing that.

Mr. Sutton would sternly remark, "You kids are giving my dog fits, and I don't want you getting hurt on my property either!"

He didn't know we fed the dog many times, and it became friendly to me and Jack after a while. We figured the air didn't belong to anybody in particular and he had no right to tell us where we could swing while on that rope. Besides, every once in a while it was a quick and easy way to swing over to retrieve a baseball and avoid climbing over his chain-link fence.

I had decided to go fishing today and figured Jack might want to go. As I approached the treehouse, I yelled, "Jack, I'm going fishin' down at the old wooden bridge!" He didn't pay me any attention, having so much fun swinging down on that rope. I kept up with my persuasion, remarking, "The water should still be up high now, and the fishin' will be really good. There's a big channel cat', just waitin' to be reeled in. Come on down, let's go fishin'. You said you would go with me today!"

After swinging down the last time, he climbed back up again, and disappeared inside the treehouse. In frustration, I loudly exclaimed, "What are you doing in there, Jack? Come on down... Let's go fishin'!"

Finally, Jack popped his head out and replied, "Okay-Okay already. I heard you the first time Bean." He swung down the last time, digging in the ground with his feet, kicking up a pile of dust everywhere, including on me. He quickly let go of the rope, stopping right in front of me, as I was spitting out some of the dirt. Then, like it was his idea, he remarked, "Well, whatcha waitin' for Bean? Let's go fishin'!"

We started collecting our rods, extra hooks and sinkers, and other fishing supplies. We decided for bait, to take a few slices of light bread, and a good supply of worms. Sometimes, there were spots around the yard we could find to dig for worms, but we always had a good backup plan. We had our own worm bed that we had made out of an old wash tub. We kept it in a shady spot, next to a corner behind the house. Along with the dirt, we would put in oatmeal, coffee grounds, other food items and we watered it often to keep it moist.

If you neglected it and the dirt got dry, all the worms would die. What a delight to simply scoop in that moist dirt with your fingers, grabbing a handful of lively, wiggling worms for free anytime you wanted them. Those same few handfuls, would cost a quarter at the store and our homegrown worms were far better than any store-bought ones. Plus, half of the worms in the container you bought would be dead, and the ones still alive would be so small, you couldn't get them on a hook. In our worm bed, we mostly farmed the bigger, fat earthworms we could dig up around the yard to put in the bed to multiply. Some of our earthworms were almost a foot long, not like the skinny red wigglers they sold at the store.

If our worm supply did happen to get low, bread was an easy alternative. Plus, carp and buffalo especially loved the dough bait. To use bread for bait, we rolled it into a little ball, and used treble hooks to hold it on longer.

For some reason, more often than not, we referred to bread as light bread and I never asked why. But it certainly came in handy if we got hungry. If we fished for a long time, we could always sacrifice some to eat ourselves.

Mama was always remarking, "You boys sure do go through this light bread, faster than anyone I know!" We never let on that we used it for bait too. Finally, with our rods, our bait and fishing supplies, we hopped on our bikes and off we went, headed for what everyone in town referred to as 'the old wooden bridge'. When we arrived, luckily no one was fishing there and we were glad to have it all to ourselves.

This bridge was indeed old, wooden, and built on something like stilts. Cars had to go very slow in crossing it. The old boards always appeared to be way past replacing. It was so shaky, I was always a little spooked myself, while going over it in a car as you could feel the entire structure wobble. Also, not having any sides made it that much scarier to go across.

If you leaned against the pilings underneath, you could feel the vibration caused by the cars going over the bridge. Cars crossing it, would make this unmistakable, rhythmic noise, TaDum... TaDum... TaDum, that you could hear a mile away, all day long. If you were there, fishing underneath, it was particularly loud and pieces of wood and dirt might hit you on the head, falling off the underside of the bridge.

Once under the bridge fishing, we hated being bothered by passerbyers. If they saw us fishing underneath, they would often proceed to come down to see what we were catching or only want to yap about something. We were there solely to fish and would hide as best we could when we heard someone walking over the bridge. I guess it also made for a fun way to play hide & seek, with people passing over.

So we liked to get underneath the bridge, staying out of sight as much as possible. If other kids saw us having any luck, we knew they might get their fishing stuff and come back. We surely didn't want that, having others show up and ruin our fishing. Fishing to Jack and me was a real art. We knew exactly what bait to use, which kind of hook to use, depending on what we thought might be hitting that day and always talked quietly. If we didn't walk gently, those darn fish would know people were walking around on the bank and that would scare them off. Fish might have little brains but they sure knew how to use every speck of the little brain they had. Most kids that would see us there would come running down the bank, making lots of racket and scare off our likely catch. That always would put me and Jack in a bad mood with any visitors showing up.

Then there was always the three Torry boys. Of course they were our good friends with whom we usually played baseball, fished with, squirrel hunted and messed around with most of the time.

But today, however, Jack wanted it to be only me and him. Brothers are like that sometimes. At times you feel like you almost hate 'em for maybe something they did or said to you, and then the next minute you feel the need for some brother time.

Today was one of those days. I wanted to spend some time with Jack. I didn't want anybody else to come along, not even the Torry boys. Besides, we would want to later show off all the fish we caught and make 'em jealous. It was always like a friendly competition thing with the Torrys, to see who could outdo the other in whatever venture it was, especially fishing.

Every time the river would swell like this from some rain, we could always count on catching all kinds of fish; carp, catfish, drum, buffalo, and perch. We considered all of them good eating fish, except those troublesome gars that looked like little alligators. They had all these rows of really sharp teeth but were always a fun fight. You had to be careful while trying to get 'em off your hook though, as those teeth could really do damage to your fingers while messing with 'em, if you happened to reel one in.

Now with catfish, Jack and I also loved eating the tails, but only catfish, not the others. Catfish tails would cook up all crispy, and tasted like eating French fries. Jack and I would always fuss over who would get to eat the last catfish tail when we had catfish for supper. Those tails were that good.

I dared Jack to try eating the eyeballs once. We fried a few up, but Jack said they were so small, and went down the pipe so fast, they didn't taste like anything. Jack was always willing to try just about anything on a dare.

We were finally settled in under the bridge, and luckily, no one was bothering us. We were having some really good luck. Jack had caught two catfish, our favorite, and I had caught a pretty nice size carp. We had put them on a stringer in the water close to the bank, to keep them alive until we would get through fishing. I decided to put on a brand new sharp treble hook after the last carp I caught, so the dough ball would stay on my hook better.

With the fishing starting to slow up, the sound of the water and the wind, along with the chirping of the birds, it was a relaxing symphony put on by nature. It was making us both sleepy. My little brother had already nodded off, lying comfortably on the bank.

I was fighting sleep myself, letting out some awfully big yawns. I was about to take a break to catch a nap myself, when, bam, my rod bent over double and awakened me out of my slumbering state. I knew that I had hung a really big one this time and couldn't wait to get it in, and show him off. I figured with that sharp new hook, I had put on, hopefully he was hooked really well.

It was all my little reel could do, to not let the fish take out any more line than I was reeling in. It finally felt like he was beginning to wear out, and I was winning the fight, when the fish hung my line up on something in the river bottom. I didn't want to pull too hard and let this one get away or break my line. I finally had to give it some slack to see if the fish was still on but to my disappointment, he appeared to get off.

Now I just wanted to get that new hook back and get a bait back out there but I was still hung up on something in the river. I was pulling and yanking hard, but it was hung up solid. With all the commotion, Jack woke up, and strongly admonished, "Quit pulling on your line so hard Bean, you're gonna break it!"

While straining and grunting, I decided to give it one last hard pull. That stubborn treble hook finally came loose and popped out of the river like a fired missile, going straight into the top of Jack's head.

It must have gone in deep, as Jack went completely berserk. He ran up the river bank so fast, I didn't have time to get something to cut my line, as he's now hooked like a fish on my reel. Jack went off running and screaming, straight down the road toward the Coleman Brothers gas station. All the while, I was feeding him more line from my reel to keep the line slack, while trying to catch up. The gas station was a few hundred yards back toward town, close to Main Street. Jack was a very fast runner, and having a sharp treble hook buried in his head, didn't slow him down one bit. I think it was the fastest I had ever seen him run.

He is running and hollering loudly as he could, with me chasing behind him, trying to keep up. I kept giving him more line from the reel, hoping it wouldn't run out before he would stop.

Still screaming, Jack finally got to the Coleman gas station and I finally caught up. I was still holding the rod in my hand, with that hook still buried in Jack's skull. There was fishing line all over the place, all in tangles, so I couldn't reel any of it up.

Mr. Coleman, the old gas station owner, had never seen such a sight, and it took him awhile to realize what had happened. When he got us settled down enough, to really look at the situation, he cut the line from the hook, and the tangled line that was wrapped around our legs.

When he got Jack still enough to sit down to examine his head, Mr. Coleman said, "I can't believe there's a treble hook down in there. I can only see the top of the eye sticking out. I don't think I better mess with trying to get this out myself."

He put me and Jack in his truck, and drove us to the closest doctor, Dr. Holmes. He had a little three room office that I had been to a few times, and only once do I remember him having a nurse there. I think it may have been his wife at the time. We went on in, with Jack hobbling along like he was going to pass out with blood streaming down his head. We saw Doc Holmes laid back, in an office chair with his head propped back, breathing out of his mouth, with it wide open. I figured he was taking a nap or resting.

I had often wondered if he was a real doctor but we weren't in any condition to be picky about our choices right then. As time went on, while trying to wake up the doctor, we realized that he was a little more than sleepy. We realized by now that he was drunk as a skunk.

With each persistent interruption from us, he was constantly stretching his eyes and mouth, shaking his head back and forth, trying to focus and stay awake. As Mr. Coleman was explaining the situation, Doctor Holmes started to come a little more to his senses. He was struggling to stay alert, but finally seemed to understand why we were there.

After being able to keep his eyes open, he grabbed a special doctoring tool that resembled a pair of needle nose pliers like we used for fishing. I thought to myself, those are the neatest set of pliers I had ever seen. They looked brand new, like they had never been used before. They were very long and so shiny, they seemed to almost blind me with the light they reflected. They had really big handles to hold them by and weren't straight on one the end, like the ones we had for fishing.

Here I am, with all that was going on in that serious moment, and I was thinking how those pliers would make a great pair to have around for fishing purposes. I was picturing it in my mind. I would be holding a fish and using those nice pliers to get the fishhook out with ease, all the while admiring my new shiny pliers as I nodded in approval. At that moment, the real situation with Jack and the doc was slowly fading in my mind, giving away to dreaming about using that fancy tool for fishing down at the river.

With Jack still hollering, I finally managed to snap my head out from my dreaming world about those stupid pliers, and to pay attention to the serious dilemma immediately at hand.

That's when I heard Doc Holmes saying in heavily slurred speech. "Well now, this don't look bad at all, seen a lot worse... Don't worry, son, I'll get that hook out of there."

The other problem was that he would close his eyes intermittently in a drowsy fashion, like he was nodding off while standing up.

Finally, when he opened his eyes, he had grabbed onto me instead of Jack and was fiddling all through my hair, looking for where that hook went.

"Now where did that dang hook go?" He inquired.

Mr. Coleman grabbed his hand and put it back on Jack's head, keeping him straight on whose head he was supposed to be working on.

When the doc realized his mistake, he only remarked, "Oh... Right... Yeah!"

After getting him settled on the correct head, he was holding those fancy pliers, waving them around in the air like a baton of an orchestra leader and in slurred speech still, said, "Okay, I got it now.. Trust me boys, this hook's coming out."

All the while, Jack was still hollering and we were trying to hold him still, so maybe we could get this ordeal over with. Doc kept probing and digging, yanking and pulling, like a dentist trying to pull a stubborn tooth not wanting to come out.

Finally, he managed to get the hook out and Mr. Coleman and I breathed a sigh of relief, but I'm not sure how much better Jack felt when it was all over.

Jack began to calm down, got patched up and Mr. Coleman told the doc he would get us home and talk about settling up later. On our way out, Doctor Holmes didn't say anything at all. He slouched back into that same chair he was in when we got there at the beginning. He stuck his hand out over the top of the chair, in a weakened attempt of a wave, as his head appeared to quickly droop once again, to a state of slumber.

We all got back into Mr. Coleman's truck under much calmer conditions this time, thank goodness! He took us back to the old wooden bridge to help get all our stuff we had run off and left. He told Jack to sit still in the truck, while he helped me load up our bikes in the truck bed.

Mr. Coleman said he should take us home and let my mama or anyone there know what had happened but no one was there when we arrived a few minutes later. He helped unload everything and made sure Jack got in the house okay and told him to take it easy and maybe lie down for a spell.

He wrote down his phone number for anyone to call the station if they had any questions about what happened. He made sure I understood and said, "Beanie, if Jack gets to feeling bad or something, before your mama gets home from the clothes factory, don't hesitate to call me."

I thanked him for all he had done for us that day. I don't know how it might have turned out if Mr. Coleman hadn't been there to help us. That night, when I finally got to sleep after thinking about all that happened, all I could dream about was that nice, shiny set of doctor pliers used on Jack's head.

I always thought Jack was the toughest kid I had ever known. He was a lot tougher than me, that's for sure. But I would never admit it. From all his hollering from that incident, one might not think he was tough. But then again, I wasn't the one with a big treble hook buried deep in my skull, with a drunk doctor cutting and digging into my head.

When mama got home and I recounted the entire story, she almost couldn't believe what happened. Jack was lying on the couch asleep. She began to comb through Jack's hair, examining the evidence and said, "I'll call Mr. Coleman to thank him and figure out if I owe him anything for doing what he did."

I told her the doc didn't take any money and agreed to settle up later. She said, "Okay, I'm just thankful that the hook didn't get in Jack's eye. This could have turned out real bad."

I replied, "It's a good thing Jack's got such a darn hard head."

"Yeah, good thing huh," she replied with a smile.

I commented, "You know, I think Jack may have finally done something to overshadow me getting the name Bean. Once word gets around town about a hook in the head, they may start calling him Captain Hook or something."

Mama said, "Yeah, but knowing Jack, he would probably love a name like that and would wear it as a badge of honor."

The very next day, Jack was feeling a whole lot better. He wanted to get our fishing stuff together again and head back to the old wooden bridge, while the fishing was still good.

We loaded everything on our bikes again, and as usual, we rode by the gas station on the way there. We saw Mr. Coleman putting gas in a car and we gave him a big smile and friendly, thankful wave. While he was using one hand to put gas in the car, he halfway raised the other in a hesitant, reply of a wave, with a surprised look on his face. I don't think he could believe we were heading back fishing, again, that very next day.

We sure were thankful for Mr. Coleman, and everything he had done for us. We hoped he would always be close by, there at his gas station, for any future emergencies.

Plus, for a nickel, his station had the coldest grape sodas in town!

CHAPTER TWENTY ONE
Catch A Ride

One thing about life is that it goes on. At least that's what mama would often say after dad's passing. She had a way of explaining things in down to earth terms you could easily understand.

"Life is like a train... We're all just along for the ride," she always had the habit of saying.

Mama loved trains. She grew up in the mountains of North Carolina, in a family of tobacco farmers and loggers. She would recount to Jack and me how she would sit on the front porch of her mountain cabin, and watch a train going around the mountain far down below. She would listen to the whistle of the engineer as a long, rising pillar of black smoke, trailed behind from the locomotive smoke stack.

I would listen to her describe that scene so many times, I would envision myself, sitting on that same front porch, listening to the fading sound of the train whistle, as it disappeared around the mountain. I would often dream of catching a ride on that train, gleaming happily down at the valley below and going to wherever it would take me. In my dream, the train never stopped, nor did I ever see the destination and that was the best part. I didn't want to. Like mama was always saying, I was along for the ride, not the destination.

It had been a year since dad had died. Somehow mama had managed to keep from losing the house and pay the bills. She had to work long hours and sometimes do what she called overtime shifts to make more money. Things were definitely tight, but we were getting by. I was almost thirteen by now and in the seventh grade. Jack was still in elementary school, three years behind me. Like always, we looked forward to the weekend during the school year, so we could play baseball, go fishing at one of our favorite spots on Little River, or just ride our bikes all over town.

Today, Bobby and I were throwing the baseball behind his house in The Greenfield when all three Torry brothers showed up a few minutes later. We had just enough people to have a pitcher, a catcher and a batter with two outfielders. We made up this game where you batted until you made three fly ball outs or you struck out once. If you fouled the ball after two strikes, it counted as strike three.

I was first up to bat. John was pitching first and went to the little hump of dirt we had built up for a pitcher's mound. Sam knelt down as the catcher, behind an old piece of a rug we used for home plate.

After a few warm up pitches, Sam told John, "Whenever you're ready, let her rip."

John replied, "I've been working on a new pitch. I want to see if I can throw a few of 'em!"

I responded, "You know how good a hitter I am. If you can get it passed me, you know you've got a good pitch."

I got ready at the plate and John let go of that first pitch. It was coming hard and right at me and then suddenly broke right over home plate. I backed out of there, falling down in the dirt. I couldn't believe my eyes.

"What the heck was that? That ball must'a broke two feet at least! I thought it was going to hit me for sure."

John proudly said, "That's my new breaking ball pitch. Don't know if you call it a slider or just a curveball but... Well, guess I got it working pretty good if it scared you."

I didn't want to interrupt the game right then, so I asked him if he would try to teach me how to throw that pitch later. He showed me his grip and said it had a lot to do with how you held the wrist and placed the fingers on the seams. I couldn't wait to learn how to throw that pitch.

After embarrassing myself by striking out on those dang sliders, it was my time to pitch. I didn't want to embarrass myself anymore by trying something new right then, so I decided to stick with my fast ball.

Sam said, "I'll stay catching. Y'all can do most of the batting and pitching." For some reason, that was his thing. Sam always liked doing the catching, without any protective equipment whatsoever. No catcher's mask; no shin guards, nothing. It was a wonder that he never got hit in the head or something broken but he never did. He occasionally got plunked with a back swing of the bat too and I couldn't count how many times he got stung with foul tipped balls. But he'd get right back in there catching. Baseballs seemed to not hurt Sam or he never let on if they did.

We switched out positions, so John took Bobby's place in the outfield and stayed out there with Barry, while Bobby came on in to bat. I was now getting ready to do my warm up pitches. I began digging my right foot into the dirt, just like a big league pitcher does before settling in to deliver his heat.

Sam, still behind the plate, held his glove steady right over the plate, giving me a good steady target, and yelled out, "Put her right here, Bean!" I began to fire 'em in there, right over the plate, with Sam not having to move his glove.

He exclaimed, "I've never seen you throw that hard before Bean. You're gonna wear my glove out!" He took his glove off, stood up and exclaimed, "This ol' glove's got no padding and it's all worn out... I gotta get me a real catcher's mitt."

Sam crouched back down ready to catch again, as Bobby got in his batting stanz at the plate.

Bobby said, "Bean, throw that fastball of yours in here. I'm feeling good today. I bet I can hit one all the way out to the alley."

Now the alley was an automatic homerun when we played a game and was a big deal to hit one that far. Hitting in baseball is all about timing and balance for the batter. If you can fool a batter with a slower pitch when he is expecting a fastball, it messes 'em all up and they can look really silly in their swing. Besides, I surely needed company looking silly like I did, trying to hit John's fancy slider.

That's when I thought of trying to be a little tricky. I had been practicing throwing this really weird pitch that Sam had shown me how to throw before. It was really hard to get a good grip on it and took a lot of practice to throw it the right way. It was called a knuckleball.

You really didn't use your knuckles to throw it. You actually would dig the tips of your fingers into the hide of the ball and not snap your wrist at all. Hopefully, if thrown correctly, the ball would spin very little and almost float up to the plate, and have this weird wobbling action that was hard to hit. I wanted to impress Bobby with my new found pitch I had been working on, thanks to Sam.

So I dug into the mound, stuck my fingertips into the ball as hard as I could and let her fly to home plate. It was so slow that Bobby saw it coming, waited back on it and drove it all the way across the alley on the other side, hitting a tree. Bobby was jumping up and down, shouting, "Home Run... Home Run... Home Run!"

After he got through celebrating his majestic feat, we had to go find the ball before we forgot where it landed. We got to the spot we thought it went and Barry found the ball in the bottom of the little ditch. It was sitting in some water.

Bobby remarked, "That is the farthest I have ever hit a baseball!"

"Yeah, you don't gotta rub it in Bobby! Looks like I'm gonna need some work on throwing that knuckleball. I better stick with my fastball for now."

Bobby picked up the baseball and said, "Is that what that was? It did look like a weird kind of pitch but I sure blasted the heck out of it, didn't I?"

We were drying off the ball and started heading back with the intent to keep playing. Bobby said he was through batting after hitting the big home run. So that made it Barry's turn to bat. He didn't quite love baseball as much as the rest of us but could hold his own as a player and we always needed five to play. Barry's favorite part was getting to bat so he was excited about getting his turn to hit.

That's when Bobby stopped, and almost in a panic said to me, "Bean, isn't today the 15th?"

"I think it is Bobby... How come?"

"Last time he was here, the train engineer told me the 15th was the day he would be coming back on the 202."

Bobby didn't say it very loud so the Torry boys wouldn't hear. We knew we better hurry getting there, to not miss the train. We told them we remembered something important we had to leave to go do.

Barry disappointedly said, "Dang it. Y'all will do anything to get out of letting me have my turn at batting. Y'all like having me around only to stick me in the outfield and chase the balls around. When it's my turn to hit, you wanna quit all of a sudden."

Bobby said, "No Barry. We really have to head to town. This is really important. We just forgot about it... You get first dubs up next time we play, I promise."

"Well what is so important then?" Barry asked.

I said, "We don't have time to discuss it now. We'll tell you later but we gotta get going."

Then off Bobby and I went running, to get our bikes and headed to town.

We always loved catching the freight train coming into town whenever we could, so we hopped on our bikes and headed that direction as fast as we could. We hadn't heard the 202 whistle, so we figured it hadn't got here yet.

We got to Sutton's gas station on the corner, right across the street from the tracks. We figured the gas station would be a good place to hang around to wait and watch for the train to get there. We didn't have any money, so we could drink water from the water hose at the station if we got thirsty. So we sat and patiently waited.

It was usually the 202 locomotive that would make a stop in Little River about two or three times a month, depending on the time of year. It would drop some railroad cars off and then pick some up. Bobby and I always wanted to be around the tracks when it would come to town. We never wanted to miss it.

Catch A Ride
(A poem by the author)

I can hear that whistle now it won't be long
Coming up that hill as its chuggin' along
Got it in my sight, comin' round the bend
Can't miss that train, it ain't comin' again

I gotta reach on out, I gotta grab a' hold
To catch that train while its moving slow
If I don't act now, I'm left standing here
Better get onboard while my chance is still here

Now I've taken a seat and the tracks are clear
I ain't lookin' back, 'cause the past ain't here
And where she goes, I don't really know
But I'm awfully glad I didn't miss this show

Don't stand there staring at your toes
Don't you wait too long, the train will soon be gone
Don't get left behind, stranded in the cold
Gonna catch a ride to find out where she goes
Gonna let that train take me on down the road
Gonna take that ride and find out where she goes
Gonna let that train take me on down the road
Gonna let that train take me on down the road

We were sitting down and leaning outside against the side of the service station building about half asleep, when we heard that familiar whistle. We hurriedly ran over to the tracks and stood as close as we safely could to the train coming in. Soon as we saw the engineer, we would do our ritual. We would make a fist, holding our arm up and yanking our elbow down into our side. He replied with that loud train whistle. I figured we might drive him crazy by getting him to repeat doing that so many times when he came to town but I think he had a lot of fun interacting with us. Every time we did that signal with our arm, he would never fail us. He always replied by blowing that train whistle. It gave us the biggest delight.

The train tracks came to a dead end in our town, so the engineer would have to go in reverse when he got ready to leave town after switching out cars. He would always be sitting right next to the open side of the locomotive, with his arm propped up on the open ledge, waiting for cars to be switched out. When he didn't have a lot to do but sit and wait sometimes, Bobby and I would get right below him, looking up, what seemed like a story high, to carry on a conversation with him. He loved talking about trains and how much he loved his job. Bobby had gotten to know him a lot better than I did.

We learned his name was Mr. Ed, like the talking horse in the movies. We were always asking him lots of questions about trains. I had at one time asked him, "How do you get to become a train engineer?"

He told me most people in the business call what he does a loco pilot or train driver but engineer is fine and that's the term most people use. He said the main thing is you have to have a lot of stamina to do the job. He went on to explain that meant being able to stay awake for long periods of time and also to be in pretty good shape.

There was this one time he let us get on the train with him in the engine room. He told us to not tell everybody we got to do that, as that might get him into some trouble. We could tell that he was proud of his engine and how much power it had.

He pointed to the most important part he had control over, as he said, "See that handle right here where I sit. I have to be able to push and hold that lever down for a long time. It's what makes the train engine go. A train engine doesn't have gears like a car, it just gets more and more speed as I hold that down. We call it the power handle."

Bobby said, "A train engine must have a lot of power to be able to pull a mile of boxcars loaded down, especially up a hill?"

Mr. Ed replied, "You boys sure know how to ask a lot of questions. But, they are good questions. My engine has around 7000 horsepower, where say a car...might only have 200... And, I can go hundreds of miles on a single gallon of fuel. See how far you get with that one gallon of gas in a car!"

Another thing he told us was that all locomotives have it set for the engineer to always be on the right side of the car without exception, so he could lean out and see oncoming signals. Bobby and I learned everything about trains and how they worked from talking to Mr. Ed. I did a report in school on the subject once and got an A grade. Mr. Ed was proud of that when I told him.

He would let us play in an open car if there was one, until he got ready to leave with the train. As a warning, he would blow the whistle three short blasts and one long one to let us know to get out of the boxcar, as he would be preparing to depart.

Bobby had told me that Mr. Ed had promised to sometime let him take a ride to the next stop on his route, which was Marked Tree. It was a ten mile trip by the highway. The route for the train was much longer as it had to go a long way around to get there. It had to avoid a fork of Little River as well as the St. Francis River that ran through Marked Tree. He said it was about thirty miles by train.

Well, this was my lucky day. Bobby wanted to do it today and Mr. Ed said we could catch a ride today if we wanted to. He told us we couldn't ride in the locomotive with him but we could hop in an open boxcar. He told us to stay out of sight until he got a little bit out of town.

Being so excited about catching a ride on the train, we forgot about our bicycles and left them across the street at old Suttons' service station. It was too late anyway as Mr. Ed already had the train moving. When we got a short distance out of town, we emerged from the dark inside corner of the car and sat next to one of the open sides. We had no water, no food or anything on us at all, but we didn't care. This was one unbelievable feeling. The train was going very slow, maybe 20 miles an hour. We didn't care how long it took to get to Marked Tree. Bobby and I were thinking; heck, the longer it took, the longer we got to ride.

For a while the tracks ran right alongside the banks of Little River, of which I was very familiar with.

I said to Bobby, "I think that wild turnip patch is coming up on the other side of the train that is close to our good fishing hole down here."

We knew that turnip patch was located around a line of these big cedar trees that led to our favorite spot on that part of the river. Some days in the late spring or early summer, on our way out here, we'd be digging all around in the ground there, pulling up raw turnips, blowing off the dirt and devouring 'em right on the spot, peeling and all.

"Yeah, the last time I helped myself to a few of 'em, I got an upset stomach, I ate so many." Bobby said.

I replied, "Well, fishing is hard work and a fella's gotta eat!"

"I guess eating too much dirt with 'em didn't help the situation any." He replied.

Bobby saw the big cedar trees coming into view and said, "Bean, our fishing hole's coming up soon."

As it slowly came into view, I saw the Torry boys in our old spot, all three of 'em, John, Barry and Sam and they hadn't noticed us yet. I couldn't believe it. We had left them only a couple hours earlier at The Greenfield, telling 'em we had something important to do. Now here they were, already at the river, in our good spot and us on that train.

They finally turned our direction, watching the train go by and they suddenly saw us come into view as we began to pass them. In somewhat of a shock, you could see them standing frozen in disbelief. We waved at them with a proud, showing off expression on our faces. Their heads appeared to be turning in the slowest, methodical motion, as their eyes couldn't quite believe what they were seeing. They returned a half-hearted parting wave, as we watched them disappear in the distance.

Being that the tracks were up higher, and together with the movement of the train, it added a different perspective to my view of the river. I felt more like the river's equal, being part of this huge monster machine passing by on its banks, eventually leaving it, and the Torry boys behind, as we made a slow turn in a long, big curve. It was now mostly open fields, crossing a few gravel and dirt roads on our path to Marked Tree. The train was going so slow, it took over an hour to get there.

Giving us specific instructions on when to get off the train, Mr. Ed said, "The train will come to a stop just on the outskirts of Marked Tree, close to where the highway from Little River comes in. Watch for this big red barn, close to a big curve in the St. Francis River that would come into view. You can't miss seeing that red barn and when I stop the train, that's when y'all get off."

He told us he would talk to us about our little adventure the next time he sees us, when he gets back to Little River.

We explicitly followed his instructions when we saw the red barn and the river come into view. We wanted to say goodbye but we figured he didn't want anyone finding out he let two boys catch a ride on his train. Fortunately, we got off close to the highway heading back for the ten mile trip to Little River. It was getting late in the evening by now, around seven o'clock. We had a long walk to get back home ahead of us.

There was little traffic on the highway, as only a couple of cars passed us and they didn't stop. It was getting dark with no moon that night, so it was hard to see, except by an occasional street light. We were hungry, tired and thirsty by now. For the rest of the time, we couldn't believe that not a single car came by to give us a ride.

We ended up walking all the way home and that was with us taking short cuts across some fields. It took us three hours to walk that distance, with a few little breaks we took. We figured we would be in big trouble when we got back as late as it was getting. We spent our time trying to come up with what to tell our folks about what we did. We didn't want to get Mr. Ed in any trouble either, so we decided to say we snuck on the train without anyone seeing us. We figured a little fib with the purpose of keeping our friend like Mr. Ed out of trouble, surely wouldn't hurt anything.

It was around 10 o'clock by now and we were crossing the bridge on the west side of town, when none other than Sheriff Mason slowly was driving by in our direction. Yep, he spotted us, and as soon as those headlights shined on us, he knew who we were.

"Okay boys... Where in the dickens have y'all been? Both your mamas got worried after neither of you showed up around supper time and it got so late. Mr. Sutton told Belle y'all had left your bikes at his station earlier today and then went messing around the railroad tracks but y'all never came back. Me and the deputy was out there on the tracks looking for body parts all evening. I told Belle, and your mama too Bobby, that I was sure y'all were out playing somewhere and just forgot about time. I thought I would drive around a little to see if I saw you anywhere and well... Here you were."

Bobby and I looked at each other trying to determine who was going to start with probably telling the biggest lie either of us was going to have to tell in quite some time. Good ol Bobby jumped right in.

"Well, you see, Mr. Mason...it went like this. Bean and I were close by on our bikes when we heard the train whistle and you know how me and Bean love trains. Well when the train got here, it stopped for a while, sitting there on tracks without moving. Bean dared me to climb into one of the empty boxcars. So, when no one was looking that's exactly what I did. I told Bean how cool it was in there and for him to hop on in too. We mostly hid in the corner so no one would see us. We had the idea of us riding a little ways and then hop off, while it would still be going real slow. Well the train started moving and then got going a lot faster, before we could jump out. Being stuck on the train, we ended up riding in that boxcar all the way to its next stop, which was Marked Tree."

All the while, the sheriff is leaning his head sideways, with a little squint in one eye and some doubt of skepticism on Bobby's story without saying a word.

Bobby continued with his story... "The train took several hours to get to Marked Tree. That darn train is slower than my grandma in house slippers, on the sidewalk on a snowy day in the middle of winter. By the time we got off and headed back on the highway to Little River, it was already getting late and nobody would stop to give us a ride. Bean decided it would be better to take a short cut across these fields about half way back and we sort a' got lost for a while but eventually made our way back to the highway. We were so thirsty we started looking for some place that might have some water. I saw this barn that was off the highway down a dirt road and we headed for it, hoping to have a water hydrant somewhere around it."

By now, as Bobby kept talking non-stop, the sheriff was leaning back, and his head was cocked all the way over to one side with his arms crossed, repeating over and over, "Mm...huh... Mm...huh," while slightly shaking his head up and down a little with a hint of a sarcastic grin on his face.

Bobby continued... "Well, we finally found a faucet by that old barn, got us a good drink and were resting for a bit before continuing on. Then this pack of mean dogs came out of nowhere and started chasing us, growling and barking, figuring we'd be eaten alive. So we went runnin' across the fields, into this patch of woods, not knowing where we were headed until we finally got away from them dogs. It was a close call. Anyway, that took us a while to get outta them woods as we were going in the wrong direction and we finally came out into some open fields and got lost again for a spell, being all turned around. We finally figured out which way it was and got back on the highway... We went along fine for a while but with no moon, it was hard to see where we were walking. Then Bean stepped into a hole on the side of the road, kinda hurt his ankle a little and we had to stop as it took a spell 'till he started feeling better. So that slowed us up even more but we finally got going again, back on the road when he could walk better... We were never so happy to see that ol bridge come into sight and were celebrating when we got there. Then we saw your lights and here we were when you found us."

I couldn't believe how much of a tale came out of Bobby's mouth. Bobby stood there and finished with the most matter of fact expression on a face you would ever see. He told it so well and convincing, heck, I was wanting to believe it. More than that I couldn't believe how the sheriff sat there and listened to that whole spiel.

With one raised eyebrow, after staring at us for a minute on figuring out how to respond, Sheriff Mason concluded, "Well, I guess... If that's the way it was! Then that's the way it was! Just don't let me catch you boys ever hopping a train again. You know in some cities they will take you straight to jail if they see you trying to catch a ride on a train like that. Let this be a lesson to ya...to not ever do that again. Anyway, time's a wastin'. I better get y'all home before I get in trouble myself with your parents for sitting here and jawing."

We both told the sheriff we were sure glad he didn't arrest us and thanks for taking us home. We were both so tired we could barely walk anymore. When the sheriff dropped me off, he had a big grin on his face, and in parting said, "Bean, now don't let no mean dogs get you tonight!"

I answered with only a smile and waved goodbye.

Of course, we both got into big trouble at home for pulling that stunt. Neither one of us got a whipping for it, just a good scolding and told to never do anything like that again.

Jack was still awake with hearing all the commotion of what had happened but mama told us both to go on to bed.

Of course, Jack was wanting to hear all the details.

"I'll let Bobby tell you later," I said and chuckled!

As we were heading off to bed, Jack told me that as soon as he was big enough, he was going to hop that train because he couldn't wait to; 'Catch a ride'.

CHAPTER TWENTY TWO
The Pinball Wizard

Jack was becoming less dependent on having me around all the time. He began to find things to do on his own. I was glad for that, as I was growing older, having my own friends, but I would always be there whenever he needed me. Jack didn't seem to need friends like I did. He would be off on his bike all by himself and I might not see him all day. So sometimes I would still worry about him. After all, he was only going on ten, but he was a lot tougher than me at three years older. He would often get into fights with kids much older and he might not always come out on top, but most kids knew better than to mess with him. He was really stout for his smaller stature and younger age.

Today, I didn't see him around anywhere and I figured he might be at the drugstore in town. Going there to buy medicine was usually the last thing kids thought of for being there. When someone mentioned going to the drugstore, our thoughts turned to ice cream floats, cold sodas or sweet treats. The biggest reason kids loved our drugstore was to go there to only play the pinball machines in the back. If you played enough you could get really good, and if you scored high enough, you would get extended or extra games for free. You might play for an hour on just one nickel.

It became Jack's favorite thing to do. If he had any money to spend, he would often be at the drugstore, getting a soda, a float or an ice cream cone but mainly to play a pinball machine. He was still too short to really see the action as well as he wanted, so he used a stool that got him up higher. The machine was really designed for adults or teenagers. So that stool helped him reach around the sides of the machine for better control of the buttons that worked the flippers. Using the flippers was like hitting a baseball with a bat in a way. It was all about timing. You used them to keep that steel ball going 'round and 'round the machine, hitting bumpers and other objects to keep adding up points. The machine started out by giving you five steel balls. When the last ball fell through the gap between the flippers, then the game would be over. He loved the pinball machine called Circus Town.

It had a lighted display of a clown's head with big orange hair. If you can land a ball in this certain spot, the clown's hair would explode off his head with smoke coming out of his ears and you would hear this loud, funny "Yowh Wee" noise the clown would make. It was Jack's favorite thing to accomplish while playing and he would crack up every time he did it, seeing the bald head of the clown after getting his hair blown up. It was really funny when that happened.

The machine would let the person that scored the most points in a game, set their initials at the top of a list of all the best scores. Of course, the initial that was displayed most of the time, at the very top was, yep... JB.

It became an obsession with Jack and he got to where he preferred pinball over playing baseball, fishing or anything else. He played so much he became a regular pro at it. He would constantly go by there to proudly make sure his initials hadn't been replaced by someone else's.

We might be out fishing and he would suddenly exclaim, "I better go see if anyone has beat my high score yet! I got a reputation to keep up!"

If he was gone very long at all, I knew someone must have beat his score, as he would be there trying to get back his champion status. That is of course, if he had any money to plug into the machine. But that didn't happen very often, as he was hard to dethrone as pinball king most of the time. Jack loved being known as the pinball wizard around town.

I was never jealous of him and in fact, I had a little pride for him getting recognition for something. I think it gave him even more pride, when I would sometimes comment, "I think being a pinball wizard around these parts, is a lot cooler than being known for doing something dumb in an old bean trailer like what I did."

"I don't know about that Bean? That is something that might be hard for you to top anytime soon!"

I didn't know if that was supposed to make me feel better or feel worse, but I reluctantly agreed, "Yeah Jack, I think you may be right?"

I did get a little solace though for being good at baseball. When we played ball in The Greenfield, everyone always wanted me to be on their team, since I was the best hitter around. So at least, I had talent in something.

One problem with Jack and his pinball playing was that as time went on, he began to play hooky from school and where would he be found? Yep there he would usually be, in the back of Holmes Drugs, running up another top score on one of the two machines that were there. It had gotten to be such a habit, if the owner was there, he would call the school and let them know Jack was at it again during school hours. Jack stayed in a lot of trouble by doing that.

Sheriff Mason got to know Jack very well as he would get the call that Jack was there during school hours and would go by there, pick him up and take him back to school. The sheriff knew mama was at work and couldn't leave. Time after time she tried dealing with the problem but working all day at the clothes factory didn't allow her to do much about it.

So Jack got away with skipping school quite often. I think he didn't mind too much getting picked up by the sheriff. Sometimes the sheriff would have to run back by the police station, right after picking up Jack with only an hour or two left for school and Jack would end up hanging around the station for a bit.

When that happened, later at home he would ask me, "Guess what I did today Bean? I sat around talking to the folks at the city hall, drinking free cokes and eating peanuts all afternoon. It sure beats sitting in class."

Jack could eat four or five bags of those peanuts that came out of those dispensing machines and out-drink anybody in sodas.

Now I guess it made me a little jealous. I saw myself sitting bored in study-hall, while Jack was having fun playing pinball and later sitting around city hall getting refreshments, talking with folks in town that dropped by.

Jack and I had known Sheriff Mason for years from coming out to the farm, ever since I can remember. Of course, many of those times had simply to deal with theft or an incident having to do with one of the tenants dad was looking over. But there were also those times, when dad had been drinking, that the sheriff would simply bring dad home instead of arresting him. He would always talk to us kids back then and sometimes drink coffee with mama for a while before he left. So, Jack and I had grown up regarding the sheriff as more of a friend, or like an uncle in many ways, and not like a policeman to be scared of.

This particular week, since it had been raining for several days, we couldn't play outside much anyway. So Jack had plenty of an excuse after school to go play pinball. But I couldn't wait to get outside, having been cooped up all week in either school or at the house because of the weather.

I was so delighted when the rain finally stopped. But the summer heat and humidity were starting to kick in and it was almost intolerable right after any rain. Your clothes would feel like they were glued to your skin, like wrapped in plastic, from staying so wet with sweat. But that didn't matter. After being stuck in that house every afternoon, I was ready to do something, anything outside. The Greenfield was still a muddy wet mess and so naturally, fishing would be the next best thing we could do. So now, with the weather clearing up, it was a great opportunity to go to our favorite fishing spot down at the old wooden bridge. From experience, I figured we would catch something with the river filled up from the rain that week. Jack would know that conditions like this, was what we had been waiting for. It was at just the right level with enough room left on the river bank to set things up. Since it was still too wet and muddy to think about playing baseball, I thought that would make Jack's agreeing to go fishing that much easier. Plus, we hadn't done any good fish-eating for supper in quite a while. I was hoping Jack would be ready and raring to see if we could scrounge up one of those tasty channel catfish.

I checked all around the house and didn't see him anywhere. But to not waste time by going looking for him, I thought I would go ahead and get everything ready. So I proceeded to get the bait, check our reels and make sure they had good hooks and sinkers tied on before heading to the river. Then I'd go find Jack.

One important thing in fishing is keeping your equipment in good shape. A rusty hook or ragged line could cause you to lose that one nice fish, and sometimes the only fish you might manage to catch on a certain day. I was always fussing at Jack about leaving bait on a hook after quitting fishing or leaving a tangle in a reel. His worst habit was leaving an old, dried piece of hardened bait on a hook, from fishing days before.

Being the organizer and prepared type I was, I always kept my things in tip top shape, ready to go. But Jack wasn't like that. He usually did stuff at the last minute, while I would be ready at a moment's notice. So usually by the time we would get to a fishing spot, I would already have been fishing for several minutes before he was ready to make his first cast. He would still be messing with a tangle in his reel or changing out old hooks on his line. Those were the times I would look his way without speaking a word, nodding with a little cocky smile already having a good time, while he looked frustrated, still fiddling with stuff.

I would get on to him about being such a procrastinator but he didn't like folks telling him what to do, especially his older brother.

Sometimes, after getting his fill of my elderly brother advice, he would exclaim, "Bean, you ain't my mama and I wish you would quit acting like it, always telling me what to do... You do things your way and I'll do 'em mine!"

Of course, he was right, I did pester him a lot about little things, but I thought, what's an older brother for anyway, if it ain't for sharing all his vast learning?

It was starting to get later in the afternoon and I was getting impatient to get on our way to the old wooden bridge. With everything ready, the only thing left needed was to round up Jack and get him to come home to help carry all our fishing stuff.

So I set out to find him. I thought he might be at John Torry's house down the alley, but the opposite way from town. It was close by, so I thought I would check there first. Sam was out back throwing the ball with Barry when I stopped with my bike on the street by their house.

I shouted, "Have y'all seen Jack around anywhere?"

Barry yelled back, "I think I saw him go by a little while ago on his..."

Sam interrupted, "Bean, you want to work on that knuckleball, seeing how you need the practice on learning how to throw it?"

I didn't want them to know we were going fishing, so I said, "Appreciate it Sam but I don't have time right now."

Sam, while trying to muffle the biggest giggle sarcastically inquired, "Well where ya going? Gotta catch a train or something?"

"Real funny there, Sam, but I don't think I'll be catching a ride on any train for a very long time."

Mama had told Mrs. Torry about Bobby Jansen and I catching a ride awhile back on the 202 to Marked Tree, and getting brought home late that night by the sheriff.

Mrs. Torry had told me how she couldn't believe how we had worried our mamas like that but said our trouble was good, compared to a lot of meanness that some kids get into.

I told Sam and Barry that maybe I'd see 'em later and said goodbye. They both were acting as if they were still trying to control laughing. I only responded by shaking my head, while deciding to head to this little store called Louis Grocery, since Barry saw Jack heading that direction earlier.

It was only a short distance down the road past the Torry's house. Mr. Louis always had the best tasty, homemade bologna sandwiches. Jack would sometimes hang around there drinking his favorite soda, a grape flavor, and maybe having one of those good sandwiches, that is, if he happened to have any money on him to pay for either one.

I thought there might be a good chance of him being there. I went in and asked the owner, Mr. Louis, if he had seen Jack.

Mr. Louis said, "Yeah, he had come by about an hour ago, got a bologna sandwich and said he was going to go play some pinball at the drugstore in town with a couple nickels he had leftover."

Then looking a little lost in thought, he quipped, "Maybe I ought to think about making some room in the back of the store to put a couple of them machines in here? Kids need something to do around here anyway and they tend to play on 'em for hours sometimes."

"With Jack, you would sure have a steady customer," I replied.

Mr. Louis, being the consummate salesman I suppose, said, "Bean, I'll make you a good deal today on them Red Wigglers. I'll sell ya two containers for the price of one," as he somehow figured we might be going fishing.

"No sir...thanks... We still have plenty of 'em in our worm bed at the house." He sold crickets too but Jack and I preferred catching grasshoppers for free, plus they stayed on the hook better.

Mr. Louis was always the real talkative type. I never wanted to make eye contact if I was in a hurry when I went into his store. Once he looked at you eye to eye, he would go on and on in whatever he was talking about and it would make you feel rude to just walk away. He was telling me today how his wife had been bugging him about getting a new refrigerator.

He said, "We were getting our TV fixed at Mr. Henson's Appliance store when she saw this new-fangled refrigerator that automatically makes ice for you. I told her that ain't worth spending hundreds of dollars on, when we are doing fine with using ice trays." Continuing as he chuckled, "I swear, these modern conveniences are making people downright lazy. I suppose one day they will have cars that do the driving for ya!"

"Yeah... That'll be the day!" I skeptically replied.

As he was educating me on the likes of married life, I kept staring at the ice cold looking grape sodas in that refrigerated soda box. Feeling trapped in conversation I interrupted, "I think I will have one of those cold grape sodas. I always get thirsty riding my bike."

I had about twenty cents on me and figured I could spare six cents. I didn't want to spend my last dime on that tasty looking bologna sandwich, even though I really wanted it.

The sodas were in this big metal cooler box that you looked down into, with this clear, flip top lid you'd lift way up to get out a soda. After dropping the required nickel and a penny into the front coin slot, you were ready to grab that wet, ice cold bottle. You had to pull the soda bottle by the neck, down to the end of a row, then up and out of the box. It was a real process to get the bottle out of there but it also added a little fun while getting one to drink.

"Yeah... Everybody's putting in them new stand up coke machines but they don't keep 'em cold like these old cooler boxes do." Mr. Louis commented, as I was getting my soda.

I was so thirsty I killed off one grape in about one minute and then decided to spend another six cents on a second one.

"You must be more thirsty than you are in a hurry."

"Well I guess so, but I got a reputation for holding a lot of liquid!"

After talking to Mr. Louis for a little bit longer while taking my last gulp, I was about to leave but I asked him if I could get two cents back for the empty bottles.

"Sure Bean... I'll get my money back when they come by to pick up the empty cases."

I looked at it like I made a little transaction of business. He made some money and I ended up getting my drinks cheaper.

Finally, after enjoying my time talking with Mr. Louis and refreshing myself with those two cold sodas, I told him goodbye, hopped back on my bike, and headed straight for the drugstore in town. I was paddling fast and every time I hit a bump or a hole in the road, I could feel the liquid from those sodas, sloshing around in my stomach.

When I arrived at Holmes Drugs, as soon as I opened the front door, I could hear the sounds of bells and that unmistakable, rapid ding-ding-ding-ding of a pinball machine. I would have bet a hundred bucks it would be Jack in the back.

Yep, there he was, pounding away on a pinball machine. He had an almost crazed determined look on his face, constantly bumping the machine with his body and I knew it would be a hopeless situation to get him to leave.

"Jack, I got everything ready at the house. The reels, bait, everything we need to get to our favorite spot and catch something before dark. All we have to do is go home and grab our stuff real quick and head to the river."

He had a really high score and didn't want to leave. I timidly kept attempting to entice him with how good the fishing might be today but he just wouldn't hear it. Without taking his eyes off that steel ball he was slapping around inside the machine, looking down the entire time, he kept responding to my pleading with, "Bean, I'm close to a twenty thousand score, a new record high. No way I can leave now!"

I knew by then, there wasn't any way he was going to quit anytime soon, so I gave up prompting him. Without him ever looking directly at me, I sadly shook my head, and said, "Okay, guess I'll go by myself then but you'll be disappointed when you see me come home with a couple a' big ol catfish later."

Jack still never looked up or responded in any way. I slowly walked out, hopped on my bike and reluctantly rode back home alone. By this time, I was thinking I should have asked one of the Torry boys if they would have gone fishing with me but it was too late by now. It was even later by the time I got back home and mama was in the kitchen starting supper, having gotten in from work.

I told her I was hoping to get in a little fishing, after I had already spent a lot of time trying to get Jack to leave the drugstore to go with me.

Putting her arms on her hips, in a very stern tone she said, "Bean, you go back and tell Jack I'm cooking supper and to get his little pinball hiney home this instant or a switch 'ill be a' waiting!"

She always did have a way with words and how to get her point across directly.

"Mama, I just got back from wasting time trying to get him to leave the first time. He barely paid any attention to me. You know

Jack... Once he gets to playing pinball...it takes an army to pull him outta there!"

"Bean, don't you argue with me! Just do as I say and go tell him exactly what I said," she said, in a very stern voice this time.

So, I left again for town and hoped by the time I got there, he might be through playing. Mama was tired from work, not in a good mood and I certainly didn't want that to get any worse.

When I arrived at the store, the clerk was closing the place up and Jack was walking outside, down the sidewalk, with a sad look on his face with the store having to close.

I told him mama was cooking supper and I repeated her exact warning; "Get your little pinball hiney home this instant or a switch 'ill be a' waiting."

"Yep, that sounds like our mama alright. She's got a way with words but they're always meaner than their bite. But, I guess we best be getting back before we really do get into trouble. Besides, I'm starving anyway."

"We... Don't say... We...get into trouble Jack... I am just doing what I was told... I'm not the one she's threatening here with a switch."

"Well you know what I mean," Jack snapped back and together we hopped on our bikes, and paddled fast as we could for home.

Jack would have to wait another day to get his record high score and I would have to wait at least until tomorrow to complete my plan of going fishing at the old wooden bridge. But we had the best supper I could remember in a long time, and Jack got lucky.

That pinball hiney didn't get a switch... At least this time!

CHAPTER TWENTY THREE
Dr. Thombs Pond

Summer school break had finally arrived and we were ever so glad to see it. Although it wasn't yet officially summer by the calendar date, the classrooms were unbearably hot. Of course, with no air conditioning in those days and only these little tilt windows to open for any air circulation, we counted on fans to help keep classrooms as cool as possible. All they seemed to do though was blow around the wet, hot air. The high humidity that came with summer approaching, combined with the occasional late spring shower, made for some awfully sultry conditions at school. I think the teachers were as glad as the students when school let out, perhaps more so. Like me, most of my friends had no air conditioning in their house and so we did things outside as much as possible. It gave us that much more reason for spending time around the river too. Heck, anywhere away from the dry, hot and dusty conditions was an improvement from the heat. Being around any water at all, made you feel as though it was a cooler place to be, although I'm not sure if it was simply more of a mental thing than actual physical relief.

It was already unusually hot for early May and had been quite dry conditions for the last several weeks. As a result, the water in the river had gotten to a very low level and made the prospect for some good fishing not very encouraging. The branch of Little River that ran behind Main Street and at the old wooden bridge was so low, it had developed an island out in the middle. You could practically walk across the river there, so we thought to try the branch of the river on the other side of town toward Marked Tree. There was a spot there, not far from the bridge, that was much deeper than the branch back in town. Hopefully, the water level at this location would still be good and we might be able to catch something there. I went down to the

Torrys' house to see if they wanted to give fishing there a shot with me and Jack. Bobby had left early that morning to go to Jonesboro with his parents.

We had tried our favorite spot there and others, up and down the river, but we were having no luck at all. We had given up on catching anything, were gathering our fishing stuff and had begun to walk down the dirt road going home.

We were all talking loudly at the same time, when Sam interrupted and said, "Listen! Y'all be quiet a minute! I can hear the peacocks from Doctor Thombs pond."

John commented, "Yeah, it's amazing how far you can hear 'em hollering like that. I can sometimes hear 'em as far away as the highway back by the bridge. I wonder how many peacocks Dr. Thombs has? They sure can't be cheap. Only a doctor can probably afford to own 'em."

"Well one thing for certain. John, you ain't never gonna be no doctor, but you can always have a few chickens." Barry replied.

"At least I'd have free eggs for breakfast and chicken dinners. You can't eat no peacock, at least in this country."

Sam, one to always be straight to the point said, "Will y'all shut up for a minute. I want to hear the peacocks!"

That's when Jack jumped in with the biggest glow on his face like he had stumbled upon gold in our backyard. He said, "I got the best idea for something y'all ain't gonna believe. I don't know why we have never done it before."

"What are you talking about Jack, idea for what? Hope it ain't to go back to the river and go swimming. The last time I did that, a water moccasin swam right past me and I ain't got in the water since."

"Oh no! Nothing like that. I know how we can easily catch a lot of catfish, right here, right now. If we got the guts to do it?"

As I listened to the continued cry of the peacocks in the distance, I knew what Jack had in mind and it definitely had nothing to do with catching fish from the river, especially since he mentioned catfish. I knew he was talking about sneaking into the doctor's catfish pond behind his house.

Everyone in town knew about the doctor's pond that was said to be loaded with thousands of catfish. Jack was always the one to take a dare and everybody knew if they prodded him on, he would more than likely follow up on his own wild idea today, even by himself, if no one else would do it.

The doctor's house was in an area that was very secluded, off the last paved street in that area, down a gravel road that ended at his house. It was only a few hundred yards from the river where we were at and not far from where we were walking. Behind his house was a huge pond and yard that was the talk of the town. It had all kinds of beautiful, maintained plants and flowers and specially planted trees and shrubs that surrounded the pond. He had gardeners to maintain the area and the pond to keep it in pristine condition.

Of course, none of us had ever been inside to see it but we often peeked through the fence to get a glimpse of it. The doctor had planted so much shrubbery between the tall metal fence surrounding it and the pond, it helped to make the fence a more effective barrier to any unwanted intruders like us. The metal fence was ten feet tall and had that very thick shrubbery just on the other side. It would be almost impossible to carry anything with you, if you attempted to climb over the fence. The pond was protected like a prison fortress.

Jack told us his plan. As he went on explaining it, you would have thought he had been thinking about it for quite some time and not simply on the spur of the moment.

Jack spelled it out like this. "Look, since me and Barry are the smallest, y'all can help push us up higher with a head start to climb the fence. Once on the other side, we can work our way through all the thick shrubs easier too. There are so many catfish in his pond, I heard they come right up to ya like a herd of cattle when you feed them. We don't even need our fishing poles."

"Jack... What do you mean we don't need our poles?" Barry asked.

"Poles... Where we're going... We don't need poles! All we need is a few feet of fishing line, some hooks in our pocket to tie on and some bait."

Barry said, "I don't know Jack. It sounds like a lot of fun but I sure don't want to get into any trouble."

Jack assuredly said, "With the dark, cloudy skies and all the shrubs and bushes around the pond, it will give us cover and no one will ever know we are there."

With that one simple statement, Barry was easily convinced of Jack's plan and like he never had any doubt about it at all, replied, "Shoot, I can already taste a big ol plate of those catfish, sitting in front of me at supper time!"

I added, "We hardly used any of our bread for fishing today, so we got plenty of it left. I'm sure once that piece of bread hits the water, you'll have ten catfish fighting for it. It should be an easy thing to just jerk 'em in on the bank."

John inquired, "But if y'all catch as many fish as we are thinking, how are you gonna get 'em back over the tall fence with so much shrubs, some of 'em like trees and stuff?"

Sam said, "Oh, that's the easy part. As y'all catch 'em, just throw 'em over the fence to us like you're throwing a baseball hard. Me, John and Bean will put 'em on a couple stringers. I got two or three long strings of cord that'll do just fine. It'll work."

So now our plan was coming together. Jack and Barry used Sam's shoulders to help get a good start over the fence.

By now, I had gotten up a little nerve and decided I didn't want to miss out on the fun of the easy catching of a lot of fish. At least I hoped so. I wanted to climb over that fence too.

I said, "If we catch these fish as fast as I think we will, two of us can be jerking 'em in doing the fishing, and that'll leave one of us freed up to throw the fish we catch over the fence. I got a good arm and I can get 'em over the fence the easiest of the three of us."

Jack said, "That's good thinking Bean and that is just like you. You always think a plan through to make sure everything goes smooth. That will work a lot better."

Jack went over the fence first, then me and then Barry. After Jack and I had gotten all the way down on the other side, you could hear Barry complaining, "Dang it, some of these bushes got sharp thorns on 'em, poking me all over. I think I might be bleeding some."

Sam heard him and said, "Don't be a wuss Barry. A little pain for all the fish we are fixing to have is all worth it."

"Yeah, but you ain't the one over here getting cut up all over and bleeding to death."

At that point I quietly snapped back, "Sshhh! Y'all don't talk so loud. We gotta stay quiet!"

Barry finally worked his way down the fence, through the thick bushes to the ground. Jack assured Sam and John, "Okay, we all made it over and don't see nobody around."

About the same time, a peacock let out a loud cry not too far away and Barry jumped so hard he knocked Jack in the chin with the back of his head.

"Dang it Barry. It's only the peacocks. You almost knocked my head off... I think you knocked a tooth loose!"

"I'm sorry. Those peacocks are so loud, that hollering they do can scare the dickens out of ya when you're this close to 'em and not expecting it. I just hope they stay on the other side and don't come this way. I see one there on the side of the pond we should keep an eye on. They sure are some beautiful creatures though, all green and blue…just beautiful. I wish I had one as a pet to keep around the house. Of course, they are too big to keep in the house but…"

"Barry quit your yapping and let's get to fishing," I interrupted.

We had rigged up a short piece of fishing line for each of us to use with only a hook on the end and no weight at all. We had extra hooks in our pockets, in case we needed 'em.

Then I got as close to the fence as I could, to tell Sam and John, "Okay, we found a good spot on the bank to start fishing. All we need is the bait. Y'all throw us that loaf of bread over the fence now."

Sam reared back, let go of the loaf to heave it over the tall fence and it almost made it but instead, the bag got caught just past the top of the fence and was dangling about a foot or so down on our side.

In an almost angry voice, Barry exclaimed, "Dang it, Sam. You didn't throw it hard enough. Now one of us has gotta dig through those darn, thorny bushes again and get up to the top of the fence to get it loose! That's just gonna make that much more racket. I'm starting to get more nervous about this whole thing over here, not to mention…

I've climbed over a security fence like they keep around prisons… trespassed on someone else's private property attempting to steal their fish and could end up in jail after all this is over with…that is if we don't get shot first!"

Jack assured Barry, "Don't worry. The sheriff and me, we go way back. He's a friend of mine. He even lets me call him Dean most of the time. He might scold us as his job is to do, but he ain't taking us to no jail. Besides, we're too young to get arrested."

Barry replied, "For some reason that sure ain't making me feel any better in this particular situation."

Jack said, "I'll do it. I'll climb back up there and get the bread loose."

He fought his way through the thick, thorny bushes again, climbed back up and finally got to the top where the bread was stuck. He carried the bag with the bread all the way down this time, to make sure nothing went wrong. He didn't want it to fall and get stuck inside the bushes somewhere.

Now with the bait in hand and our lines with only a hook on the end ready to go, we were prepared to sneak out to the bank and see what kind of luck we would have. We practically crawled on the ground, to keep as low a profile as possible, getting to the edge of the pond. We surely didn't want to be spotted by anyone that might be looking out from a back window of the house or something.

Jack was the first to give our fishing plan a go. He got out the fishing line, put a little piece of bread on the hook and slung it out only a couple of feet past the bank. It was amazing what happened. So many catfish jumped all over that bait, they almost pulled the line out of his hand. Jack was not ready for such a quick response. It was instantaneous. As soon as that piece of bread hit the water, those fish went crazy, fighting over the bait. Jack and Barry started jerking in fish as fast as they could slap on another piece of bread and get it in the water. I had never seen anything like this in my life. It was one fish, after another.

"Jack, let me have some of that fun," and he swapped out with me for a little while. Soon the fish began piling up on the bank, so it wasn't long before I went back to grabbing the fish and working as fast as I could to throw 'em over the fence for Sam and John to string up. I could not keep up with how many and how fast Jack and Barry were bringing 'em in. They were almost all the same identical size but plenty big enough for some good eating.

I heard Sam say, "Bean, you're throwing us so many, so fast, me and John can't keep up with you."

"We just want to get 'em over the fence. We can string 'em all up later when we get through fishing if we have too," I replied.

Sam had turned his back facing the fence messing with one fish I had thrown over. That's when I threw another bigger one, and it hit him smack dab in the head.

Sam exclaimed, "Bean. Watch where you're throwing 'em. These things have got some prickly fins you know. Could have hit me in the eye."

"Sam, I'm just throwing 'em over anyway I can to get 'em outta here. I can't help where they land. You gotta keep an eye out."

"My eye… That is exactly my point."

It was the most beautiful vision I had ever seen gazing up at the sky, watching those fish streaming through the air gracefully flying over the top of that fence in an almost rhythmic, musical display of nature. I could hear an accompanying symphony, playing in my head,

After only about thirty minutes tops, we had run out of bread for bait. Toward the end, having thrown so many fish high in the air, my arm was worn out and that fence felt like it had grown to be twenty feet tall. A bunch of fish didn't make it over and landed back on our side in the bushes but I wasn't about to crawl through the thick brush to get 'em.

Everything so far went according to plan. All we had left to do was for us to get back over the fence and make sure we had all the fish loaded up on the stringers and get our prized catch home.

I told Sam, "Okay, that's it. We're heading back over now."

Jack went first with no problem and got back down on the other side. I followed closely behind and was almost at the top of the fence about to go over and looked down to see Barry frantically appearing to be fiddling with something in his pocket.

"Barry! What the heck are you messing with? We gotta get going!"

"Oh man! One of those extra hooks is digging in my leg and it hurts. It's sticking through my pocket and it's stuck... I'm trying to get it out!"

That's when it happened... A peacock came out of nowhere right behind Barry and he didn't see it while messing with that hook in his leg. Just as Barry turned around to look, it charged right at him, half flying and jumping through the air, poking his neck out in sudden, quick attacks, back and forth at Barry. I noticed how much bigger these birds appear, when you see 'em up close and those previous beautiful, peaceful looking birds take on a whole new demeanor. This one was making this horrible, loud, repetitive scream and was scaring the daylight out of not only Barry, but me too, although I was safely way up on the fence. This peacock was definitely in an attack mode. It kept on jumping at Barry in that menacing manner and would not let up.

As Barry turned and was frantically struggling to get to the fence, that peacock stayed right on his tail, chasing him through the bushes, all the way to the fence. I don't know who was screaming louder...the peacock or Barry? With all the ruckus going on by now, all the other peacocks were joining in with their loud cries and heading our way.

Barry finally got through the bushes to start climbing the fence, when the peacock appeared to bite him on the butt as he started his climb. Now Barry is really screaming bloody murder.

Sam, Jack and John are now hollering, "Barry... Get out of there... Get out of there!"

All the peacocks are squawking so loudly by now, I figured the entire town was going to know something was going on. I'm at the top of the fence trying to keep my cool to help grab Barry to help him over the fence. Any hope of remaining quiet has been long gone by now.

Barry finally got to me where I could grab him and we both were just getting over the top of the fence, when we heard some nervous voices shout out from the back of the house.

I knew it was the doctor's daughters that I went to school with; Matilda, Alyssa and Sally.

They were shouting, "Who's there...what are you doing on our property...are you messing with our peacocks? Y'all better get out of here...we're calling the police!"

They were all very pretty girls and I always had a crush on Matilda in particular. She was in my same grade and I would be totally embarrassed for her to find out it was me on top of that fence and that I had been at the pond. I felt trepidation about having to see her again, or any of her sisters, at least anytime soon after this escapade.

Especially with our presence being discovered, we are now in total panic mode. We knew to get away from there as quickly as we could.

Barry and I hopped to the ground and Barry said, "Oh no...my glasses got knocked off and I don't see 'em anywhere... Mama's going to kill me if she has to buy me another pair... I've only had these glasses about a month."

I yelled back, "Don't worry about the glasses Barry...We'll come up with something... Just say you lost 'em down at the river while fishing...it won't be a lie."

When Barry dropped down to the other side, he looked to be a total mess. His shirt was all ripped up with blood all over it and his face too, from being pricked by the thorny bushes. He was soaking wet with sweat too, looking completely miserable.

Thankfully, Sam and John had already strung the last catfish and we hurriedly made our escape from the pond to get back on our way home. We all breathed a big sigh of relief, once we got a little distance between us and Thombs pond.

In spite of the ordeal, we couldn't believe how many fish we had but didn't want to stop and do any counting until we got farther away. We took the best route home that would help us avoid being noticed. It was getting much later by now which helped a little to not be seen, but it would be quite obvious to try explaining away catching that many fish in Little River at that time.

What a sight to see though as we all began to get calmed down. Sam and John were holding on to each end of one huge stringer of fish, while Jack and I were carrying another one also loaded with fish, walking down the road in plain sight.

Although the manner and circumstances of us catching all those fish wasn't exactly due to our fishing prowess, I think we all had a little misguided pride in showing off the fish to anyone passing by. Several people that drove by stuck their head out their car window, and only gasped in awe of the huge stringers of fish we were struggling to carry. Surprisingly, not one of them said anything or inquired much about all those fish. The stringers were so heavy, we couldn't go very far without having to stop and rest some. Each stringer must have weighed at least thirty pounds and it was almost a mile back to our house. We were finally getting close, and becoming more confident in getting away with our little criminal adventure.

Finally, we made it to my house and all five of us were completely worn out. We plopped down on the back stairs, and were still breathing heavily from our toil of carrying those fish.

I finished filling an old wash tub we had out back with water and we carefully counted every single catfish, and then double checked our count, as we put them in the tub. We wanted to be sure of our bounty and had counted fifty two catfish.

I looked at Sam and said, "There's more fish here than how many digits of Pi you know how to recite Sam."

"You sure about that Bean?"

As we were figuring out how to divvy up the fish between us, Bobby showed up.

"I've been looking for ya Bean. Just got back from Jonesboro with my dad and we..." He stopped in shock at all the fish he was seeing and exclaimed... "Holy cow...what in the world...where did y'all catch all those fish...darn it, on the very day I had to go out of town with my family, y'all do a killin' fishing."

I debated whether to tell him the truth about what we had done but decided to be honest. I couldn't lie to my best friend. So I began to tell Bobby about the entire episode, all that had happened in quite detail. Bobby was laughing so hard when I got to the part about Barry being attacked and chased by that peacock.

Barry said, "Well, it wasn't funny at the time but it kinda is now when I hear you telling it."

I was thinking Bobby might get on to me for doing something that I knew was pretty devious. Instead, he enjoyed the story and said, "Wow Bean. I didn't know you had it in you to do something like that. But you know what? Sometimes I myself get tired of being the good kid all the time. Once in a while, you have to go off the rails. Do something no one would expect you to do. Ain't talking about killing nobody. Just some innocent fun. It's only human and ain't none of us perfect! Besides, it wasn't like stealing somebody's prized possessions. It's just food and somebody is going to do some awfully good eating! Besides that, them peacocks got a little even with ya anyway, especially Barry!"

Bobby always had a way of using logic that most folks could never argue with. He was like that guy from the planet Vulcan, in that new TV series about a spaceship traveling through the galaxy. Just like that guy on that show that used only logic, no one could ever win an argument with Bobby either. Besides that, I always joked with Bobby that his ears were a little pointy like the guy on that TV space show.

But I was the only one that could joke about that, just like he was always funnin' with me…calling me a knucklehead.

Now there we were. All of us standing there, staring at that huge tub of fish, looking at each other and I think we were starting to read each other's mind. We suddenly realized how much fish cleaning we had to do, especially being as tired as we already were.

Being the consummate business person, I said, "I got a great idea! Here is our chance to make some quick money. We could spread out, go around to our neighbors and sell 'em some good eating catfish. Let's say fifty cents for each fish!"

Knowing Sam was a walking calculator, I asked, "Sam, how much would that come to with fifty two fish at fifty cents each?"

"Twenty six dollars," Sam quickly stated.

"Divided by five people," I just as quickly asked.

"Five dollars and twenty cents each." Sam answered.

"Too bad we are honest criminals. We could make a good living doing this," I proclaimed!

CHAPTER TWENTY FOUR
Whispers

As the months passed, the memories of the farm began to fade somewhat from memory, but not forgotten. Of course, nothing could ever match the freedom of living in the middle of countless acres of open fields that changed so much between planting time and those mostly white fields at harvest time. But the biggest change of living in town, even a small one I think, is the people, your neighbors. On the farm, most neighbors would do anything to help each other if needed, but a tenant's life was so demanding, most folks didn't have much time to spare, except for working, eating and sleeping. As the expression goes, everybody tended to their own business.

Living in town, you live close to everyone by design. You live close to your school teachers and your schoolmates, whether you like them or not. You run into the same people all over town, all the time, so your life is never an isolated one and it is difficult for any family to harbor many secrets. When you leave your house, your neighbors probably notice. When you get home, they usually know. Of course, if any big event happens, word just travels that much faster. Usually by the time you hear it again, after making the rounds, it may not even resemble the same story. It's not always a bad thing in every case, as we all need other people at times, but human nature does usually tend to lend itself to the darker side of things. People are curious creatures and there usually isn't bad intent on their part to get things wrong, they simply end up that way and are mostly harmless.

The story about Bobby Jansen and I hopping that train to Marked Tree, only ten miles away, had really become a whopper. In no time at all, the story went that we ran away from home, hopped a train to Memphis and got thrown off by some hobos after getting beat up. Then we ended up in West Memphis, got picked up by the police and spent a night in jail to teach us a lesson. That was only a few versions of what happened.

My bean trailer incident from years ago, became that I spent a month in an ICU at the Baptist Hospital in Memphis, where I was given up on by doctors to even live, but somehow survived. Of course, one could look at it like… Well it all just adds to a reputation…so what's the harm? I suppose it's better than never been talked about at all. Maybe it's a good thing, if even falsely, that people care about you in some unreal, abnormal and perhaps self- promoting way.

But secrets within a family, between the members themselves who live in the same house day by day, are often much more easily contained than the community rumors. It is beyond one's control in the community but in the family, it can be. So perhaps the easiest way to learn of something of which otherwise you might be the last to know, would be to tune your ears to those of the community. Of course, for me, that close, immediate community to hear something was from my classmates, having to spend a big part of the day sitting elbow to elbow with them either in class or at the cafeteria. Unfortunately, sometimes the whisperer's intent is not for an incidental comment that might be overheard in conversation but rather for a more devious, hurtful effect on someone else. That whisperer's sole purpose today, was to shake up the world of a happy middle schooler, and that middle schooler was me.

I was sitting in science class and Mr. Huggins was continuing teaching about the subject of anthropology and in particular, the theory of evolution, as he had been doing all week.

At the beginning of class, like he had reiterated all week, he explicitly repeated, "Class, this is a theory and only a theory! It is not proven but in science we must look at all sides of a question and not be afraid to examine them, regardless of our beliefs."

He had given us the assignment to read some material on evolution. Every student during this week's class had to at some point give an oral report on their thoughts about what we were assigned to read. Mr. Huggins had randomly assigned several students on each particular day this week to be ready for their interview and to answer some questions he would ask. He had told us that by knowing the day of our interview, we couldn't have the excuse of being unprepared since we each knew in advance when to give our report. He had written out the names of five or six students on the blackboard, for each day's session. On that list today at the very bottom were two names, Bobby Jansen, and lastly me, Benny Barnes.

I was ready to get it over with and was hoping the bell didn't ring so I could get mine done. I had decided in my own mind that evolution was exactly what Mr. Huggins called it, a theory and what I believed about it or anyone else for that matter would not change what the truth was. I was going to tell him that I didn't believe it and that people having evolved from apes or monkeys never made much sense to me, although knowing some of my classmates like I did, I might have to re-examine my beliefs. I thought adding a little sarcastic humor wouldn't hurt anything, especially after Mr. Huggins had to engage in such serious discussions all week!

He had a small table set up in the front corner of the class, off to the side of his desk where he would do the interview one by one, giving the student a little more privacy. I was glad for that, as I didn't want the entire class hearing my answers.

Mr. Huggins told us, "I want every student to be honest when I ask you questions and whatever you tell me will remain private and have nothing to do with what grade you get. I simply want to know what you honestly thought about what you were assigned to read and any conclusions you made. I want to be assured that you actually read the material and I will know by the answers you give to the questions I ask."

Most of the students whose turn it was that day to be interviewed had gone through the routine of going up to be interviewed by Mr. Huggins and not a lot of class time was left today. All the students' names were crossed off the list on the blackboard, having given their report, except those last two, my name and Bobby's. He was called up first, and most students were sitting and bending their ears trying to hear as much as possible of what questions Mr. Huggins would be asking. You could hear enough to know that the student would talk a bit about what he thought about the theory of evolution, and then Mr. Huggins would follow up with questions, though you couldn't quite make out what he was asking.

I was sitting in front of James Hatterson, an older student who had been held back a year in elementary school and Monk Bond, who was sitting right next to James, both behind me. They were both large boys and known for picking on kids that were younger or smaller. They hung around together and most of the other students tried to stay out of their way. They did a lot of mean things to other kids but rarely got into any trouble for it. Most kids were too embarrassed to tell on them and were afraid what they might do, if they found out you were the one who told on them. I surely didn't like that they sat right behind me in science class, often having to sit and listen to them talk in a bad way about other students.

I was trying to listen to Bobby doing his report and heard enough to hear Mr. Huggins say, "This is my last question, Bobby." Now I was getting my thoughts together and preparing to answer the call to go up front, when I heard one of those whispers that would shake up my world forever. James, as if speaking to Monk, quite loudly whispered, "Did ya hear that old lady Barnes was screwing around with the sheriff. Rumor is that little Jack is the sheriff's son, and not really a Barnes at all and that's why Bill Barnes killed himself?"

Monk repeated similar words, "Yeah, I heard that had been going on for a long time. Guess that makes Jack a bastard kid."

I immediately became frozen in place in my seat. My shoulders felt like they had drooped down to my knees. My eyes would only stare down at the floor, fixed in place, as if losing all ability to even blink. I felt as though the eyes of the entire class were upon me, as if I had committed some great terrible act. I knew those words were not some unfortunate whisper and were pronounced with full intent of an effect on the person right in front of them. Me! I felt more pain in those words than any I had heard since hearing the words ingrained in my memory forever, spoken over a year ago by mama telling me, "Your dad is dead, don't make me say it again."

I wasn't able at that moment to be angry or get mad. I suppose being shocked with the revelation of what I just heard, there was no room left in my brain for anything but dealing with the reality of those words, and how much of it might be true. I felt totally humiliated as those whispers had done their intended damage. The physical effect was obvious, as my body became raging hot and actual sweat dripped from my forehead. It took all my effort to hold back crying and I felt like a baby for feeling that way, asking myself, "Why don't I get up? Why don't I say something back? Why don't I fight back?"

But what could I do or say in that situation? I was never a fighter like my little brother. How could I respond to something verbal that had wounded me more than I could ever suffer in a physical fight. I was trying to figure out what to make of the words I had just heard, and not so much about dealing with who said them.

Besides me, several people were close enough to hear those whispers, including Mr. Huggins as Bobby was getting back up to return to his desk and it was my turn to go up. I could not get the words I had heard out of my head. They slowly repeated themselves, over and over in my head like a stuck record player, as I walked toward Mr. Huggins. While passing me, Bobby touched my shoulder with empathic, saddened eyes, as he was sitting down. He couldn't really say anything at that moment, but he knew.

I managed to get up, which actually made me feel a little better, if not only by getting some distance from where those words were spoken. I took my seat at the little table across from the teacher, with my eyes filling with tears but not visibly crying.

I was still looking down, holding back so much emotion and Mr. Huggins said, "Bean, look at me! I heard what they said and I will deal with them later. Don't let them succeed in what they were doing. They were trying to make themselves look superior but in reality, it just shows how immature and mean they can be. You hear what I'm saying?" Then he continued, "You are going to make something great out of your life. All the teachers are always saying that about you and don't let anyone take you off that path, okay? Remember, you have done nothing wrong!"

In broken speech, with my nose constantly sniffing while fighting back crying, I remarked, "But is it true...what they said...do you know if it's true?"

Mr. Huggins replied, "Bean, to be honest I don't know. There are rumors about everything in this town. There have always been rumors that I've been messing around with another teacher and it's not true at all. I think it was because the two of us are always meeting to discuss school events and all the clubs that the both of us are in charge of this year, so people start talking. People will use any excuse to talk about other people. I learned that the best thing to do was to simply ignore it."

Finally, the class bell rang and while putting a hand on my shoulder, as if to signal me to remain seated until the class cleared out,

Mr. Huggins shouted to the departing class, "We will continue with reports tomorrow!"

As I got up to leave, I asked him, "What am I gonna say at home after what I heard? How can I even bring something like that up?"

"That is a tough one Bean and one you shouldn't have to deal with... I've learned that most things come out on their own sooner or later anyway... Just try to manage it the best you can for now and see what happens. In the meantime, you can talk to me anytime you need to and maybe you should contact Reverend Chamblis. He is a great listener and I can call him for you if you decide to talk to him. I know he has put up with having to deal with all my infirmities, and I have a lot them. He has helped me through some rough times. Sometimes just having someone to listen, can help heal a lot of things. So keep that in mind, okay!"

That was a lot to think about for a young kid but I really appreciated the time Mr. Huggins took talking to me. It actually helped and in a quiet, somber tone, I answered, "Yes sir, I will," and I slowly proceeded out to the hallway.

Bobby was leaning against the wall, waiting outside in the hall, knowing what that was all about. But now, the thought of going home made my body quiver all over. In a soft empathetic voice, while putting one arm around my shoulders, Bobby said, "Come on Bean... let's get outta here."

As soon as we opened the door and stepped outside of the school building, Bobby stopped us both in a deliberate motion and turned and looked directly at me. It was a gesture to make sure there would be no doubt believing what he was about to say. Then in the most assuredly, stern voice, unlike one I had never heard him use before, he added, "I'm gonna beat the crap outta those two boys later! You wait and see!"

CHAPTER TWENTY FIVE
Winning Ain't Losing

Jack, Bobby and I usually would meet up after school to walk home together. Most days it would be a group of us walking together that lived in the same direction and today wasn't any different. This time it was the Torry brothers, Ricky Louis, Bobby, Jack and me in a mostly strung out party, making our way down the alleyways we used as shortcuts to our homes. We never took the nicer paved streets as the more comfortable, secluded dirt alleys that lined the back of houses, was always our preferred route home.

The less traveled back alleys offered isolation and escape from the hustle of the main thoroughfares, especially right after school let out and that comfort and peace was exactly what I was needing after today's events. Being very distraught, I purposefully kept back from intermingling with the group or anyone else that happened to come along on our way. John Torry was wanting for everyone to meet at The Greenfield around four o'clock, after we would have a chance to get home and get our baseball stuff.

Sam jumped in saying, "Yeah, I finally got me a brand new catcher's mitt I need to try out... I got it oiled up real good but need to get it broke in...the sun is shining...the field is in great shape and is a perfect day to play some ball."

Any other time, I would be excited to get to play some ball, but not today. I was hanging back, not saying very much and was in a noticeably somber mood. My depressed disposition was very evident to everyone, realizing that I had a bad day at school but not really knowing the reason why. As a result, everybody was avoiding saying anything to me except of course, Jack. He finally noticed that I wasn't responding to anything he was saying and finally said, "Bean...

You've barely said a word... I've never seen you this quiet. Did you get in trouble at school or something?"

"No Jack. I don't feel very good and I just want to get home."

"Well, okay Bean. I think I'll head on down to Holmes Drugstore and play some pinball. I haven't played in two whole days. Sure don't want to get rusty!"

Barry heard Jack and replied, "I don't think there is any worry of you getting rusty Jack. You must have a million hours on those machines down there. You could buy a lot of baseballs and fishing stuff with all the money you spend on those machines!"

We were still in the alley and getting close to the intersection with Sycamore Street, not far from home on Elm, when I saw in the distance, none other than James Hatterson and Monk Bond. James, looking very relaxed, was puffing away on a cigarette and was holding out the pack for Monk to take one. Neither of them had yet noticed our little band of misfits heading their way.

The Torry brothers also had their encounters with them before and although they weren't really intimidated by them, they still preferred to not engage them. At this point we had no choice but to either turn around, cut through someone's yard or keep going straight ahead and take our chances. We outnumbered them after all, being that there were five of us and only two of them. So onward we marched feeling confident and we approached the two bullies with the intent of paying them no mind.

Of course, right on cue, as Monk lit up a cigarette of his own, they looked at our little band and stood across the width of the alley to block our path. James, blowing out a huge puff of white smoke and holding the cigarette to his side, said, "Well lookie here... I knew I smelled something that stunk and now I see what it is!"

Monk added, "Yep and there's little bastard Jack too!"

James in a commanding tone said, "Y'all not thinking of crossing this here street are you? You gotta turn around and go back the way ya came. This is our corner and we don't allow stinking losers to cross here!"

I was still thinking of what they had spoken in class earlier... "Old lady Barnes screwing around with Sheriff Mason...makes Jack a bastard kid!" I was still trying to deal with that in my mind, as it repeated over and over in my head. Those words might as well have been stamped on my brain like an address on an envelope. I could not blot them out, no matter how hard I tried.

Jack heard James call him a bastard kid and misunderstanding, asked me, "Bean, why did he call me a 'Baxter' kid? The Baxters live on the other side of town and I don't look anything like any of 'em anyway?"

I replied, "No Jack, they called you a bastard, not Baxter. It's like a bad cuss word you call somebody that you don't like, just to put them down... To make them feel bad about themselves."

Jack didn't really understand the meaning of the word like they had meant it but I was happy that he seemed to accept my explanation.

I wasn't scared or intimidated by now but I also thought it wouldn't solve anything to get into a fight. Bobby and I were never ones to solve problems with fighting if it could be helped. It wasn't ever because we were scared or sissies, we simply always thought there was a better way to solve problems with other people.

Shoot, Bobby could talk his way out of any situation. I think he could convince a bank robber to turn himself in, walk into a jail cell on his own and then turn around and deposit some of his own money in the same bank he had robbed.

He was always saying, "Bean, I can use my brain to solve most problems with people and I never have to get into a fight. It's just never worth it. Even if you win, you lose!" I don't know if I agreed or ever totally understood what he meant by that losing by winning philosophy, but since I didn't like fighting either, it sounded like a good one to me.

By now, other kids from school walking this way had taken notice of something going on and stopped to see what was going to happen. Of others, Monk and James made it point to show their power by granting them permission to pass on through. There began to be a large gathering of kids and this only seemed to encourage Monk and James to demonstrate their authority even more.

In a frustrated voice, John relented, "Let's cut through here and leave it be. This ain't worth getting into it with 'em."

We were all preparing to simply turn around and go another way, that is, everyone but Bobby. Up to this point, he had remained completely silent. But now he walked right past me, breathing heavily with his face taut and turning red as blood. He went right up face to face to Monk and said, "Y'all have bullied kids around here long enough and it's gonna end, one way or another! Besides, nobody talks to my friends like you did today and gets away with it!"

I couldn't believe what I was hearing and seeing. Monk was a huge boy, the tallest kid in school at over six feet tall. Bobby's head came up only to Monk's chin and now I was beginning to fear the worst. Monk looked straight down at Bobby, and with knuckled fingers tapped several times right on top of Bobby's head, in a manner imitating knocking on someone's front door, except this was Bobby's head.

Monk said, "Jansen...Why do you bother messing around with these losers? I know you got more brains in that head of yours to know better than that!"

Then, in the blink of an eye, it happened. Bobby leaned back, cocked his arm back in a tight fist and with one swift blow landed a punch into Monk's stomach before he had time to react. Monk instantly fell to the ground as if being downed by a prize heavyweight boxer in the ring. We all stood there in shock, looking at each other, not believing our eyes. Not only seeing this huge body of a bully lying helplessly in the dirt moaning and groaning, but from witnessing Bobby doing something we never thought he was capable of.

Bobby stood over Monk breathing heavily, perhaps assuming he would eventually get up and would have to continue to fight. But Monk didn't and instead he began to cough profusely and we assumed it was the result of only the blow to the stomach.

As he continued to lie there, he began pointing at his throat with his mouth open and making these awful gagging noises.

I said, "I think he must have swallowed his cigarette and is choking on it."

John said, "Is that possible? Can you swallow a cigarette?"

Sam said, "Heck, I've seen on TV where people swallow a cigarette and other things, and then it comes out of one of their ears. I've seen 'em do flaming swords but I don't know if they were really swallowing it or if it was some kind trick sword or an illusion. I was always wondering how they do all that stuff but they sure know how to make it look real but swallowing that two foot long, flaming sword was the one that always got me."

Barry added, "Well, I don't think the sword they swallow is really two feet long. It has to be some kind of a trick sword. They probably..."

John jumped in and said, "Oh no, they really do swallow that sword. They really do. I've read about that somewhere and it ain't trick."

Sam said, "John. There's no way a man can get a two foot long blade down his throat like that. It has to be some kind of..."

Interrupting, I said, "Guys! Monk is starting to turn a little blue in the face and we ain't got time to be discussing TV shows and sword swallowing tricks right now. We gotta deal with this situation at hand."

We knew by then, Monk wasn't getting much air at all if any. Bobby wanted to inflict pain but he certainly didn't want to kill him. James stood there in silent astonishment, not knowing what to do either.

Bobby, having by now returned to his usual calm disposition, said, "Bean, help me get him to sit up and try hitting him on the back like your dad did when you swallowed that big bug…maybe that'll work?"

After about a minute of the ordeal, Monk was really looking weak, his eyes were almost closed and we knew it was getting serious. Sam and Bobby kept him sitting up and I was slapping him repeatedly on the back.

John said, "He ain't looking so good Bean. I think you need to do it a little harder." So, I extended my arm high in the air and as far back as I could, to give one last final hit, hoping it would work.

I had never hit anyone that hard in my life, but now at least, it was for a good cause. With that one last, hard slap on the back, it worked. Monk began to take some deep breaths and sat there for a while.

Apparently, that last hard slap made him swallow the cigarette on down. He began regaining his color and his composure and looking up at us, simply gave us a nod in a seemingly apologetic way of acknowledging our help. However, without saying a word he slowly got up and walked away with James, looking back over his shoulder with one last glance.

The kids that had gathered began to disperse, going on their way as some were giving us nods, letting us know they liked the outcome. Some kids patted Bobby and me on the back, as if giving an approval for what we did. I wasn't sure if their signals of congratulations were for taking a stand like we did and not backing down or for showing some unexpected mercy for helping a defeated opponent. Maybe it was for both? One thing for certain, it was a far better outcome than the one that was going through my mind at the beginning of the confrontation. Everything happened so fast it seemed like the entire event was over as quickly as it started.

Things began to settle back to our normal conversation of gathering our baseball stuff and going to The Greenfield to play some ball.

Thinking about what Bobby had said earlier, I asked him, "Whatever happened to that whole spiel you gave me about how fighting never solves anything...how even if you win, you still sometimes lose?"

With a big ol grin from ear to ear, Bobby said, "Don't you know how full of crap I am half the time?"

By now the Torrys started discussing sword swallowing again.

Barry said, "I don't see how you got people that can put a whole dang sword down their throat and here we had somebody choking on a little o' cigarette?"

Reaching down on the ground, I couldn't believe what Jack found. He picked it up, held it high in the air, carefully observing it and for everyone to see what he had found.

He was showing us a moist, dirt covered cigarette and while blowing off the dirt, he pretended to stick it in his mouth and mockingly inquired, "Anybody got a light?"

In disbelief we were all staring at the cigarette that almost choked Monk to death.

Jack said, "Since Monk didn't get to finish this here smoke...figured there was no need to let it go to waste!"

Sam added, "Guess we save it and give it back to Monk the next time we see him."

Jack concluded, "I guess we're all just a bad bunch of bastards," and we all went to laughing our heads off.

CHAPTER TWENTY SIX
Revelation

There were only a little over two hundred students in the entire Little River middle and high school together. Being such a small school system, the middle school classes, which consisted of the seventh and eighth grades, required only six classrooms. They were all grouped together in a little wing of the high school that had been added onto the main building. Both had the same principal Mr. Hayes and mostly the same teachers. As a result, there wasn't any big space to separate where the students hung out in between class time, like lunch or any break periods. Of course, most middle schoolers hung out together in groups as did the older kids.

I was still in middle school, the eighth grade by now, and that next day at school proved to be unlike any other I had ever experienced, as word had gotten around about the encounter in the alley. Kids that before had barely paid me any attention looked at me in a totally different way. Toward the end of the school day I asked Bobby, "Have you noticed anything funny? Have people been looking at you different?"

"Oh yeah! Most kids before hardly noticed I was ever here and would never say anything to me. Now it's like they're seeing me for the first time. It's a strange, weird feeling."

"Yeah, the same here. I'm hearing things like... Hey, Bean... Great day! How ya doing?"

I usually went around school, minding my own business, not bothered by anybody and I had liked it that way but now, as weird as this new found attention was... I thought I could get used to this.

The day passed quickly and it was time for our last period... Mr. Huggins science class. I had some trepidation as I took my usual seat in front of James and Monk, who were already seated. With all that had transpired, I had no idea what to expect. Were they going to give me trouble every day from here on out? Were they going to gang up on me after school and teach me a lesson? The one thing I realized, as Mr. Huggins began to continue this week's lesson in anthropology, I wasn't embarrassed anymore. I wasn't feeling humiliated. I hadn't at all forgotten the hurtful words but now I wasn't carrying them like a heavy load over my head or a burden to weigh me down. I had put them away, like a note tucked away in my back pocket that I would take out and examine when I would determine the time is right. I decided that I would be in control, not let some outside force dominate my life.

As I sat there listening to Mr. Huggins, I heard absolutely not one peep out of James or Monk behind me. It was total silence! I was beginning to wonder if they were still seated behind me.

Mr. Huggins was discussing what makes humans different from animals, which of course is a broad subject. He was saying how we can make rational decisions and learn to control our emotions. He was talking about how the beasts of the field kill each other in order to survive and although humans sometimes do that too, we can decide to do good things to benefit one another and, in the end, improve our own lives, as well as society as a whole. By now, I wasn't sure if I was listening to a church sermon or a science class. However, the class did seem very interested.

Finally, the bell rang and as everyone began to leave the classroom, the strangest thing happened. As I was going out the door, I looked back at Mr. Huggins and he displayed a quick thumbs up with a little grin erupting over his face. I knew exactly why he did that and I never shared that with anyone, not Jack, not Bobby, no one.

The previous night at home, Jack and I didn't say anything about the confrontation we had in the alley that afternoon. Neither Jack or I, brought up any hint of it. We figured what would be the point in discussing it, especially if I was asked what had started the ruckus with those boys. I certainly would never be able to even begin to ask mama directly about what I had heard in class. That was something I was going to have to deal with on my own, in my own mind. It was the type of thing I knew I would never bring up with anyone, mostly because of Jack. He would always be the closest person to me in my life and nothing could ever change that. I reasoned it all out in my brain. What if the worst was true? What if we were only truly half-brothers? I knew that wouldn't change anything. Things would still be exactly as they were the day before, so I put that part of the question to rest.

The other part, however, was very troubling to know what to do about it. Did mama have an affair with the sheriff? Did my dad know about it and it somehow contribute to him killing himself?

I asked myself. "Is there any way I could possibly bring the subject up to mama? Should I even try? What would be gained if I did? Could I bring the subject up in some roundabout way that might lead her to give some hints about it?"

All these questions ran over and over in my mind like a stuck record player. I finally decided to put that stuck record back in its sleeve and tuck it away on the shelf where its contents would remain safe and protected, at least for now. That was my plan! But plans have a way of meeting real life head on, as that next night at home demonstrated.

We had just finished supper, was helping mama clean up the kitchen and I was drying off the last plate, storing it back in its place.

That's when mama said, "You boys come take a seat here. I need you to talk to you boys about something."

Jack and I proceeded into the living room, plopping ourselves down, almost swallowed up in the pillowy softness of that old worn sofa; the same old couch we still had, from back on the farm.

Jack and I weren't sure what mama had on her mind but we could tell it was serious. I had figured by now it was probably about that confrontation in the alley.

She began to speak. "Boys..." And, with a long pause, glancing up at the ceiling as if to pick her words carefully before looking back at us, she continued... "I thought it was time I talk to you both about something. You boys are growing up and I don't want you hearing all kinds of rumors about your dad...me...the sheriff and be worried about anything you might hear. So it's best I let you hear it from me, as people like to talk and that's when things get all twisted around."

I knew mama was about to talk about the very thing I had decided only a few hours earlier to hide away in my mind, like that record on the shelf until the appropriate time to bring it up. I soon discovered I was right, as she began to go into more details.

"I know there have been a lot of rumors going around town. People always love to talk and gossip, especially in Little River. If the newspaper printed all the rumors and gossip going on in this town, it would be the size of an encyclopedia to hold it all. There is usually a little bit of truth to things and then it gets all blown up into something else."

She continued... "I know about the fight in the alley... First, I was worried about you getting into a fight but then Mrs. Torry told me some of the things that those boys said and I can't imagine what you thought."

I interrupted at this point and interjected, "Mama, we didn't get hurt and it all ended up being okay in the end."

"Yeah, I was glad it turned out like it did but I want to talk about what you heard. But before I really get into that... I have to go back, way back to the beginning, of how I ended up here in Little River and how I met your dad."

I was fascinated as she began to recount to us that story. As she went on, I couldn't believe how I had never heard any of it until now.

This was her account:

As you know, I grew up in the Appalachian Mountains of North Carolina, miles from any city. I've told you many stories of living on that tobacco farm with my family, who also did logging and for a short time operated a saw mill. I had four brothers who went off to fight in the war against Germany, so I had to give up high school to help out on the farm. My father told me I could continue my education after the war was over. I was a young girl, about seventeen and very isolated from other people with only my parents, and I was very lonely. I felt like I was no different than the animals we were keeping caged up until the time for slaughter to have meat to survive.

It was a life of hard work and not much else. My only relief was reading in a magazine that my father had for keeping up with the war. I would often look at it but only after he would be through reading it. He usually had a pile of those magazines lying around, before he would throw any away. I was looking at the advertisements in the back of one for various things for sale, when I came across something that seemed to jump off the page at me.

It was an advertisement for another, different magazine put out by something called, Lonely Hearts Magazine. It was offering a free subscription for a limited time to help out lonely soldiers in the service, or veterans after they got out, who might want some other lonely hearts to write to. I knew your grandpa would not approve of it, so I ripped out the part to fill out, snuck a stamp and put it in our mailbox. I couldn't wait until the day I would see that magazine come in our own mailbox.

Of course, from that day on I volunteered to walk down our steep hill to the road to get the mail and climb back up. It was quite the trek down and back up to do, so dad was happy to let me do it most of the time as his knees were getting pretty bad.

I was so excited the day I opened that mailbox and there it was. As soon as I opened the box, I saw part of a big, red heart on a rolled up magazine, jumping off the cover at me. I couldn't contain my excitement as I felt I was getting a letter of reprieve, like a prisoner hoping to receive a commuted sentence for a crime he committed.

Later that night, I began to read the names and addresses of men, mostly telling something about themselves and looking for a pen pal. I found a couple of them interesting that I began to write to but only one, your dad, Bill Barnes, continued writing back. As you know, your dad was fifteen years older than me and that would make the situation worse if your grandpa ever found out.

Jack and I both sat there in complete silence, intrigued with this story that I thought more resembled listening to a well told fairy tale. But this was real life, my mama's life and her story that somehow she had kept secret all these years.

She then reached down and placed a small old looking, cherry wood box on the coffee table, opened it and began to gently shuffling around its contents. "These are the letters that you dad wrote to me and some of what I had written to him that he had saved. I guarded every single letter he had written. I would read each letter over and over, sometimes a dozen times."

I interrupted, "Mama, what happened after that. How did you finally meet dad?"

She told us she was getting to that part and continued with the story:

… Your dad was well into his thirties by now and had been out of the army for several years. He had hurt his back while serving, well before the war, and was honorably discharged. He sent me a picture of him in his old army uniform and I thought he looked like a kind and quite handsome man.

We kept on writing back and forth for several months and he wanted to come and meet me and my parents. He wrote that he lived in northeast Arkansas, not far from what he called the foothills of the Ozark and Ouachita Mountains. He said he loved the mountains but the only thing he knew how to do was farming, like what his dad, his grandad, and family did for a living.

So he moved to the small farm, in the Mississippi River delta country, just outside of Little River. This wasn't far from where his brother, your Uncle Remus and Aunt May had started sharecropping at the time.

C.J. Potter owned most of the farmland around Little River, and needed a manager to look after his sharecroppers, so he hired your dad. He knew your dad had a great reputation for his knowledge of farming.

About the same time that your dad moved to the farm, your grandpa found out about the letters we had written back and forth and he put a stop to our communication immediately. He instructed me to write to your dad one last time, to tell him our relationship was over with.

But your dad wouldn't take no for an answer. Not long after, your dad showed up on our doorstep, introduced himself and told my parents he was in love with me and was asking permission to marry me and take me back to Arkansas…

Jack inquired, "What happened then mama? Did you run away with dad? Here to Arkansas?"

Mama laughed, "No, son… I couldn't believe what your grandpa told him. He was actually quite impressed with your dad and by the courage it took to show up there. He told him to come visit twice a month for the next six months and he would have his permission then if we still wanted to get married. Besides, my dad knew I was turning eighteen soon and I could do whatever I wanted to do by then anyway. So, your dad came and visited every other weekend, until we got married by a justice of the peace in nearby Vilas, North Carolina and on the very same day, he took me away with him to the little farm at Little River."

By now, though totally intrigued with mama's story, I was wondering what all of this had to do with what she had started out saying she was going to talk about.

So I asked, "How does this get back to you talking about the fight we had, the rumors and all that other stuff?"

"Yeah Bean... I sort a' got carried away with that story didn't I? I have never told anyone except you boys that much detail about me and your dad. Mrs. Torry and Mrs. Jansen know some of it, but not many others do as far as I know. I guess it is nothing to be embarrassed about. It is exactly what happened and how I ended up here. Nothing bad! But let me get back to how it relates to today's events. Dean Mason and his wife were some of the first people I met when I moved here. Dean wasn't the sheriff yet and he ran one of the cotton gins for C.J. Potter. We all hung out together on weekends or as much as farming life allowed. Dean had married a lady named Phyllis Cade right out of high school. Without going into too much detail, Phyllis eventually had some kind of mental breakdown and one day shot Dean, her own husband, while he was sleeping. He survived but would not press charges against her. Her condition got worse and she was put in a sanitorium in Hot Springs, where not long after that, she killed herself. Bill and I had become good friends with Dean and his wife, and we were always there to console him after that tragedy. It was tough on him for a long time. Dean eventually ran for and won the Sheriff's job and has been re-elected ever since. Once the farm began to fail, your dad started drinking and that's when all those episodes with Dean bringing him home began. Of course, that started rumors about me and Dean, way back then. When your dad died, Dean and I both had spouses that suffered the same fate, each by their own hands, so we had that in common. It was something that no one else could ever understand. I was never unfaithful to your dad, he knew that and it had nothing to do with his passing. Dean and I began seeing each other only a few months back but not so openly, as enough rumors were going around already. I know there will always be those rumors about me and Dean, going back to when your dad was here, but they are just not true. Some people are always going to believe that and there is nothing I can do about it. We had planned on taking it real slow but we finally decided to go ahead and get married and that will be the end of it we hope. It will be over and done with. That's the final thing I wanted to talk to you two about...us getting married. I wanted to make sure it was okay with you boys..."

Jack interjected, "Mama, I like Sheriff Dean. You can marry him if you want too. I think he would be a great stepdad. I am already his favorite kid in town!"

Mama replied, "Yeah, I think you're right but you may have to lay off of some of that pinball a little bit, especially during school hours. You know he has that big jail cell to use if he needs to!"

Mama looked at me and said, "Well, Bean... What do you think about all this? You have barely said anything."

I stoically replied, as if still in thought, "Mama, I was so intrigued with your story, it makes me want to be a writer one day. That story of your and dad's life and up till now had me completely spellbound. I didn't want it to end, especially a down to earth, personal journey of one's own mother, told in her own words. It doesn't get any better than that."

"Bean…That is one of the rare times you have ever referred to me as mother instead of mama… I like that and you know what else? I don't want it to end either… Our story is just beginning!"

Be watching for Dadfire's book of poems
coming soon!